The Greatest Prize

Lynn Shurr

A Wings ePress, Inc.
Regency Era Historical Romance Novel

Wings ePress, Inc.

Edited by: Jeanne Smith
Copy Edited by: Rebecca Smith
Executive Editor: Jeanne Smith
Cover Artist: Trisha FitzGerald-Jung

Wings ePress Books
www.wingsepress.com

Copyright © 2020 by: Lynn Shurr
ISBN 13: 978-1-61309-559-1
ISBN 10: 1-61309-559-7

Published In the United States Of America

Wings ePress Inc.
3000 N. Rock Road
Newton, KS 67114

What They Are Saying About

The Greatest Prize

"Shurr is a wonderful storyteller."

—The Romance Studio

"Very easy reads, well written, combined with conflict, believable plots and secondary characters that make the story come alive."

—Jane Lange, *Romances, Reads and Reviews*

"I love the picture the author paints of the town and the way of life, and the characters are strong and interesting.

—Joan Conning Afman
Author of *The Cheetah Princess*

"Lynn Shurr breathes life into the characters and allows each turn of the page to lead up to a pleasurable ending."

—Cherokee
Coffee Time Romance and More

"I love how deep and well-written the characters are."

—Juliette Brandt
Paperbacks and Frosting

"You can count on Lynn Shurr to deliver interesting characters and great romance."

—A.C. Mason
Author of *Deadly Bayou*

Dedication

For Kathy Guidry, friend and swim buddy

The progeny of Pearce and Flora Longleigh,

Duke and Duchess of Bellevue,
as recorded in the family Bible:

James Logan Longleigh, Storm Cloud, born in the Ohio Territory, April 12, 1784?

Thalia Amabel Full Moon Woman Longleigh, b. March 1, 1785.

Iris Emily Doe Eyes Longleigh, b. October 16, 1787.

Twins, Calliope Constance Corn Tassel & Clio Judith Small Turtle, b. June 22, 1789.

Joshua William Big Paw Longleigh, b. January 24, 1791

Jason Samuel Benjamin Rattler Longleigh, b. January 24, 1792

Pandora Jane Black Wing Longleigh, b. September 15, 1794

Euphemia Dorcas Little Dove Longleigh, b. December 31, 1795

Justinian Giles White Bull Longleigh, b. July 10, 1800

And all made the lives of their parents very interesting.

One

Bellevue Hall, North England, March 1813

"Oh, do look at them, dearest. Joshua and Kate courting exactly as I predicted ever since The Incident." The diminutive Duchess of Bellevue squeezed her husband's brawny arm and then squeezed it again simply because she enjoyed doing so.

"Had they been any older when The Incident occurred, they would have been married long since," the duke grumbled as he watched the young couple strolling in the garden from his vantage point by the glass terrace doors. "To be quite honest, I am not sure what a sensible girl like Kate sees in our second-born son. Since going up to London to study law, he has become a complete dandy. Why, he could put an eye out on that high, starched collar, and I doubt he can sit in pantaloons so tight, nor put on his jacket without the help of a servant. As for the waistcoat of lime green and gold, it dazzles the eye to the point of blindness."

"He comes by his love of finery honestly, darling. I seem to recall a youthful viscount who had a penchant for white satin and other frippery."

The duchess flicked the froth of lace at her spouse's wrist with the tip of her fan. "Josh merely wishes to be stylish unlike others I could mention who cleave to knee breeches and greatcoats." She eyed her husband.

"Which are a damned sight more comfortable than what he's got on."

"To each generation their own, but I am sure you would look stunning in such snug pantaloons."

The light patter of ladies' slippers sounded on the marble of the hallway as the two youngest daughters of the Longleigh brood dashed for the terrace doors. The duchess held up a staying hand toward Pandora, her most difficult daughter, and Euphemia, her most biddable.

"Halt! Pandora, return to your chamber for your deep bonnet and a parasol. Your complexion is quite dark enough. Phemie, you as well. Be slow about it. Give Joshua and Kate some time together before you descend upon them."

"You should have called us when Kate arrived, Mama. She would much rather see us than Josh, I am quite sure. He's such a prig." Pandora held her ground.

Her mother's large, gray eyes darkened to the color of steel. "If you want Kate as a member of this family, go upstairs at once and remain there until summoned."

Small Phemie took her taller sister's hand. "Yes, Mama. Come Panny, we shall visit with Kate soon enough."

"I don't see why—"

"Go!"

Shaking off her sister's hand, Pandora went stomping off as hard as she could in her light footwear. Phemie, delicate of form like her mother, skipped after her, raven curls bobbing.

The duchess sighed. "When did I become so like my mother, fretting over complexions and parasols?"

"About the time we started having daughters with complexions only slightly lighter than my Shawnee skin. Boys, now, boys are much less trouble—some boys. We should have allowed Josh to join the military." The duke eyed his son's attire again.

"As I've said before, I have no heirs to spare! Besides, some of those uniforms are just as gaudy," the duchess replied sharply. Softening her voice again, she added, "And I still find every inch of your complexion alluring, my love."

She turned to the garden view again. "See how Joshua leans so solicitously over Kate. He has your height, your dark good looks. Her cheeks have turned rosy, and her eyes sparkle as she gazes up at him. Now that is love in bloom."

"Forgive me for saying so, beloved, but I believe they are quarreling."

~ * ~

"I'm only stating the facts, Kate. We've known each other since childhood, and I feel I must be candid. Compared to the ladies of London, you are a pleasant enough country sunflower, but you cannot compete with the golden orb itself. Your dowry is only fair to middling. You shouldn't set your sights too high when you come out this season."

Joshua Longleigh adjusted the complicated tie of his cravat, trying to loosen the knot a bit for more comfort. Kate's big brown eyes blazed up at him. He swore he could see little flashes of gold in them, like tiny lightning bolts.

"I hope you strangle on that thing. To think I have regarded you as my knight, my savior, ever since The Incident—and you say such things to me. Three years in London and all your chivalry is gone."

"I was not your savior. When your mother ordered you laced into that corset to correct your posture, the maid simply became overzealous and tied you too tightly. If you had stayed in the house, you would have been fine. But no, you and Pandora had to chase after me and Jason. You ran out of air and fainted face down in the gravel path. Of course, I cut you free with my penknife. As a mere lad of fifteen, I had no idea how to undo a lady's undergarment properly."

"And now I suppose you do!"

His cheeks heated, flaring as red as hers beneath his dark complexion. "This not a proper subject for a girl taking her first steps out of the nursery."

"To think my mama wanted us betrothed on the spot, though I was only twelve. I thank heaven the duchess put her off and suggested our affection should grow naturally as we were so young. I might have been stuck with you forever." She'd become so wroth with him, tears gathered in the corners of her eyes.

"Now don't cry. You aren't all that bad. Someone will want to marry you. We must be grateful to *my* mama for her good sense and her opposition to tight lacing. Didn't she convince yours that posture could be improved by walking around with a book placed on your head? Jason and I got a lot of amusement out of watching that."

Kate stamped her foot down hard. Whether by intent or not, her shoe landed on the tip of his highly polished and very pointed boot, increasing the agony of his already throbbing toes. A sturdy girl and curvaceous, she'd grown a fine bosom in the three years since he'd seen her. He enjoyed the bounce of her breasts when she struck, despite his pain, but Kate would in no way qualify as a sylph-like beauty. He suppressed a grimace.

"I am not crying! I am angry with myself for adoring you these past six years when there is too little to admire. Whoever would want a man so shallow, so ridiculously dressed? No wonder you have not passed the bar as yet. The barristers must regard you lightly."

"Not so! They are simply a murder of old crows that have yet to recognize my eloquence and sharp legal mind. As for whom I shall marry, I plan to win the affection of Camilla Sharpton, the Duke of Strictly's only daughter. She is a nonpareil, the brightest star in this year's firmament. Her golden curls shimmer. Her blue eyes are wide as the sky itself, and her form is that of the fairest nymphs. Her accomplishments are as numerous as the leaves on the trees. She is the greatest prize of the season."

Kate watched his eyes leave hers and gaze off at the ornate fountain of Triton decorating the gardens, as if the peerless Camilla stood in the midst of its spray and wore only a wet, diaphanous gown. Scowling, she demanded his attention again.

"You call that eloquence? I call it trite twaddle."

Joshua Longleigh sighed as if the bright bubble of his daydream had burst. "Well, Jason is the would-be poet in our family, though Papa despises his verses. My eloquence is more of the argumentative type, a great asset for a barrister."

"And you think this nonpareil would wed a second son? I doubt she'd look lower than the heir to another duke." Kate punctured his inflated self-opinion once more.

"My prospects are very good to inherit, considering how my brother, James, is always running off to foreign countries in search of antiquities. If the climate doesn't kill him, some savage will."

"How entirely callous of you."

"I simply repeat my mother's words, but Papa insists a man must live his own life as he sees fit. Evidently, that is fine for James, but I am not to be a soldier. With four sons, the Longleighs aren't likely to die out, and with four daughters between James' birth and mine, we are not close. He went off to Eton before I became aware of his existence."

"Very well, or I should say very ill, of you. Regardless, tell me, who is the male catch of the season?"

Joshua frowned and looked down that aristocratic nose he'd inherited from his maternal grandfather. "I suppose I would say Harold Brumley, Viscount Astin, the Duke of Martindale's heir. If I said myself, I suppose you would accuse me of conceit."

"Yes, I would. Describe Brumley for me."

"Oh, I don't know. He has yellow hair and curls, a rather willowy form for a man, I'd say. Tall, I suppose."

"Taller than you?"

"No, shorter by an inch or so and not nearly so wide in the shoulders. Physically, I am his superior. He ranks me only by accident of birth."

Kate rocked back on her heels and removed her foot from his toes. She had a cunning look on her face like a vixen about to snatch a goose to feed her young. "I propose a wager."

"Nonsense. Men do not wager with young ladies."

"Are you afraid you might lose?"

"Lose what?"

"Why, the greatest prize. I will bet you that I with my bumpkin charms can wring a proposal from Harold Brumley while Lady Camilla will turn you down flat."

Joshua blinked his brown eyes, far darker than hers, more like deep mysterious caverns set in the perpetual bronze of his face that revealed his Shawnee ancestry, he'd always thought. Perhaps the sunlight striking his garish waistcoat reflected into those eyes and caused him to squint at her more closely.

"Hmmm," he said. "You wouldn't do anything immoral to gain him? Use women's trickery?"

"Of course not. I shall use my intelligence to win his regard."

"Then you've lost the wager already."

"Are you calling me stupid?"

"No, I'm saying intelligence is the last thing a man notices about a woman—which shows exactly how naïve you are. If that is your only weapon, then I've won. What do you want to bet?"

"The true reward would be to marry as happily as the duke and duchess."

"Ah, yes, my parents. How their constant displays of affection have embarrassed their ten offspring, far, far too many children."

"I find your parents endearing, but I suppose you feel they should have stopped having babies with you."

"No, I'd miss my younger brother, Jason, but I'd place another wager they wish they had stopped before having Pandora."

Kate leaned forward, crushing his toes again. "Panny is my best friend in all the world."

"Even so, I'd suggest you not stand near her at Almack's. She will frighten off any men who approach you, and Astin will not so much as cross the room."

"You are horrid. I will wager half my middling dowry that I can bring Harold Brumley, Viscount Astin, to heel before the end of the season. And what will you give me if you fail to gain Lady Camilla as a wife?"

Caught at a disadvantage since he had no income other than the stipend his father granted, Joshua Longleigh hesitated. "Half my quarterly allowance."

"You do think I'm stupid. Two quarterly allowances in full."

"A man must have something to live on, Kate."

"If you gain Camilla, your money problems will be over. I hear the Duke of Strictly has settled forty-thousand pounds on his daughter."

"Yes, Mama has complained about that, but Papa says Strictly has only one daughter, while he has six. Of course, he should offer more to get someone to take Pandora off his hands."

"Again, you insult my friend, your sister. The bet is on, Joshua Longleigh. The bet is definitely on."

Two

"Stand aside, my dear. She's coming on like a ship under full sail." Not waiting for his wife to comply, the duke placed his large hands around her tiny waist and lifted her to safety as the terrace doors crashed open. His hands lingered.

Kate failed to notice. Her cheeks blazed, and her bonnet had fallen back by its ribbons as she'd dashed full of anger back to the Hall. Her good manners anchored her. Upon seeing her host, she dropped her curtsy. "Your Grace, thank you for allowing me to accompany Pandora to London. Mama sends her deepest thanks for this service, and deeply regrets she will miss this season."

The duke acknowledged her with a nod, but failed to release his wife from his grip. "No bother at all. Rather less than usual, with only two daughters and their belongings to cart around. We do pray for your mother's swift recovery from her illness."

The duchess gently removed her husband's hands from her waist. "Do not stand on ceremony, Kate. The duke has been Uncle Bear to you since early childhood, and I your Auntie Flora. You are cousin to our near neighbor,

Sir Guy, and how we have missed you romping in our gardens since you've grown up."

"I've missed coming here, too, but Mama insisted I be sent away to be finished. Sometimes, I feel as if they finished me off entirely. I was grateful to have the company of Pandora and Phemie at the female academy."

"Yes, well, I had to pay the head mistress double to take Panny back year after year, but never heard an ill report of you. Kate, you have grown into a fine young woman," the duke replied.

"Yes, she would make a wonderful addition to any family. I will see you are successfully launched into society along with Pandora. Of course, Phemie will not be out until next year, but she will benefit from being exposed to culture in London."

The duchess glanced over Kate's shoulder. Kate turned and smiled. She'd definitely gotten under his dandy skin. Josh stood chucking pathway gravel wrathfully at the statue of Triton and one of his buxom sea nymphs. His mother called out the open door, "Stop that at once, Joshua. You will clog the fountain," but the breeze carried her light voice away.

The duke put his fingers to his full lips and issued a blasting three syllable whistle. His son straightened immediately and looked toward the house. "Your mother says to cease throwing gravel at her statuary. You aren't a wee lad anymore."

Joshua acknowledged the order with a tip of his tall hat. He turned and strode away from the Hall, digging his black lacquer and gold walking stick into the ground as if he wanted to spear the life out of Mother Nature.

"Did you have a pleasant conversation with Josh, my dear?" the duchess inquired.

"As you suggested, the exercise did me good after the long carriage ride. I feel very exhilarated, but I never did find Pandora and Phemie, only Joshua."

"How silly of me to forget they chose to wait for you in their bed chamber. You shall have the twins' room right next to theirs. Your boxes have been taken up. Go along and refresh yourself. We will have some tea shortly. I am sure Joshua will be joining us."

The three of them watched the Longleigh's second son turn onto a side path and whack the heads off several early daffodils with his cane as he went.

~ * ~

Lady Pandora Longleigh sprawled on the huge canopied bed she shared with her sister. Often on very bitter nights, they curled together under the covers, the kitten and the wildcat as her father liked to say. Now Phemie sat primly on a side chair across from Kate.

"You will wrinkle your gown, Panny, and put Mama out of sorts."

"Oh, blast gowns and the London season. You do know our mother intends to marry you off to Joshua, Kate."

"And you know that has been my fondest desire since I was twelve. Now, I've finally grown up, and I find him—"

"Insufferable."

"Yes. What happened to the gallant lad who cut open my corset and put his lips to mine to breathe air into my lungs? I believe he must still exist under all that ridiculous affectation."

"Ha! Now he has only London air in his. Or should I say airs. Even Jason considers him a snob, and you know they are as close as Phemie and I."

Kate looked down at her folded hands. How she loved the eccentric Longleigh family and desired to become part of it, living far from her own straight-laced parents. That hope had fled in a single conversation.

"In fact, I won't be marrying Joshua. We've made a secret wager that he can win Camilla Sharpton, and I shall gain a proposal from Harold Brumley, Viscount Astin."

"Who in hell are they?"

"Panny, your language!" Phemie exclaimed.

"I thought I was among friends, not in the drawing room. But a wager, you say? Suddenly, I find my first season of more interest. Tell me more." Pandora slid off the bed and left behind a few hair pins. Several straight black locks cascaded down her shoulders.

"Evidently, Camilla and Harold are the greatest prizes of this season's marriage market. Your brother says my appearance and dowry are inadequate to attract a superior man."

"The nerve of him! Get up, get up!" Pandora drew Kate with her to stand before a full-length mirror.

"Look at us. We are splendid examples of English womanhood with rounded hips and bosoms. Our teeth are good, our complexions unspotted—

though I would trade for your rosy cheeks and milkmaid's skin. I am so dusky, thanks to Papa. Your hair is thick, waving, and a lovely rich brown, an exact match for your eyes, which do have a sparkle to them. I think I would trade your locks for mine, too."

"Nonsense, Panny. Your hair is as black, straight, and shining as a bolt of the finest silk. It becomes the tone of your skin, the dark of your eyes. I believe this year's crop of suitors will find you very exotic." Kate slid a finger down Pandora's loose strands.

"Exotic, perhaps, but they will run straight to dance with the skinny waifs so malnourished and undeveloped they die giving birth on the first try. Next year, those widowers will be back seeking exactly the same kind of bride. Tell me, are women nothing more than pleasing ornaments and brood mares? No! We have intellects and talents the same as men, but not their rights."

"She's been reading Mary Wollstonecraft again," Phemie explained. "*A Vindication of the Rights of Women,* one of Mama's favorite works."

"I'm not familiar with it," Kate confessed.

"With a mother who trussed you up in a corset at twelve, I would think not. I, thank heaven, was born into an enlightened family. Papa says I need not accept any half-wit lords or drooling old nobles or self-aggrandizing dandies like Joshua. I may remain single, if I wish."

"But Mama says no matter what our intelligence, we should never cease being ladies," Phemie added. "We should find love within marriage like her and Papa."

"Says the girl who begged extra tutoring in Latin and Euclid. What good will that stuff do when you are squeezing out baby after baby? Don't be deceived by her petite figure; Phemie is like Mama in every way but her coloring. I'll wager she'll give birth to a dozen."

"With the man I love, who will allow me my Latin and Euclid. Besides, I am not entirely like Mama. Papa says Panny inherited all her fierceness while I am—"

"His Little Dove. Sickening. If any man called me that, I would skewer him with my stiletto."

Kate laughed, all her misery over Joshua dispersed. The Longleigh girls always raised her spirits. "If you had a stiletto."

"But we do. Show her, Panny."

Pandora raised her skirt and petticoat to show the weapon strapped to her leg. "Papa says we must not go unarmed to London. Should some cad attempt to have his way with us, we are to stick him between the ribs. He showed us how."

"Getting to the weapon is a problem to be solved, however. Mama would not allow us any open seams."

"Listen to the innocent. Our skirts would be thrown up by our attackers."

Kate held in her merriment. How freely the duke's daughters spoke. She had to thank them for all manner of forbidden knowledge. They read freely and received very candid advice from the duchess, though recently her own stiff mother had surprised her with a salty comment. She shared it with Phemie and Pandora.

"My mama said I should simply knee them in the ballocks. You see, for a country girl, I am prepared for London, but I shan't need a knife or a knee to deal with Harold Brumley."

Phemie's round black eyes, as curious as a robin's, widened. "You don't mean to let him seduce you in order to win the bet?"

"No, as I told Joshua, I plan to use my wits to wring an offer from Viscount Astin."

"Marvelous. Phemie and I shall help you win your wager with Josh in any way we can," Pandora said, her dark eyes alight with the challenge. A servant scratched at the door.

"Enter."

The timid maid, a girl near their own age, curtsied and delivered her message. "The duchess requests your presence for tea in the drawing room." She hesitated. "Immediately." She bobbed again and scurried off.

"I do believe I frighten her." Pandora checked herself in the mirror again. She smoothed the wrinkles in her high-waisted muslin gown sprigged all over with a delicate pattern of ferns and tucked in the scarf across her bosom to cover her breasts. "Phemie, tie my sash. Kate, stick some pins in my hair. The two of you are perfectly presentable. And off we go."

The three fine specimens of English womanhood left the bed chamber, linked arms, and descended the wide staircase.

~ * ~

Joshua barely glanced their way as they entered the drawing room. Careful not to get soot on his tight buff trousers, he stood by the fireplace and balanced his cup on the mantle.

"He probably cannot sit down," his wretched sister, Pandora, said loudly enough for him to hear. The truth stung. He suffered to be fashionable, to be different from his old-fashioned father, to show the old man he had a mind of his own, even if he was kept from the war in case James expired in foreign parts.

Panny had set the young ladies off into gales of giggles. They filled a settee, fluffing out their white skirts as they perched. His sisters were attractive, he supposed, all dark, flashing eyes and shining black hair. Panny looked like the unkempt hoyden as usual, and Phemie far more demure than he knew her to be. Kate sat between them, every bit their equal, but rosy and wholesome.

The smoky pall of London would soon pale those cheeks, and the grinding round of balls and fetes would trim her figure to a more popular size. In a way, he hated to see that happen. He'd tried to warn her London would not suit her, nor she London. Why did she have to change everything by coming out? Why couldn't Kate simply stay in the country and marry some good-natured fellow like her cousin, Sir Guy, who sought a bride immediately upon reaching his majority. True, he and Guy Appleton had attained the same age, but if he could not have Camilla, he would wait until he grew as old as James to wed.

The duchess prepared tea for the three young ladies, knowing them so well she had no need to ask their preferences. The duke thrust out his cup for a refill, and she larded the beverage with cream and sugar to his liking. She added only hot water and lemon to her own brew.

Josh cleared his throat, drawing attention back to himself. "Ahem, as I was saying before my sisters arrived in their own good time, I don't see why you summoned me to Bellevue to escort the ladies when I take my law studies seriously and Jason merely dawdles and writes sonnets to tavern wenches and women as old as Mama."

"Older women may have charm and experience to offer." The duke patted his wife's knee fondly. "And tavern maids youth—and experience."

"Young ladies present," his wife rebuked.

"Ah, yes. The point is, no Longleigh male would ever deny a lady the safety of his escort."

How he tired of hearing what Longleigh men did and did not do. "You have footmen aplenty for protection on the road."

"They are not skilled with weapons."

"Then why did you not summon Jason as well for extra protection?"

"Two Longleighs can take on four ordinary men and are quite enough for an escort."

"I still don't see why Jason got off from this duty and not me."

"Because your mama requested *you*," his father roared. "Enough said."

Josh took refuge from his father's temper by taking a sip of tea seasoned only with lemon and found himself wishing for sugar. Silence settled on the tea party like a cozy over the pot. Kate Morely did her social duty and refreshed the conversation.

"Tell me, Auntie Flora, what do you know of Harold Brumley?"

"Viscount Astin, Martindale's heir? Why do you ask?"

Kate leaned forward in her eagerness to learn of Astin and showed far too much bosom, in Joshua's opinion. Camilla never bent over in such a way. She remained properly erect no matter what the situation.

"I hear he is the most sought-after match of the season. Tell me of him. What are his likes and dislikes?"

"Some call him an Adonis, very fair, handsome features, graceful figure, though I prefer less grace and more substance in a man." The duchess touched her husband's arm. "My sons, Joshua for example, have more manly attributes and are taller. Outside of himself, I'd say Astin's only great interest is snuff."

"Snuff? Powdered tobacco?"

"Yes, the gossips say he has a magnificent snuff box for every hour of the day and every costume he wears. He spends a fortune on various kinds of tobacco, three pounds for a pound, to suit his whims, Brazil or Macouba, or scented with attar of roses. Blends his own mixtures, as well. A filthy habit, no matter how fashionable. I am grateful the duke takes only an occasional pipe."

"But haven't I seen an entire curio cabinet filled with snuff boxes here at the Hall?"

"Those wishing to impress the duke make gifts of them. He merely puts them on display."

The urge to interrupt overtook Joshua. He'd heard quite enough of Harold Brumley. "Astin has yet to learn to appreciate a fine cigar taken out of doors. Trent Heaton brought back a supply from the Spanish Peninsula last time he came home on leave to visit his ailing mother." He slipped a slim leather case from his gaudy, striped waistcoat. "Papa, if you would care to give them a try, let us retreat to the terrace and leave the ladies to their conversation. I believe you will find these pleasing."

"Splendid idea, boy. Ladies, please excuse us."

The gentlemen left, intent on their cigars. Kate continued to probe for information regarding Harold, but got little more as the duchess seemed determined to point out at every turn that Joshua was the better man, despite becoming dandified.

"He will return to normal once he settles down with a good and sensible woman and starts his nursery. We did teach him that people matter more than fine dress. Yes, he will come around. Do not be discouraged."

"Why, I have nothing to be discouraged about. I embark on my first season with optimism and in hope of a fine match. I should love to see the snuff box collection close up."

"Certainly, though that is hardly much entertainment for a young lady. Some of them are quite risqué, I warn you."

All the women rose and sought out the gilded curio cabinet sitting on gracefully curved legs. Though she had to stand on her tiptoes to do so, the duchess took a key cleverly hidden inside its finial and turned it in the lock.

"Now here's a pretty one with the nymph, Daphne, being turned into a laurel tree." She handed it around.

"I wish you had named me Daphne," Phemie complained.

"Euphemia was a saint who tamed lions, not some helpless female who had to be saved from Apollo by Mother Earth. This one is rimmed with small diamonds."

Pandora reached into the cabinet and made a selection. A painting of a single, innocent white feather ornamented the enameled lid. She snapped the golden catch.

"Oh, this one portrays the swan having his way with Leda, which led to the birth of Pollux and Helen of Troy. Do you think that is possible, swans and women?"

She passed it to Kate and Phemie and watched their eyes widen. "Seems so," said Kate.

The duchess snatched the box and replaced it in the cabinet. Phemie, being short, took a box from the far corner of the lowest shelf. The face of a beautiful woman with golden curls wreathed in flowers smiled up at her. Beneath the portrait, the name Flora stood out in golden script.

"Not that one!" the duchess squeaked, but Phemie danced away as she sprung the lock. "Why Mama, you are entirely naked."

"That is not me, but a representation of the goddess Flora. My nether limbs have never been so heavy."

"Would a goddess have a tattoo of a butterfly on her hip? A strange portrayal," Phemie queried as her mother pressed the lid shut and put the box back in its place.

"Here are some lovely cherubs and sweet birds to view."

At the opening of the lid, the box emitted a chirp. The other, the sound of harp strings.

"How cunning! May I have one to take apart?" Phemie asked.

"Certainly not. They are quite valuable."

"May I borrow a few to take to London? Not the bejeweled ones, of course. I have a new acquaintance who would be charmed by their music, I'm sure. I will take good care of them," Kate promised.

"You have always been a responsible girl, unlike my own. Take your pick of the more modest ones."

"Oh, the birds and the cherubs will do quite well. Thank you, Auntie Flora."

"Now, young ladies, you must find your own amusements. I have copious details to attend to before our departure for London tomorrow." The duchess took her leave of them.

Pandora leaned close to Kate's ear. "I divine your plan. You will lure Astin by feigning an interest in his passion."

"Exactly," said Kate.

Three

Joshua Longleigh, burdened by packages, stood fuming before Madame Castille's Chapeaux Boutique Extraordinaire on Bond Street. As if the journey back to London had not consumed enough of his time, now he had been pressed into service as an escort for the ladies' first shopping spree. His mother had servants enough to do this duty, and he saw through her every mention of how charming Kate looked this afternoon in her bonnet of deep rose velvet trimmed on the inside with lace. If the hat was so becoming, why did she need another?—or his mother or his sisters, who now seemed determined to try on every item in the store.

Bad enough he'd neglected his law studies while riding beside the coach that bore the family to London for the season. Followed by an older carriage brimming with indispensable servants, a wagon filled with baggage, and several stable hands mounted on the extra riding horses, their procession moved at the pace of a funeral cortege. Their party took over entire inns and emptied out the kitchens as the Longleighs crept toward the city. Somehow, he always had to hand Kate down from the conveyance or help her up into it again. Why ever did they have footmen clinging to the coach if he was to do their job? Because his mother wanted them to touch, that was why, her way of trying to forward a match he refused to be forced into accepting. Besides, Kate, a quite healthy girl, really needed no assistance at all.

What rankled even more—his father and Jason had absconded to Gentleman Jackson's boxing saloon down the street, leaving him to the scant mercies of women shopping. He stood so near the Prince Regent's own tailor, Mr. Weston, he could practically feel luxurious fabrics passing between his fingers. Enough of this manipulation! Joshua entered the hat shop and reached up one long arm to keep the bell above the door from ringing. He beckoned to an apprentice of Madame Castille, who attended his mother personally and dumped the packages into her arms. Indicating the bundles belonged to the Duchess of Bellevue, he managed his escape to the tailor's shop for a few moments of freedom.

As he fingered a rich brown superfine wool with a yellow fleck that reminded him of Kate's eyes, he chanced to glance out the tailor's window and saw a rose-colored bonnet bob past. He expected to see his sisters pass, too, in pursuit of him, but they did not, nor his mother. Kate was up to some ruse or other. She'd fooled him many times at childhood games. Thrusting the cloth at the clerk, he ordered, "Have it made up into a jacket of the latest style. You have my measurements and the direction for delivery."

He reached the door just in time to see Kate's nicely rounded rear enter the dim interior of a tiny tobacconist's shop impressively ornamented by a half-naked wooden Indian maiden holding sheaves of the dried leaves in her arms like a beloved baby. The window of the store sat small and high, perhaps to keep sunlight from injuring the products sold within. He could go inside and catch her in the act of whatever she planned, or lurk by the door and pry the information out of her afterward. The second idea of sparring with Kate seemed so much more appealing. He loitered, waiting for her to emerge.

~ * ~

Kate had never been in a tobacconist's shop, nor had many women. Her mother loathed any form of tobacco and did not permit the substance in her house. What she knew of snuff was as little as the grains of the fine, brown powder. Thankful she remained the only customer, indeed, the only person in the place as she browsed among the tins and the pipe racks hardly knowing where to begin. A wonderful aroma that bespoke of foreign lands where the sun cured the leaf in lofty barns filled the place. She lifted the lid of a Chinese jar and the odor of violets drifted out.

"Excellent choice, my dear young lady," a voice piped up from behind the counter.

A dwarf tidily dressed in a tailcoat cut to his size, climbed up onto a long-legged chair. Had he been there all the time and had she rudely overlooked him? If so, he took no offense.

"Barnabas Small at your service. Like myself, my shop is also small. However, I assure you since I sell only the best, not a great deal of room is needed. How may I serve you?"

"I am seeking a small amount of snuff—as a gift."

"For a gentleman or a lady?"

"Some for both."

"You cannot go wrong with the variety before you greatly favored by Queen Charlotte herself. The more elegant gentlemen do like a good Macouba if you want a scented brand, or the Brazil or Spanish Bran if not." He quoted the cost for each.

"So dear. An ounce each of the violet-scented and the Macouba, I suppose."

She could not linger making up her mind or the duchess would miss her. Pandora and Phemie could be very inventive, but Lady Flora was not easily fooled for long. Nervously, she waited as the dwarf measured out her order and placed the snuff into two tiny sacks. He tried to sell her some rather inferior snuffboxes as well, but she declined, keeping an eye on the small window lest the duchess spy her out. No, the duchess was not tall enough to peer inside, but she recognized the top of a lofty gray hat last seen on Joshua Longleigh. Cocked at a rakish angle, he wore it very well. Found out so soon! What to do? If he revealed her purchase to his mother, she would surely take the snuff away and scold Kate for wandering Bond Street alone.

"Have you any cigars?" she asked the proprietor urgently.

"Not very fashionable as yet, but they might be the coming thing. Yes, I have box or two in from Spain," he admitted.

"I need only two, not an entire box." Kate doled out her coins. At least they were cheaper than the Macouba. She plunged the sacks of snuff deep into her reticule, but accepted the duo of cigars wrapped in a packet of brown paper. She kept them in her hand as she emerged blinking into the sunlight and bustle of Bond Street again.

"My, my, I wonder what my mother would say if I told her that her protégée frequented tobacconists' shops," Jason drawled. "Back to the country with you, I'd suppose, my wager won for me."

Kate cocked her head at him. "To think I meant to make you a gift of these for your patience with us today, and you would send me into exile." She held out the packet of cigars and enjoyed the flummoxed look upon his face.

"Ah, very thoughtful of you." He broke open the paper and sniffed the contents. "A very good choice. Thank you."

Smiling impishly, she asked, "Would you be so kind as to escort me back to the hat shop? I know I should not have come alone, but I did so want to surprise you."

"That you did."

They had only a short way to walk, but the crowds were such Kate was jostled a few times and glad of his company. The bell over the door of the hat shop tinkled as if laughing when they entered. The duchess, her face completely obscured with the heavy veils of a large chapeau, turned to see them enter.

"Kate? I thought you had gone to the necessary." Lady Flora cleared her face of the veils. "And Joshua, I never thought you would set foot in a ladies' establishment." Still, she appeared very pleased to see them together and rattled on. "I was showing the girls the sort of hat I wore in my youth to save my complexion. We had to go in search of one in the back room. What fun their father made of my hats, one of my favorite stories."

"Yes, we do enjoy hearing it again and again, Mama," Pandora said with minimal sarcasm in her voice.

"We do," insisted Phemie. "But you must take the magnificent purple turban and the packet of gold-dipped plumes."

"Purple, do you really think so?"

"Only you could bring it off with flare, Mama," Phemie added.

"I will take it then. Joshua, you have been so very patient."

"That is why we stepped away for a moment after I returned from out back. I wanted to reward him with a pair of his favorite cigars." There, would he squeal that she had gone alone?

"Smelly things, such clouds of smoke. I hope the duke will not take to them."

"I would never smoke them in your house, Mama. Now, can I treat you all to an ice at Gunter's?" Joshua offered graciously.

Evidently, the wager would continue.

Four

With his brother at his side, Joshua Longleigh lounged against a wall at Almack's, that stuffy but well-lit hall glittering with gaslight and mirrors and the newest debutants trotted out for the marriage market. He covered a yawn with a gloved hand and raised his quizzing glass to peer at the perfection of Lady Camilla who stood across the room.

"Pinched Papa's old quizzing glass, have you?" Jason Longleigh chided.

"He won't miss it. Papa loathes these affairs. That is why you and I have been pressed into service as escorts. There goes Mama now, scurrying to pay her respects to the patronesses, and leading Kate and Pandora like fillies on a lead up for auction. How I hate being forced into knee breeches again simply to satisfy the rules of this antique institution."

The brothers observed the flurry of courtesies and bobbing plumes among the duchesses and princesses who held the keys to Almack's. Kate and Pandora dropped deep curtsies as his mother presented them.

"At least you accompanied Kate. I had my sister on my arm. We are in for an evening of country dances and weak refreshments, I fear."

"I wouldn't have come at all except for the hope that Lady Camilla will grant me a dance."

"Defy Mama? I would have liked to see that."

"She insists on pairing me off with Kate simply because of The Incident. I have my own mind when it comes to the perfect wife."

"Ah, yes, The Incident, one of the highlights of my youth. Even at twelve, Kate had a promising bosom, and that corset pushed it even higher. When you cut the strings, I thought her little apples would tumble right out. To my disappointment, they did not, but you were quick enough to cover her lips with yours. Your first kiss, if I am correct."

Jason Longleigh paused to offer a glittering smile to one of the older women, Lady Tartte, who fanned herself languidly across from them. With his lean face, high cheekbones, large and lustrous dark eyes, and a sweep of straight, black hair covering his collar, he looked the poet he professed to be. His neckcloth remained without starch and loosely tied in a floppy bow, no matter what the current fashion.

"Stop baiting me. That was not a kiss, and I am sorry Kate took it amiss and considered us practically betrothed. I have set her straight. She is free to find another. And you, you should find another valet."

"I have better things to spend my allowance on."

"Tavern maids and trinkets for widows who favor you."

"I can have them for a poem. However, I need money to publish my verse since Papa will not foot the bill. Remember, I'm the one who lost my virginity at fourteen, while Kate remained the only female you touched for three more years. Oh no, here comes Appleton. Sir Guy, how goes your search for a bride?"

Pleasant, round-faced and rosy-cheeked, Sir Guy shook his head. "No success yet. This bunch would consider a hereditary knighthood a step down."

"Have you given your cousin Kate any thought?" Joshua inquired.

"I have, but you know when we played Indians at Bellevue Hall and tried to capture the girls, I always ended up tied to the stake, not Kate. She is far too clever for me. I would bore her to death. No, no, I need a sweet, good-natured girl, not too demanding or intellectual."

"There's always Pandora," Jason jested.

"I believe I said not too demanding or intellectual. Sweet, good-natured, you know, like Phemie, but not so interested in science and learning."

"Why, I should call you out for insulting my sisters!" Jason Longleigh exclaimed just to see Appleton blanch.

"I meant no insult. Pandora is quite beautiful and Phemie very smart... both far, far above me in every way. Too far above," Appleton dithered until Jason clapped him on the back to show he jested.

The musicians began to tune their instruments for the first dance of the evening. Amid their squeaks and squawks, the duchess drifted gracefully across the dance floor with more purpose than any audience would assume to accost the young men and explain their roles for the evening.

"Now, Joshua, you ask Kate for the first dance before the music starts. Sir Guy, lead Pandora out. And Jason, for heaven's sake, dance with someone near your own age."

Knowing she would accept no other answer, they replied, "Yes, Mama," except for Appleton who nodded in compliance.

"Very well, then. I must not let the girls stand too long unattended. Ah, but I see Countess Langley. Hasn't she a son born the same year as Jason? I must see if he attends and introduce him to Pandora—and Kate, naturally." Off she went about to capture another partner for her protégées.

~ * ~

Briefly left alone, Kate and Pandora perused the crowd. "Do you see anyone matching Astin's description?" Kate asked.

"There, holding court in the corner. Simply follow the hopeful stares of all the young women in the chamber, and you will find him."

Kate took in the sight of Harold Brumley. Handsome? Yes, very. His golden hair waved back from a high, white forehead, and he wore his side whiskers long but close shaven, a fair frame for his face. He possessed the requisite long, straight nose and a jutting chin with a cleft deep enough to hold a small coin. His eyes—an azure so blue even the artificial lighting did not dull them.

As she watched, he withdrew a snuffbox from his painted silk waistcoat and flicked it open with a one-handed twist of his wrist. He pinched up a portion of tobacco and inhaled it into his nostrils. The box closed, the handkerchief prominently embroidered with the family coat of arms came out, and the sneeze erupted into the cloth. The young men gathered around him attempted to achieve the same effect with equal grace. Most failed.

Kate looked around at the other girls all dressed in maidenly white and waiting for a partner to appear for the first dance. Every one of them wanted that man to be Viscount Astin.

"Panny, your brother is right. In no way do I stand out from the others. Astin won't notice me, not when Camilla Sharpton stands right there with her bosom friends."

"He's not all that fine. I suspect without an excellent tailor, Astin would appear rather stringy. Padding has added to his shoulders and plumped out his calves. Taking after Papa, my brothers have no need of that. As for Lady Camilla, she is gorgeous, but I suspect she chooses less attractive companions to stand among in order to show off her beauty. The one on her left is my estranged cousin, Matilda Everton, poor creature."

"How can anyone be estranged from their cousin?

"Long family story to be told some other time. Briefly, my Uncle Roderick held Mama for ransom after she had married Papa. We do not speak to or acknowledge the Evertons. Mama says they are all vipers and penniless, too, but just look at her. Hard not to have pity."

If Kate had been asked to choose one woman from the throng that she outshone, she could not go wrong in picking Matilda Everton. She started out well enough with dark blonde hair and pale, but somewhat protuberant blue eyes. Sometime during her life, her nose had acquired a prominent bump. The masses of long curls bunched and hanging alongside her face could not disguise a receding chin, nor could a thick coating of powder expunge a poor complexion. She had a spare figure and rather large feet sticking too far out from her skirts. The one thing she did not lack was a rigid posture and a sense of her worth in the marriage mart as the daughter of an earl, impoverished, but still sitting on a high rung of the social ladder. She looked down that bumpy nose at many a potential partner.

"I wish I had her imperious manner."

"No getting cold feet now, Kate. Didn't Phemie and I distract Mama with finding that old, veiled hat while you slipped out to buy the snuff at the tobacconist? You did bring it with you?"

"Yes, some of the violet-scented Queen Charlotte favors and a stronger blend that might appeal to Astin. Who is Camilla's other friend?"

"Tomasina Murray, the Earl of Harcourt's second daughter."

"She's very pretty with that dark hair and such striking violet eyes. She is a bit plump, but in an attractive way."

"Tomasina is a brainless cow, or she wouldn't be standing with a woman who puts her looks in the shade. She'd do for your cousin Guy if she didn't think so much of herself to stoop to a mere knight."

The band leader announced the first dance. The gentlemen scattered to find their partners. Viscount Astin strode by them, leaving a wake of disappointed female faces behind. He headed directly toward Lady Camilla only to be cut off by Joshua Longleigh, who bumped him aside with a casual poke of an elbow. Astin ended up facing Matilda Everton. He did have the good manners to pretend he desired her company on the dance floor, though he secured the next with Camilla before leading out her friend. Grinning triumphantly, Joshua led his prize to the formation. Kate despaired—of winning her bet. That was all. She must put on a good face and smile as others passed her by.

Sir Guy popped up before them. "Lady Pandora, may I have the pleasure of this dance?"

Standing several inches taller than her childhood friend, Pandora looked at the top of his head and gave a negligent shrug. "I suppose. If I am here, I might as well dance. Come, Appleton, let's get it over with."

Kate remained alone. She caught a glimpse of herself in an opposing mirror. No great beauty, no large dowry, gentry but not nobility. If it weren't for the duchess's patronage, she would have no chance of an excellent marriage at all. A darkly handsome man bowed before her.

"Oh, it's you, Jason. Thank you for rescuing me from the wall."

"I am as well-known for my gallantry as Joshua is for his pig-headedness. Shall we dance?"

She needn't have worried about gaining other partners after Jason fulfilled his obligation and vanished with one of the chaperones. The duchess diverted a constant stream of young men their way, introducing them if necessary. Sir Guy stayed near and proved to be a reliable fetcher of orange-flavored orgeat and fruity ratafia when she and Panny needed liquid refreshment after the rigor of several country dances. He seemed intimidated by many of the unfamiliar ladies and hung about his childhood playmates, very much out of his element. Joshua strolled by and negligently signed for Kate's last dance, "Since we shall be riding home in the same carriage."

Known to be the Duke of Bellevue's generously dowered daughter, Pandora's card filled rapidly. Men were drawn by her flashing dark eyes and a total indifference that appealed to their competitive nature. They led her out proudly and returned with soured expressions.

"Have you offended them, Panny?" Kate asked.

"What do I care? They bore me. All their talk is of the weather or a favorite horse or some tidbit of gossip concerning people I don't know and couldn't care less about. Bring up the horrors of slavery, equity for women, or the Peninsular War, and they can't wait to be rid of me. Who's next on your card?"

"Astin." She swallowed hard. "My hands are so clammy, I'm grateful to be wearing gloves. Your mother pushed him my way some time ago, and he asked for a dance very graciously."

"As if he had any other choice with Mama standing directly behind him. Here he comes. The game begins."

Astin made his bow, never looking directly at her with his striking cornflower blue eyes. "Miss Marley," he said.

"Morely, Katherine Morely, Sir Guy Appleton's cousin."

"Yes, of course. Do pardon me. Shall we get in line?"

He managed to squeeze in next to Joshua having his second dance with Lady Camilla. During the entire sequence of steps, Astin's eyes drifted toward the stunning nonpareil. She returned a glowing smile when Josh turned his head for a moment. As for the rest of the ordeal, he had no conversation, and Kate found all words stuck dry in her throat. The music ended, and he escorted her back to her friends.

"Miss Marley. A pleasure."

"Snuff!" she blurted far too loudly. Several matronly heads turned.

"Yes, indeed. I feel the need of a pinch to restore my energies. If you will excuse me."

Within seconds, her escort was off in the corner with his cronies, pinching, sniffing, and sneezing. She hadn't managed to get hers out of the tiny bag hanging from her wrist. Kate noticed the lid of his box bore the same scene in miniature as his waistcoat. The duchess had spoken the truth. Snuff was Harold Brumley's love and delight.

"Well, I botched that thoroughly. Astin followed Camilla with his eyes and did not even recall my name at the end of the dance," she told Pandora.

"Men are a bother. I don't see why you want one."

"Fine for you to say. You can remain at Bellevue Hall all your days with your status undiminished while I must sit across from my sister-in-law at dinner and watch my brother's family grow if I do not marry. Besides, I don't want Astin. I only want his proposal to show Joshua I am not such shabby goods—though I do feel that way at the moment."

"We must devise a way to make you stand out from the herd. I've got it! Mama's gold tissue opera cloak and chaplet of acanthus leaves. We will modify the cloak to drape your gown and crown you with the gilded leaves. Rather, you and Phemie will rework the cloak. My sewing always ends in tears and tangles. Once we are done, you will appear as a goddess from Mt. Olympus."

"What will your mother say about that? Aren't all the debs at Almack's to be dressed in virginal white?"

"Mama will not know until the last minute."

Joshua approached, smug smile in place, to claim the last dance before they all departed wearily for the Bellevue townhouse. They passed Lady Camilla and her final partner as they formed up. She puckered her perfect, pink lips into a small moue cast in Joshua's direction.

"Did you see, Kate? Camilla has blown me a kiss."

"She gave Astin a languorous smile when she danced with you."

"You are simply jealous."

"Of a man who considers me second-rate or of a woman who flirts with one man while dancing with another?"

"I never said you were second-rate, simply not up to London standards. As for the other, I do not believe it of her."

"Still, I had two dances to your one," he remarked as he took Kate under a bridge of raised arms. "I believe this evening's victory is mine."

She glared at him. "What did that American pirate, John Paul Jones say? I have not yet begun to fight. Next week, I shall sink your ship."

Five

Pandora Longleigh settled the chaplet of gilded acanthus leaves into Kate's coiffure and pinned it into place since she had banned her maid from the chamber. "There, stunning. Let's try on the drape you and Phemie have contrived."

The gold tissue of the former opera cloak drifted like gossamer over one shoulder where Phemie quickly tied the strings into a neat bow. The fabric slid over one breast and pooled at her waist where Phemie had made a gather and attached tapes to secure the overlay.

"Oh, I wish I could be there to see eyes turn when you enter Almack's! You look like a royal princess, Kate. The chaplet and cloth bring out the gold flecks in your eyes," Pandora's little sister exclaimed.

"She can't enter that way, silly goose. Mama will know we've pinched her cloak and won't allow Kate to wear gold anyway. I had a time convincing her to loan the chaplet. She insists young maidens should wear only flowers and ribbons and perhaps a single plume in their hair. When I said Joshua needs to be shown that thick, lustrous brunette locks can be as alluring as blonde, she finally agreed. Mama is still determined to match you with our brother."

Kate shook her head. "No, clearly his heart is set on Camilla Sharpton."

"His conceit, you mean. He believes himself so handsome and well-connected that Camilla will overlook his being a second son. Ha! We knew her kind at the academy, so high in the instep she could bridge the Thames."

The white plume in Pandora's hair quivered against her black strands as she nodded emphatically. "Now take it off and raise your skirt. We will secure it underneath until we get into Almack's then plead the need to use the ladies retiring room and dress you there while Mama seeks out her friends and lines up our dance partners."

The timid maid who had been sent off earlier scratched and opened the door a tiny crack. "The duchess says the carriage awaits and so does she."

They gathered their wraps and with Phemie trailing longingly behind, went to join the duchess and Joshua. Clamping a big hand on his youngest daughter's shoulder, the duke waited to see them off.

"Never were there fairer maidens," he claimed good-naturedly. "Phemie and I shall enjoy a few games of chess while you dance the night away with all your beaux. Perhaps I will win once or twice."

Pandora wrinkled her nose at his mention of beaux. Immediately, her mama said, "Do not screw up your face lest it stay that way. I know your opinion of balls and fetes, and I must say you have been on your best behavior this week, enduring them very well. Not to mention your application to improving your sewing so recently. Hmmm, suspiciously good behavior."

Both the Longleigh daughters gazed at their mother with the innocence of new-born lambs. Kate knew her color to be high. Her lips, very lightly rouged, trembled with nerves.

"Because of that, I have arranged for us to attend a meeting of the Abolition Society, your especial interest, Panny. Phemie may come along as well."

Pandora's eyes lit as they never did for any man. While Kate appreciated her friend's devotion to worthy causes, she had her own problems to solve. All week long, she had practiced opening the snuff boxes with flair, withdrawing her hankie from her sleeve, and sneezing delicately while Phemie sewed and Pandora read aloud harrowing accounts of escapes from slavery. Her wrists ached from her effort. What a wonder the duchess didn't think a whole flock of birds had invaded her house with the many tweets the box emitted, but she frequently visited old friends who had no eligible sons, and so the girls were not made to go along.

With that announcement made, Joshua handed the ladies into the carriage. Kate went last, and he noted her tremor. "Nerves, Kate? You do look well this evening. The chaplet becomes you."

Kate raised her chin. "The chaplet of victory. Tonight I shall have two dances from Astin, and he will remember my name. As for you, I admire the audacity of a plum jacket worn with a green waistcoat for eveningwear. You will stand out from the crowd—as will I."

"Ah, but Lady Camilla already knows my name and most likely repeats it in her dreams."

"I do not like her for you, Joshua. For all her simpering, Camilla Sharpton has a slyness about her," the duchess said as she settled herself.

"I don't see it. Lady Camilla is the most gently bred young lady of the season, a nonpareil, perfection itself."

"Of course you don't see it, son. Men are so frequently taken in by beauty. That is why there are so many unhappy marriages. Now, your father and I based our union on courage and trust."

"But you were also very beautiful and still are, Mama." Josh smiled at making his mother flush. "Still, you must concede I am old enough to make up my own mind."

"As you know, I never concede."

~ * ~

The distance to Almack's was not great, and the jam of carriages did not occur until they nearly reached the entry. One by one, the vehicles released the current crop of debs and their keepers, Kate, Pandora, and the duchess among them.

They made their obeisances to the patronesses of the ballroom. Directly afterward, Pandora claimed a need to make use of the retiring room set aside for the ladies and drew Kate along with her. Vacant so early in the evening with no dresses to repair or cool, scented cloths needed to refresh over-heated faces, they slipped behind the Chinese screen where immaculate chamber pots sat in a row, and arranged Kate's golden drape. Rewarding the female attendants who kept the space spotless with a coin for their silence, Pandora went out to scout. She reported back within minutes.

"Mama is still engaged with the patronesses. Astin has arrived and stands with his coterie in the same corner as last week. Enter by the door nearest to the orchestra and pass by him."

"Won't you walk with me, Panny?"

"No, all eyes must turn to you and only you. Be assured, you do look splendid. Even Joshua said so."

"I know this was my plan to attract Harold Brumley, but—"

"No buts. Get on with it."

Kate raised her head and drew her shoulders back to display her more than adequate bosom. She put on her strut past the musicians preparing to play and Astin stoking himself with a snuff so strong she could scent it as she passed. As his sneeze blasted into his handkerchief, she turned slightly his way and put her back to the many chaperones. Did she hear a censorious exclamation saying, "Who is that girl in gold?"

No time to waste. She withdrew the snuff box from her tiny bag and flipped the lid. The tweet drew Astin's attention as he wiped his nose. Kate quickly raised a pinch of the cloying, violet-scented stuff to her nostrils and pretended to inhale. She snapped the case, withdrew a lacy hankie from her sleeve, and emitted a dainty sneeze. Secreting the pinch as she gently dabbed her small nose, she returned the cloth to its place and the snuff box to her bag. When she looked up, Astin stood at her elbow as if his sneeze had blown him there.

"I've never known a young lady to take snuff, Miss—ah—ah..."

She thought he might sneeze again and stepped back a bit before replying. "Katherine Morely. We were introduced by the Duchess of Bellevue at last week's gathering."

"I recall. May I have the honor of the first dance?"

"I would be delighted." Kate noted Joshua had already claimed Lady Camilla, but Astin did not appear to notice. Appleton had taken on Pandora again.

"My grandmamma takes snuff, but the habit has fallen out of favor with younger women. A pity as they do not know what they miss. Snuff clears the mind and opens the sinuses, quite healthy for a person."

"Oh, I agree. Fortunately, my entire family indulges," Kate lied, thinking of how her mother, who did not allow any form of tobacco in her house, would shudder.

"Very enlightened. And your people are...?"

"The Morelys of Greenway Grange, but I am here thanks to the patronage of the duchess. My mama is ill, and so her dear friend has brought me out."

"So sorry to hear that. But tell me, what snuff do you favor?"

She was surprised he couldn't smell it half a room away. "Queen Charlotte's favorite, though I have another with me as well."

"We must compare when the music ends—if you have no other obligations."

"None yet. I have only just arrived."

"How fortunate for me."

When the dance finished, Astin led her back to his group. They circled round her and begged to see the tweeting box. She demonstrated for them, then drew the cherub box and released the sound of a harp string plucked. Since it held a more manly variety, she offered it round. The young men indulged and signed her dance card as well.

"I would allow you some of mine, but I fear it is too strong for a woman," Brumley asserted as he displayed a case of gold matching his waistcoat right down to the piping on the edges. "If I might call upon you tomorrow, I will bring you a gentler blend, one I concoct myself."

"I would enjoy that. As I said, I reside at Bellevue House."

"I know the place."

She danced until the break with Astin's snuff-spotted cohorts and had a second round with the viscount himself. Kate felt she did a fine job of pretending not to notice Camilla's glare or the older women talking behind their fans. As Astin went off to fetch her some orgeat, the duchess bustled to her corner.

"We must go at once!"

Several of the young gentlemen expressed their dismay. Kate suspected they hoped for more free snuff. Outrageous what it cost, but she'd wanted the best to impress Astin and had spent a good part of the stipend her father provided on the tobacco. Astin returned with her cup of refreshment.

"I am so sorry, but I must leave."

"Not another illness in the family, I hope."

"No," the duchess replied sharply. "I am too fatigued to remain. Come, Kate."

"Until tomorrow," Astin said, with a longing gaze at the small bag containing the snuff boxes.

The duchess linked her arm to her protegee's as if Kate might try to escape and led her to where Pandora stood with Appleton. "I am glad you have collected an admirer, young lady, because you have been put out of Almack's by the patronesses. You are never to dance here again."

"Oh, goodie! Me, too, I hope," Pandora said with a clap of her hands.

"I should have known some scheme was afoot when you asked to borrow those snuffboxes. My own girls, I would have expected it of them, but not you, Kate. Give them over at once. I have summoned our carriage. Attend me."

Kate handed over the small bag housing the snuffboxes and walked behind the duchess with head bent. They approached the clot of young men reveling in Camilla Sharpton's beauty, if not her wit. Joshua stood head and shoulders above them being, like all the Longleigh men, long of limb and robust of build. How could Camilla not desire him? She recalled so clearly coming to her senses with Josh's full, warm lips pressed to hers. How that had stirred her even though she'd just started her womanly courses a month or so before The Incident. She'd cherished that memory, hoping to have that experience again all during her long, dreary adolescence. When Joshua left for London, much of the pleasure of a visit to Bellevue Hall had gone with him.

"We are leaving, Joshua," the duchess announced to her son.

"If you would indulge me, Mama, I have not had my second dance with Lady Camilla. I will take a hackney back to my digs and see if Jason has returned safely from his evening's amusements after the dancing ends." So easily, he deflected any censure from himself and onto his younger brother.

"Tell Jason I have noted his absence."

"Of course," Joshua said, though his eyes shifted to Kate draped in gold and looking slightly abashed. He raised his eyebrows as if to say, "What goes?"

She shrugged her shoulders slightly. He hadn't even noticed her success with Astin and his crowd from across the room, and now all was in shambles.

Under the glare of the patroness's hard stares, the women departed for Bellevue House. Once in the privacy of the coach, the duchess did not hold back.

"Your reputation and my opera cloak ruined in the same night!"

"Not ruined. Phemie used a basting stitch. One snip and the gathers will come right out. The tapes can be cut off easily. We took great care with it," Kate professed.

"I wish you had taken as much care of yourself. Really, calling immodest attention to your form by dressing in gold, and I had my doubts about loaning the chaplet. Well, all is not lost. We shall have our own ball at Bellevue House and see who attends. Let those Town Tabbies have Almack's. It's not as if everyone doesn't know Princess Lieven served as Metternich's mistress for years, yet how she mocks English ways. And Lady Jersey eloped with her husband. The rest of the patronesses are not any better, though they do like to judge others."

"I did not mean to cause so much trouble." Kate unfastened the gold cloak and folded it neatly in her lap.

"I believe you did, but somehow I think your actions have something to do with trying to pry Joshua's attention away from Camilla. So, I forgive you. A shame you did not consider the effect this might have on Pandora and Phemie. How am I to chaperone my daughter while you stay behind, when I promised your mother to bring you out? What effect will this have on Phemie when she debuts next year?"

"Punish me as well, Mama. Tell me I need never go to Almack's again. I devised the scheme with the cloak and chaplet. Kate only dreamed up the snuffbox conspiracy to attract Astin," Pandora insisted. "Please say we shall still attend the Abolition Society meeting."

"One place we should still be welcome," the duchess answered.

The coach pulled up before Bellevue House, and the footmen handed the ladies down. Pandora dashed ahead, eager to tell Phemie all. Kate walked slowly behind the duchess as they entered the hall. She trailed her hostess to the cozy sitting room where the duke still played chess with his youngest daughter by the small fire warding off the chill air of March.

He greeted them with a wide smile and a hearty, "Home so early? But I am glad to have my women back safely." One look at his wife's face and he stood, opening his arms. "Something amiss, my darling?"

"Oh, yes!" the duchess said, rushing to be enfolded.

Phemie stood, made uncomfortable by her parents' display of affection, though she should be used to it. "I believe I will surrender this game and go upstairs with Kate and Panny. Good evening, Papa, Mama."

She took Kate's hand and led her away. "Tell me everything, every last detail!"

Pandora waited for them in their mutual bed chamber. "It was a coup, a total coup. Kate in gold with snuffboxes simply entranced Viscount Astin. She danced twice with him and all his hangers-on."

"Then at the intermission, we were asked to leave because of my actions. Now I have harmed your future and Pandora's as well. Here, we might as well restore the cloak this evening. I believe we are engaged for the opera in two nights—if I am still permitted to go along. I hope you passed a more pleasant time." Kate handed the opera cape to Phemie and sunk to the footstool.

"Oh, I allowed Papa to win now and again. He is so brave and big-hearted, always sending in his knights to save his queen. He hasn't a bit of logic or forethought about him. I suspect that is how Mama won him—by always having to be rescued."

"Humpf. Mama could hold her own with red Indians and abductors, I'd say. What is your next move, Kate?" Pandora had already begun shedding her finery, plumes, and ribbons without her maid.

"Let me sleep on it, Panny, because I haven't the faintest idea."

~ * ~

Jason Longleigh, well lit but not fall down drunk, stumbled into the quarters he shared with his brother in the Temple district. Their quarterly allowance went twice as far by leasing the two-story house together. He had his privacy by occupying the second floor while Joshua kept his chambers below. His close sibling had started a fire in the parlor grate seemingly for the sole purpose of staring into it, but he welcomed the warmth after his excursion to the East End.

"Where have you been, brother? Be sure Mama noticed your absence from Almack's."

Jason hooked his long legs over the arms of a comfortable chair and lounged. "I have been to All-Max in the East where the women are dusky and the tars hold forth about their adventures on the sea for the price of Blue Ruin. With Napoleon's war to the east and our quarrel with America to the west, I feel deprived of adventure. No Grand Tour for us, no wilderness escapes."

"You could join the military if you feel a lack of action."

"That was your dream, not mine. I am a poet, not a soldier. I'd rather write of great deeds than perform them. Besides, Mama cried when I mentioned the mere possibility of joining a regiment to fight Boney. She so rarely does that. I melted beneath her downpour."

"When I proposed the same, she claimed Lady Edgemont's health had been ruined by worry over her son's service in the Peninsula War. Did I want her to come to an early death? How could I argue with that? Papa raised all his sons to be warriors, but only James has been allowed to fulfill his expectations with adventures. Damn our elder brother, who leaves me sitting here in case I might have to fill his shoes as the next heir!" Josh continued to glower at the glowing coals of his fire.

"Then abandon the law and come exploring with me. We can avoid Napoleon's many fronts, I am certain. I need to gather more inspiration for an epic poem of the sea *a la* Coleridge. If he could write *Rime of the Ancient Mariner* under the influence of opium, certainly I can without being intoxicated."

"Actually, I find I love the law, brother mine. I enjoy the arguments, the plotting, the chance to win or lose by my wits. Perhaps as a career it is a better fit, but I would have liked to have been allowed the choice."

"Speaking of which, how goes that wager with Kate you told me of? Judging by my last appearance at Almack's, I'd say you won the first pot when you left her with me and Appleton for partners."

"She did well enough that night, but danced only once with Astin and made no impression. Would that were still the case."

"What, our Kate had the proverbial ace up her sleeve?"

"No, she had snuff in her reticule and a hankie up her sleeve. I knew she was up to something more at the tobacconist than buying *me* a gift. If I had figured it out sooner, I might have stopped her. That stuff drew Astin like a dog to a pork chop. She made a great success with his cronies, too, dancing and laughing with them, handing her snuff around. I could hardly concentrate my efforts on Camilla as I had to keep an eye out for her honor. One never knows with a crowd like that, and she is like a sister to me. Mama claimed fatigue and took the girls home early. Word went round Kate had been put out of the place because of her actions. She looked amazing in gold tonight, though I suspect her gown alterations had something to do with the banishment as well."

"Ah, clever Kate has upped the ante. Fifty pounds says she wins."

"I accept your wager. If you admire her so, you should court her before she ruins herself with Astin instead of betting on her like a filly in a race."

Jason considered, one long finger pressed against his lips. "No, a strong-willed woman like Kate is not for me. When I fall in love, Cupid's arrow shall wound me instantly in the heart, a direct hit. I shall be beguiled by her purity and simplicity as well as her beauty. I won't be making bets with my beloved that she can marry another man."

"Kate is *not* my beloved, but she has probably lost her reputation and our wager this evening. Tomorrow, she will be stricken and ashamed. She should retire to Greenway Grange, settle down with some kindly country swain, and remain as she is—not begin taking snuff and lovers because she married a dullard like Astin."

Jason produced a great yawn. "If my superior brother says so. I'm to bed."

Left alone with his thoughts again, Joshua knew he would not sleep. The dark coals spitting sparks reminded him of Kate's brown eyes. They had such a history together from early childhood, as Kate visited often at the nearby Orchards. How she had trailed after him, as pestiferous as his own sisters. What fun they'd had confounding poor Guy Appleton. Not that she hadn't fooled him a time or two when playing the Indian tracking game their father endorsed. She was adept at doubling back and would be eating bread and butter with jam in the nursery by the time boys got out of a bramble patch she'd lured them into by leaving a tiny shred of cloth stuck to a cane and a few footprints pointing into the thicket.

After such an adventure, Mrs. Morely would chide her daughter for her dirty frock and muddy shoes. His own dear mother would deflect Kate's punishment by saying airily, "Children will be children." To which Mrs. Morely always replied, "But girls should be girls, staying inside and having tea parties with their dollies."

He could hear his mother's light laughter as she answered, "I never did. In my favorite game, I pretended to be a red Indian and scalped my victims. Not in reality, of course, but I had quite a collection of queues and braids I'd severed."

Having secured the interest of a duchess who might raise her family up, what else could the poor woman do except say, "How interesting."

Mrs. Morely had proved difficult, though, when The Incident occurred. Oh, how she had shrieked about her daughter's innocence being stolen and tried to demand an instant betrothal. Mama had calmed her with half-promises. Papa had taken him aside, commended his good intentions, and told him to beware of nice young ladies. He should manage his urges with self-pleasuring and light skirts until he became ready to marry.

Had his intentions been good? Kate had arrived that August at Bellevue Hall a changed girl with a blossoming bosom and small, rounded hips that showed clearly beneath her white dress when they ran through the spray of the Triton fountain to cool themselves. At fifteen, he knew all about self-pleasuring, had been doing it for years. That night, he had conjured an image of Kate naked with dark curls between her legs and breasts as rosy-tipped as her cheeks to help him along. Deeply ashamed in the morning, he'd intended to go off on a strenuous hike with Jason, and without her. But she and Pandora and Phemie had run after them. Only Kate had been trussed by her mother supposedly to improve her posture, but more likely to force her daughter into more sedate ways. Had Mrs. Morely laid a trap for a duke's son?

If so, he'd stepped right into it. Guilt over exposing Kate's small, white back and letting his lips linger against hers well past the time he knew she breathed on her own had consumed him. For the next three years, he'd kept himself pure for her, supposing he would offer for Kate as soon she reached a reasonable age, perhaps fifteen. Certainly, she'd filled his dreams and left his sheets wet come morning.

While waiting for Kate to grow up, he'd dallied at Oxford engaging in elocution and debate and discovered more than willing tavern maids before moving on to London to study the law. There, he had fallen in with a modish set who introduced him to the pleasures skilled courtesans could supply for a price. The notion of marrying Giles Appleton's country cousin had melted away under their practiced hands and ruby lips. He'd kept a mistress for a short time, but had found he preferred to spend his allowance keeping up with the latest styles. The valet he had hired did not pout or demand jewelry, but simply did his job, slept in the attic, and expected only cast-off clothes as a reward for his services. Too bad Jason had never pitched in for the servant's salary but often used his services. This evening, he'd sent the man to bed after being helped out of his plum-colored jacket and his stifling neckcloth.

More comfortable, he'd stoked the fire and settled before it with a glass of wine in hand to contemplate his plans for winning Camilla Sharpton, but Kate's eyes kept appearing in the coals. Concern for her of course—that was what bothered him tonight. He'd place another wager his mama had already worked out a plan for restoring Kate's reputation. He needn't worry. And so, to bed.

<h1 style="text-align:center">Six</h1>

"This is our plan for the day. Holding our heads high, we go walking in the park as if nothing happened at Almack's last evening. We will give out that a magnificent ball shall be held at Bellevue House and have people begging for invitations. Then, we see who calls before dinner." The duchess paused to take a sip of her tea.

The duke spread marmalade on his toast and grumbled, "Must we have a ball? You know I detest them, so expensive, so unnecessary."

"Dearest, we must face down the enemy. Surely, you understand that. We can do it by emptying out Almack's for our own magnificent fete. The girls shall start a new trend. Each will be attired in colored gowns. A pity for all the white garments we had fitted, but we might have them re-styled for Phemie next year."

"That at least is practical," the duke said. He poured more coffee and laced it with sugar and cream.

Pandora shoveled eggs, rashers, and a bit of deviled kidney on to her breakfast plate from the buffet. "Good, I loathe wearing white."

"A deep green for you, I think, with golden accents. For Kate, perhaps a bronze-toned fabric. We shall have to search the shops for just the right shade to show her at her best."

Without comment, Kate took her seat at the breakfast table next to Phemie, who begged, "May I come to the ball? Oh please, do not make me stay upstairs when everyone else is dancing. I want to wear a colored gown, too, and help restore Kate's reputation."

Kate raised her head after staring at her uneaten eggs for a moment. "You should not go to so much trouble and expense for me after what I've done."

"Don't be silly, child. The duchess loves nothing better than a good social battle. If she had been born of the opposite sex, she would be a general by now. All is not lost. Eat. Keep your strength up for that stroll in the park." The duke, her dear Uncle Bear who was hard on his sons but soft on his daughters, slathered a piece of toast with strawberry jam and passed it to her.

"I can't help but think Joshua drove you to such behavior when he spurned you in the garden. Naturally, you wanted to attract another man of his caliber," the duchess said with great kindness.

Jason Longleigh breezed into the breakfast room and paused to kiss his mother on her scented, powdery cheek. "Yes, do blame Josh. He never should have accepted Kate's wager. As he is bound to lose, I placed fifty pounds on her. He keeps a miserly table, too. All his blunt goes for clothes."

Jason heaped a plate with foods to his taste and balanced a piece of toast on the pinnacle. He sat next to Pandora, who immediately shot a sharp elbow into his side. "Now you've done it."

"Done what?" He glanced across at Kate who had gone pale and at his mother who had gone silent.

The duke, sitting to his wife's right, patted his duchess's hand. Her Grace caught her breath. "Dear Lord, please tell me you did not register a wager concerning Kate at White's Club."

"No, no. We've kept it in the family. I did it mostly to nettle Josh. He is always so full of himself lately, as if his way is the only way. Tea, if you please."

Steadied by this news, the duchess poured for her son and said, "Did you ride your hack here?"

His mouth full, Jason nodded.

"Good. You will accompany us to Hyde Park in two hours."

"Shouldn't you be studying at the Inns of Court this morning, boy?' The duke frowned down the table at his poetic son.

"Joshua will represent us. I'm sure he will take dinner at the Hall to impress the crumbling, old barristers, too, but they don't seem to like him. He's far too fashionable for their taste, even if he does get a case now and then. As for me, I do feel the need for fresh air today and will go with Mama and the girls."

"I'd rather ride than slog along the paths," Pandora complained.

"Another time. Today, we form a solid defense around Kate. Dress for battle, and by that I mean impeccably. We depart at noon."

~ * ~

Jason Longleigh walked his mount beside the women of his family. He wore one of his father's swords, partly for dash and just in case some wit gave insult to Kate. The Longleigh men were known for their prowess with arms and fisticuffs. His armed presence might ward off any unpleasantness. He tipped his hat to an Ace of Spades, the widowed Lady Tartte, nearer his mother's age than his own, but still full of life in the bed chamber as he had reason to know.

The duchess took the lead with Phemie by her left side. Pandora and Kate, arm in arm, brought up the rear. Occasionally, young men of the ton taking their exercise would canter by, note Phemie's black curls tumbling down her delicate back from beneath her bonnet and pull up to beg an introduction. His Mama invariably replied, "My youngest daughter, Euphemia. She is not yet out," and sent them on their way.

Pandora drew her share of glances. She stared them down. Joshua's nonpareil whizzed past in a red curricle sporting high wheels and drawn by a pair of matched blacks. He caught a glimpse of her mass of yellow curls enrobed in a pink bonnet covered in silk posies and intercepted her blue-eyed glance as she passed. Jason supposed she'd mistaken him for Josh as they were much alike, though he was an inch shorter and much leaner than his brother. He didn't know who held the ribbons, but with a rig like that, the driver did not lack for rhino.

Kate attracted little attention except for a few murmurs when an open carriage of dowagers passed, whispering behind their gloved hands. March was not going out like a lamb. Kate strode along in the brisk breeze ignoring the weather like a country girl accustomed to long walks in rough weather. Most of the angelics of the ton had gone in by then fearing for their complexions, but the young men still rode up and down Rotten Row calling attention to themselves in any way they could.

A fellow on a tall gray with a docked tail pushed in front of Jason's own fine bay gelding. The man greeted the duchess, seemed not to notice Phemie, and fell back to speak over Pandora's beautifully exotic head to Kate.

"Miss Morely, how fortuitous to meet you here in the park. I carry with me a blend you might enjoy. I concocted it this morning with you in mind and intended to deliver it later in the day to your residence."

Pandora stepped aside to allow Kate a private conversation, or nearly private as they could still hear every word but pretended not to. His voice drifted on the breeze to Jason, also. He recognized Harold Brumley, Viscount Astin, though they didn't run in the same circles. Mostly, he associated the man with a pale body, easily bruised, in Gentleman Jackson's boxing ring and as a swordsman better on the defense than the offense. They'd been paired up a time or two. After every match, Astin required a large intake of snuff to recover. Now, he dismounted and offered Kate a silken pouch.

"Do not open it now. The wind will carry off the treasure as surely as it brings roses to your cheeks. I would like to know your opinion of it when I come to call."

Kate, her face reddening even more, demurred. "Oh, I cannot accept such a costly gift."

"Nor would you want it to go to waste as it is too light and delicate a scent for me. Please." Astin pressed the pouch into her hand.

Jason waited for his mother to intervene, but her view was blocked by her large hat and their words by the headwind. Kate hung the pouch from her wrist. Leading his horse, Astin paced beside her. After that exchange, they spoke only of the weather and upcoming social events, whether Kate would attend them or not.

Feeling he must be on guard, Jason also dismounted and walked next to Pandora. His sister leaned close and whispered, "I believe your fifty pounds is a safe bet. Tell Joshua I'll put twenty on Kate from my pin money, as I never spend it on pins anyhow."

Their party caused a jam along the path as Astin's entourage slowed their horses to a walk to follow him. Heads did turn then, craning to see who Viscount Astin favored. Chins wagged. Kate might have been banned from Almack's, but anyone who desired Harold Brumley's attendance at their soirees would have to invite her as well. His mother, brilliant as ever. With one walk in the park, the duchess had solved the problem.

They reached the carriage waiting to take the Longleighs home. Astin availed himself of a hefty footman to throw him into the saddle again as did Jason. In fact, the viscount followed the carriage, waving off as they reached Bellevue House. Before he departed, he said cordially to Jason, "I say, Longleigh, have you any interest in the extraordinary Miss Morely?"

"No, more of a brotherly concern." Jason grinned at the double meaning. "I am far too young to be seeking a wife."

"I feel that when one finds a person so attuned to their interests, one should not hesitate."

"I do agree with you there and wish you luck, Astin." Fifty pounds worth of it, he thought.

~ * ~

It seemed they had barely changed clothes and taken their seats in the second-floor drawing room with its crackling fire than Astin returned, sending up his card, and inquiring if the duchess was at home. She gave the servant a nod to admit the viscount. As he entered, Pandora left her seat by Kate and went to sit by her mother and Phemie. Jason lounged in an armchair, getting up only to give the man his bow. Kate felt he watched her every move, protecting his bet, no doubt. Given leave to sit, Astin took the space vacated by Pandora. Immediately, he launched into his major concern.

"Have you tried the snuff I blended especially for you?"

"No. Not yet. The duchess feels I should..." She held up her wrist to show the small, silken pouch and removed it.

"You must not leave it in the pouch. You should place it in one of your boxes immediately lest it lose its aroma."

"Yes, well, I have lost my boxes."

"Did some thief make off with your reticule?"

"No, um, mislaid."

"Then you shall have mine." Astin withdrew a silver box engraved with the Martindale coat of arms from his waistcoat. The heraldic animals winked at Kate with tiny, ruby eyes. "An everyday box totally without the charm of yours, but it shall have to do."

He dumped the contents into an ornamental dish sitting on a nearby table and wiped the snuffbox clean with his rather spotted handkerchief. "But before we make the transfer, indulge."

Kate hesitated a moment, then drew a pinch from the bag. She really had no other choice if she were to show Joshua his place. She raised it to her nose and inhaled. Her nose wrinkled, suppressing a sneeze.

"What do you smell?" Astin asked eagerly.

"Why, it is very pleasant—like spring with fresh cut grass and wildflowers and perhaps a tiny hint of cinnamon spice."

"Exactly! You have an excellent nose. This is my interpretation of your fragrance." Astin took the sack, transferred the powder to his empty snuffbox and presented it to her.

The duchess intervened. "I am sorry, Astin, the gift is too costly."

"Then she may return the box when she finds her own." He tipped the contents of the dish into the pouch and made a motion to tuck it away. "Unless you would accept this as a gift for the duke?"

"He does not indulge, but thank you." The duchess eyed the mantle clock. He'd used his fifteen minutes and then some in his enthusiasm. Astin took the hint and left their company.

Kate could hold her sneeze no longer. She groped for her handkerchief and let lose a very unfeminine exhalation. Her eyes watered, and she dabbed her lids. As her vision cleared, she caught Jason's droll expression.

"What?" she asked.

"How strange that you've known Astin less than two days, and he so completely defined you with a scent while my brother who has known you since childhood has no idea what he is losing—other than his bet to me."

"I am sure Joshua thinks I smell of cow patties and pig sweat."

"No, I'm thinking haystacks and what often goes on in them. He hates to lose control."

"Jason, if you are going to be vulgar, you may leave," his mother said.

"Excellent idea. I believe I shall put in some time in the gymnasium, then borrow my brother's lecture notes. I will return to dine. *Adieu.*"

Before he reached the door, the butler arrived with two more cards bearing the names of Lady Harcourt and her younger daughter, Tomasina. The duchess gestured for them to come. Jason paused to greet the ladies civilly before going on his way. Tomasina's dark lashes fluttered over her unique violet eyes as he passed. Even Lady Harcourt gave him a second look.

So it was with the Longleigh men. They seemed to have a scent all their own that drew women like hummingbirds to nectar. Kate suppressed her sigh and put on a smile to welcome Tomasina, the best of friends to Camilla Sharpton, and her puffing mother who had gone well beyond pleasingly plump and took some time to recover from taking the stairs.

The duchess immediately began to describe their upcoming gala as she must have done twenty times in the park as she encountered her acquaintances. Tomasina quickly got to the heart of the matter.

"Will all your sons attend, Duchess?"

"No, only Joshua and Jason. Justinian is away at school, and who knows where James is. We get a letter from Italy, a note from Greece. I do worry about James among the ruins he so loves."

"As any mother would. I know one young lady who will be quite happy if only Joshua attends. You will be inviting Lady Camilla, won't you?" Lady Harcourt hinted broadly. Her brunette curls, dyed to match her daughter's, jiggled merrily as she nodded her head into her chins.

"I suppose," the duchess replied with little joy.

Kate's mood darkened. The duchess was having this fete for her sake, and now she would have to compete with Camilla.

"And Matilda Everton, too? We are dearest friends," Tomasina prattled.

Lady Harcourt inhaled so sharply Kate feared she suffered from chest pains. "We have stayed long enough. Let us go, Tomasina. Help me up."

Perplexed, her daughter did as she was told. The stairs creaked beneath Lady Harcourt's weight as they left. Pandora's eyes slanted wickedly.

"Aren't you always saying we should forgive and forget, Mama, as the Bible tells us? What is a kidnapping years ago to the Longleigh family who courts adventure every day?"

"I could forgive the kidnapping. My own fault I did not escape your Uncle Roderick's clutches, but he held James captive, too. I knew the blackguard was short of funds and would try anything, even ransoming his own sister to her legal husband. It's *her* I cannot forgive, his wife, Lady Rushmore. She had a great part in the planning, I'm sure, but worst of all she had designs on your father, unnatural designs."

Phemie, who had remained virtually silent through all the visits as a well-bred youngster should, asked, "What are unnatural designs?"

The duchess reddened. "You are all too young and innocent to understand."

"Oh, I don't think so, Mama," Pandora drawled. "Shouldn't we know for our own protection? I mean Papa gave us knives to ward off evil men."

"That woman...she continued to send your father perfumed notes long after I made it plain we would never receive her. She still desires him. I want her nowhere near us."

"But Papa is so old now," Phemie said, showing just how innocent she was.

"He is still the love of my life. There, I am too upset to receive anyone else today. Phemie, inform Busby that I am no longer at home. Pandora, find your papa and tell him I have gone to lie down until dinner."

"Shall I ask him to join you? He will at any rate," Pandora answered archly.

"Wretched child! Someday, someday, I hope you love as deeply as we do. Let that be your punishment."

"I have too much good sense to let that happen," Pandora replied.

The duchess went off in a huff, and Phemie trotted dutifully downstairs to deliver the message to the butler, leaving Kate and Pandora alone in the drawing room.

"Hmmm, unnatural desires. I shall have to ask Jason. He's as good a source as any."

Kate took the snuffbox from the table and rose to go to her chamber. Much as she loved all of the eccentric Longleighs, some days their passions were simply too much to fathom.

Seven

"You simply must invite Matilda Everton, Mama. Otherwise, you give unfair advantage to Kate who will have Astin by her side all evening. Lady Camilla told me directly at the last soiree she could not accept your invitation while Tilly sits home alone. She is our cousin after all." Joshua paced his mother's sitting room, small as a hen house compared to her spacious area at Bellevue Hall, but one did have to make concessions to city living.

Indifferent to her son's agitation, the duchess pulled a colored thread through her embroidery. "I find I do favor Kate now that I know of your wager. I cannot believe you told that lovely young woman she is too simple, plain, and poor to thrive in London."

"I never said any such thing. I did imply she could not compete with the lovelies of London and made it very clear I planned to court one of them, thus saving her the pain of rejection and false hopes. And again, she proposed the wager, not I."

"Twenty pounds says Kate wins the Greatest Prize."

"I do not accept your bet. Not when you keep me from Camilla. You allow Astin to call every day. He trails Kate in the park. He pops into our box at the opera during intermission and shows up at the Philharmonic with his cortege and takes up the entire row behind us."

"He subscribed to the new Philharmonic Society the same as we did. I did offer you a ticket."

"As if I had time to attend every social function of the season! I am studying the law. I intend to be a barrister while Jason only plays at it. I should have gone to be a soldier. But you would choose my career *and* my wife. You and Papa try to control every aspect of my life."

The duchess allowed her lips to tremble slightly. She found her hankie to dab her eyes. "I thought you understood with James gallivanting around the world, you must stand by and prepare to do your duty should he fail to return. Besides, I thought you enjoyed the law."

"I do, but why can't James be called to heel? Why must I bear his burden? Camilla hinted she found men in uniform very attractive and those working up the ranks to general to be to her taste. Her friends suggested I should be off in Europe chasing Napoleon with Wellington if I want to impress her."

A single tear rolled down his mother's soft cheek and fell, forming a dark center in the midst of a wreath of daisies on her embroidery hoop. "I wish we could summon James home, but your papa says he should have his freedom. Regardless, if you were away fighting, you would never see Camilla. I say a woman who sends a man off to die in order to impress her is not worth having. Those three young women are like the little foxes that spoil the vines. I do not care for them."

He had been round and round the mulberry bush with his mother about his career and Camilla Sharpton too many times. As a prospective barrister, Josh knew he needed a fresh argument. Unclenching his fists and taking a deep breath, he said, "You permit Kate to take snuff in order to captivate Astin, something you would not allow your own daughters to do."

The duchess drew herself up, a small, bristling tabby cat. "Kate does not take snuff! She merely carries a snuff box, one I have made a present of so that she might return Astin's container. We could not insult him by refusing the special blend he prepared especially for her."

"It tweets every time she so frequently opens it, calling attention to herself and an inelegant habit for a young lady. She offers its contents around, gushing about its pleasing aroma," Josh insisted.

"But she takes none. Women are allowed to use their wiles to engage a man they desire. Her trick to draw Astin got her evicted from Almack's, and so I am giving her a new venue in which to compete."

"Unfair," Joshua reiterated.

"Very well. I will send an invitation to the ball to Matilda Everton and her wall-eyed mother, Lady Rushmore, that unnatural vixen."

The duchess put her sewing aside, went to the small secretaire, and took out a spare invitation, a pen, and a bottle of ink. As she wrote, Joshua inquired, "Would you care to tell me why Lady Rushmore is an unnatural vixen?"

"No."

"Come, Mama. I am past twenty-one and have been in London some time. I am beyond being shocked."

"She keeps her own courtesan and shares in that woman's profits. She once invited your father to engage in a *ménage a trois* with them. Perhaps more than once."

"Offended she did not invite you as well?" Joshua expected to see his mother blush and give him a sharp reprimand for his impertinence. Irritated at her championing of Kate over her own son, he wanted to prick hard at the duchess. He should have known better than to try.

The duchess replied to him coolly as she penned an address she knew well from her childhood. "Oh, she did. Let us hope her strange tastes have not influenced Matilda or her friends. Your invitation. Have Busby arrange for delivery."

Her sharp, gray eyes peered at a small crack in the sitting room door. "You may come in, girls. Did you bring your sewing?"

Joshua, preparing to leave, flung the door open and in tumbled Pandora, Phemie, and Kate. He caught Kate by the elbow. "I suppose you heard all?"

"All I need to know of your opinion of me." Anger and embarrassment shone on her face.

"Then you should not listen at doors."

Pandora answered with glee. "Mama always says she would not have known half of what went on if she did not listen at doors."

"That does not give you my approval to do it," the duchess said hastily.

"And you think Camilla and her friends are little foxes." On that sour note, Joshua departed.

~ * ~

Priscilla Everton, Lady Rushmore, watched her daughter and friends with her icy blue eyes. Long of limb and possessing a sharp nose and a thin smile, she thought herself still a handsome woman, though she had never been preciously pretty like Camilla Sharpton. She continued to powder her hair in an older style since its original dark blonde had turned an unattractive sort of gray. Certainly, she remained thinner than Tomasina, Lord Harcourt's daughter, who never went riding, but preferred carriages and bonbons that would eventually take their toll on her figure and smile. As for her own daughter, hopeless. With much luck she might land the least of Camilla's suitors once that spoiled young woman made her choice.

The girls squealed over the invitation to the Bellevue ball. They had waited in her threadbare, lightly furnished drawing room several days for its delivery, all of them wrapped in shawls. Coal was so dear when one had a husband who had gambled away two fortunes, despite her best efforts to restrain him.

Then, there were Rushmore's other expensive vices. At least, the whorehouse she'd invested in many years ago still turned profits as well as tricks. Her husband took the little boys he purchased there, and she could have her own sort of pleasure free of charge. A small reward earned for having given the man an heir who died in childhood and then having to go through the ordeal again and gotten only Matilda. It galled that the title Earl of Rushmore might go to one of Lady Flora's sons someday. At least her enemy's family would get no fortune with it, only several drafty houses and the land.

Joshua Longleigh, so like his father in many attractive ways, had delivered the missive himself, proof positive of the young man's devotion to Camilla. Basking in the debutante's delight over the invitation, he had visited briefly and refused refreshments. Undoubtedly, the baked goods were fresher and finer at Bellevue House. Lady Flora would be served right if her delectable boy ended up wed to the likes of Camilla Sharpton, who was neither as sweet nor as shallow as she appeared. That girl, yes, that girl could be shaped into a weapon of revenge.

The young woman flexed her angelic wings and boasted, "Do you see? I told you I could outfox Lady Flora and gain you entrance to Bellevue House."

"Beauty is power, Camilla, but beware of the Longleighs. Lady Flora once tried to kill me, believing I had made advances toward her husband—as if I would want that half-breed lout." Lady Rushmore steepled her long fingers beneath her strong jaw as if praying for their safety. Still thinking of Pearce Longleigh and what she had missed, she licked her lips.

"Oh, I find the Longleigh men to be deliciously handsome in a dark sort of way. I hope when Camilla tosses Joshua aside to marry Astin, he will look to me to mend his broken heart." Tomasina selected another cake from the tiered-plate of refreshments.

Camilla's kitty-cat claws came out. "I may want to keep Joshua. He could be the next Duke of Bellevue or possibly the Earl of Rushmore."

The girl did know her successions, well taught by Lady Strictly, no doubt, and possibly one reason that duchess allowed her perfect daughter to associate with Matilda. The two of them might be weighing the worth of the title or hoping to gain access to the Longleighs, disregarding the old feud. But Camilla had gained entrance to Bellevue House on her own account and taken Matilda with her. Lady Rushmore had to admire that.

"Oh, oh, then Jason Longleigh will do for me." In her haste to appease Camilla, Tomasina sprayed crumbs from her mouth onto her gown. Lady Rushmore gave the girl a look of disgust for both her manners and her weakness.

Uncaring, Camilla raged on. "That ordinary Morely chit is monopolizing Astin. He hardly seeks me out at all anymore except for the obligatory two dances. What am I to tell Papa if I cannot win the richest man on the market and the most handsome?" She put on a pretty and pointless pout for an adoring audience.

"You need the advice and guidance of an experienced woman," Lady Rushmore replied.

"I have that in my mother. She would have me go slowly and with utmost propriety."

"Yes, she did well for herself—from baronet's daughter to Strictly's duchess, a great beauty in her day. The rest of us must use guile. For instance, if Matilda could bring a man to compromise her, she might marry. Are you listening, daughter?"

"Yes, Mama." Matilda Everton hung her head.

"Do not assume that posture. It makes you look like a turtle going into its shell."

"Yes, Mama." Matilda extended her short chin as far as it would go and clapped her hands to her acne-riddled cheeks to keep it there.

"Astin was at my feet until Katherine Morely came along. It's not as if she is more attractive than me. It's the snuff. I told Astin if he meant to please me, he must give it up."

"A tactical error, dear child. You make those demands the first year of your marriage when a husband is still in your thrall. You aren't likely to change him later. Beforehand, you must stress all you have in common and overlook their bad habits. You do need my advice badly."

Lady Rushmore took a sip of tea that had already gone cold in the chilly room. "Never fear, I shall help you devise a plan to gain Lady Flora's boy quickly. As you might have noticed, the Duchess of Bellevue favors the Morely girl and has no regard for you. She has a great deal of influence over her sons and might sway the one you want to her choice over the course of the season. The very fact that Astin prefers Katherine will also draw Joshua's attention. Men do so love to compete. As for Harold Brumley, he is already lost to you because of his adoration for snuff. You will not get him back unless you are willing to take drastic measures, but you can have young Lord Longleigh easily enough."

Lady Rushmore watched the panic spread over Camilla's face as the idea caught like a contagion that she might have neither of her first choices.

"Teach me how," Camilla Sharpton said.

Eight

The duchess was well-pleased. Carriages blocked the street before Bellevue House end to end. Inside, a tremendous crush of people made passing down the halls hazardous. Most of the guests immediately repaired to the deep, narrow ballroom across from the drawing room unless they preferred cards and sought out the tables.

She'd persuaded her sons into strict black and white. No lace for Jason and no outré waistcoats for Joshua. She bade them to watch out for Kate and their sisters but to dance often with as many partners as possible. Her husband, who would intimidate any young man not treating his girls with ultimate respect, wore his knee breeches and white silk stocking as usual. She really did not seek to change him. He was magnificent as is.

No females outshone her girls: Pandora in alluring green shot with gold and wearing the family emeralds; Kate shimmering in bronze silk beneath the hundred-candle chandeliers. Amber drops hung at her ears and a necklace of the same intriguing stones ringed her neck. A starburst broach of those gems held a plume, its edges dipped in dark gold in her thick, high-piled hair. No need for anyone to know the jewels came from the Bellevue coffers. She carried the tiny bag containing the chirping snuff box because Astin would be sure to ask her to show it off. Only Phemie pouted in pale pink with her black curls worn down and tied with a bow like a school girl, which she was. Her mother would not allow her to attend in any other guise.

The duchess turned her eyes from greeting one guest to the next and came face to face with Lady Rushmore, her long-ago nemesis. She offered a curt nod. Priscilla Everton gave the smallest of curtsies. They exchanged no words. The young ladies behind her bobbed deeply and gazed at their shoe tips. When they raised their faces, Lady Flora saw only one among them who outshone Pandora and Kate. Well, she'd seen Camilla Sharpton before at Almack's, so perfect she did draw the eye. However, it seemed the girl had gone out of her way to shine with every yellow curl in place and set off with tiny rosebuds. Her dress, white with pink accents, was so layered and swagged she resembled an especially festive, mouth-watering wedding cake. Camilla played to win, but did she seek to gain Joshua or Astin as her trophy?

The duchess caught her husband's courtly bow over Lady Rushmore's hand. He grasped that hand and said, "Priscilla, your husband did not choose to attend?"

"I believe Roderick still fears you, despite your kind invitation."

Before he could say more, Lady Flora gripped the folded fan that helped her cope with the hot flashes of middle age and flourished it backward as if to unfurl. The edge came down sharply on her husband's wrist. The end piece snapped. He dropped Lady Rushmore's hand.

"I am so sorry, my darling. You stood too close." Fortunately, she kept a copious supply of her favorite weapon. Summoning a footman with a crook of her finger, she said, "Find my maid and have her bring me another fan to match my ensemble. Priscilla, I know you must want to seek the ballroom."

Lady Rushmore quirked her thin lips as a reply and gestured to her young ladies to follow. Strictly's duchess took their place, somehow relegated to the rear by an earl's wife. Flora had nothing against this still attractive woman. Regal and trim, her hair tinted the lightest shade of blonde and her cheeks and lips rouged to replace the youthful color she had lost, Lady Strictly did not flirt or take lovers. All her energies went into creating the perfect daughter, which sadly, Flora herself had never been able to do, despite a great deal of effort. No, they all took after her in spirit and would not be subdued…all except Phemie. The duchess dared to hope with that one.

If Joshua married Lady Strictly's daughter, she hoped Camilla would follow the same path as her mother, but vain and beautiful women seldom stayed faithful among the ton. Yet another reason she preferred Kate. The Duke of Strictly, dressed in knee breeches like her husband but far more brittle and pompous in bearing, followed this procession, made his courtesies, and advanced to the card room. Stout Lord and Lady Harcourt made their obeisances swiftly and rumbled away, already looking for the dining room.

There now, the worst part of the evening was over. She could ignore Lady Rushmore for the rest of the ball, but the foxes had entered her hen house. She prayed they would take no victims tonight.

~ * ~

Kate knew when Camilla Sharpton entered the room. The eyes of every man but Astin turned that way. The viscount had taken her on a promenade around the ballroom immediately after his arrival. He bade her show the chirping snuffbox and its contents to anyone who had seen it under five times. She'd considered asking Phemie, whose small hands were very skilled, to make it mute. Perhaps the chirp would simply wear out one day.

Astin told his story of being allowed to visit the Prince Regent's room set aside especially for snuff, the blending of snuff, and snuffboxes. He rhapsodized over this honor and the varieties of snuff he'd sampled while there: Bolongaro, Scholten, and Masulipatam as well as the prince's own blends. She'd heard the tale at least a dozen times and become quite tired of nodding enthusiastically as he rattled away. The viscount had turned out to be a decent man, not as conceited as he might be, who treated her well, but was so insufferably dull. The sooner he proposed, the sooner she could give her gentle refusal and win her bet. Her eyes, too, strayed toward Camilla.

Joshua and Jason Longleigh stood directly behind her in a pack of overdressed dandies. Because she listened not to Astin and tuned her ears to Josh's voice, she heard him direct his brother very clearly.

"Keep watch on Kate and Astin. Do not let him lure her into the garden. I don't like his fast set."

"Fast set? Watching the snuff-takers is as dull as waiting for tobacco to cure," Jason scoffed.

"Kate does not know London ways. She is unwary of social intrigue and plotting."

With that said, he crossed the ballroom to tender his bow before the beauty. Exactly how innocent did he think she was? Heavens, she'd grown up with the Longleigh girls as her best friends, and little went undiscussed in *that* household. Much as he infuriated her, Kate could not hold back her admiration of his masculine grace, of the broadness of his shoulders as he dipped before the woman he courted. If he dressed every day in black and white, the barristers might take him more seriously, she conjectured. Of course, if he gained Camilla's fortune, he would have no need of the law as a career. He would be bored as Camilla's husband, as bored as she was now. How she wanted something, anything to happen.

The duke and duchess took their place to begin the dancing. Astin led her out as usual. He would pass her along to his cronies so she never went unpartnered and then dance with her again in the course of the evening. In a matter of weeks, they'd fallen into this pattern while Joshua struggled to get his two dances among the mass of Camilla's admirers. *He* never danced with her unless prodded by his mother.

The time passed pleasantly enough. Intermission came along with a lavish cold buffet. As vigorous dancing built the appetite, a virtual stampede of guests made for the first-floor dining room. Kate stayed Astin with a hand on his sleeve.

"Really, you need not fight for a plate for me. I'd rather have a breath of fresh air."

"And a pinch of snuff." Her companion waved back his hoard of followers. "I would have a moment alone with Miss Morely."

Astin escorted her to the balcony overlooking the small, narrow garden mirroring the ballroom in size and leading back to a rear gate and the mews where the carriage horses were kept. Two sets of stairs on either side swept down into the greenery. Low-cut box hedges rimmed the beds of Dutch tulips, yellow, red, pink, and white, that the duchess would later have overplanted with summer flowers. Light from the ballroom spilled out and lit half the space bearing only a single statue of wing-footed Mercury on a slender plinth in its center, leaving little room for any mischief. She and Astin remained in plain view of any in the ballroom.

Kate accepted an offering from Astin's box and went through her charade of sniffing and sneezing again. All the while, she gazed back to where Camilla held court with her maidens in a set of chairs as they waited for gentlemen to bring them food like helpless nestlings. Jason Longleigh leaned negligently against the back of Tomasina Murray's seat and engaged her in desultory conversation. He paid no mind to Kate on the balcony. No sign of Joshua, who had probably rushed off to bring his lady the best of the buffet.

She turned toward the dark garden, preferring that sight. Astin placed his hand very close to hers on the railing. Obviously nervous, he fingered the deep cleft in his chin and raked the golden curls from his forehead before addressing Kate.

"Do you know I feel very comfortable with you? I am well aware that many young ladies this season seek my company, but you do not press for my attention other than to share a few dances and some convivial snuff. Then, there are those gentlemen who trail me everywhere, always wanting something." He nodded toward the coterie awaiting his return.

Astin continued. "I've been blessed with my mother's beauty and my father's chin, I've been told. Mama passed away when I was very young. Of course, I had all the best tutors in all manner of things. Still, I cannot compare to those Longleigh men in the martial arts. How they go at it even when fighting each other. Frightening, actually. I do not care much for violence. I have heard that Joshua Longleigh has some claim to you, an understanding between your families. Is this true?"

Kate observed Josh placing a brimming plate in Camilla's hands and her demure that he brought too much. "The agreement was very loose, never written down, simply a childish affection they hoped might blossom. It did not take root. As you can see, he courts Lady Camilla."

"Then, I might hope, Miss Morely." Hesitating, he paused, stoked his nostrils with snuff, and inhaled deeply. Fortified, he continued. "Might I ask you a question?" He blew into his vast, white handkerchief.

Kate turned toward the garden to hide her face. So soon? True, she could not wait to be free of the wager, to have proved herself the equal of any London nonpareil, but she had not quite worked out a carefully worded rejection of his proposal. Shouldn't he have approached the duke for permission first as he served as her guardian? Panic assaulted her stomach, making her very glad she hadn't eaten yet. She hesitated as she grasped for words. Finally, she gave the simple answer, "Yes, of course."

An elbow slammed into the viscount's back nearly putting him over the rail.

"Beg your pardon, Astin. Blinded by the light of the ballroom and didn't see you there. Just going out to have a smoke," Joshua Longleigh claimed.

"Snuff is far more healthful, Longleigh. Won't you try some of mine?"

"My thanks, but no."

Josh continued down the stairs and paused at the bottom to withdraw his cigar, perhaps one she had purchased. He put a glowing splint cadged from one of the fireplaces to it. He took a few puffs before strolling directly below the couple on the balcony. The aroma of fine tobacco drifted upward to where Kate and Astin stood so close together.

"As I was saying, Miss Morely, might I address you by your first name? I would be most pleased if you would call me Harold."

So relieved her knees weakened, Kate answered at once. "Oh, Harold, do call me Kate. I prefer it to Katherine."

"Kate, then. Kate," her suitor repeated joyfully.

Below them, Joshua Longleigh coughed on his cigar and moved away to the darker end of the garden. In a minute, they could locate him only by the glowing tip of the cigar when he inhaled.

"Cigars, disgusting. Now, may I bring you some refreshments, Kate?"

"I would like that, Harold. I will wait here."

His very handsome face alight, Harold Brumley went in search of food. He passed the cluster of young women who gathered around Camilla Sharpton and nodded to them in passing. Kate observed Camilla's glare at his indifference after he went by.

The nonpareil rose and announced, "Come, let us stroll in the garden."

The three brushed by Kate on the balcony without so much as an acknowledgement of her existence. Skirts held up daintily, they descended the garden stairs. Whispering and giggling, the young ladies drifted toward the plinth where Camilla parted from them. With Tomasina and Matilda keeping watch, she moved toward the scent of a good cigar. Without thinking,

Kate descended the stairs and hurried to join Pandora's homely cousin and the violet-eyed Tomasina.

"Where is Camilla going? She should not walk in the garden alone. Someone could come in from the mews and…"

Tomasina smirked and simpered. "She has gone to join Lord Longleigh and will be well protected by that gentleman."

"I see." She did. They laid the parson's mousetrap for Joshua, and she would not allow him to step into it. Kate moved forward only to be blocked by tall, solid Matilda.

"They do not want your company, Miss Morely. You have Astin, after all. He should be enough for you."

Kate's hands came up. She shoved Matilda aside. Taken by surprise, the other woman slipped in the gravel of the path and tripped over the low hedge. She went bum down with a snapping of tulips' stems. Tomasina shrieked, but Kate strode on. She found the couple by the rear gate illuminated only by the glow from Joshua's cigar held low in one hand while the other rested atop the wicket. She watched as Camilla's slim, white form, hands clasped behind her back, leaned forward to allow a swift brush of her lips against his. Joshua did not move at all.

"So sorry to interrupt your conversation, but Matilda has fallen and needs you," Kate improvised.

Camilla's hands flew to her cheeks. "Oh, what you must have seen, Miss Morely."

"I saw nothing. You may depend on me to say to that. I fear your friend might be injured. Do hurry."

Camilla flounced away, her anger evident in the set of her head and shoulders. She reached her friends and said more loudly than she knew, "You were supposed to discover us, you idiots, not trample the shrubbery."

Kate covered her face to suppress her laughter. Joshua stomped his cigar out in the gravel and pried her hands apart. He raised her chin. "You did see nothing. Her kiss was as dry as the wings of a dead butterfly."

"Inferior to the kiss of a very young girl gasping for air?"

"Yes. A lad does remember his first stolen kiss with fondness."

"Really?"

"Indeed, it felt like this."

Joshua's large hands cupped the back of her head. His lips descended, angled, and merged with hers. A gasp left her mouth parted. His tongue skimmed the tip of hers, no dry kiss this. He continued pressing against her, but went no deeper. She would have allowed it, allowed anything he wanted in this moment.

A dog began yapping on the other side of the gate and would soon draw attention their way. He stopped and released her, steadied her by a hand to the elbow. Kate caught her breath.

"I don't recall it happening exactly that way."

"You were half unconscious. How would you know?"

"I know I kissed you back, though not so expertly. Josh, you could have won your wager by kissing Camilla exactly this way and letting her friends witness it. Why did you hold back?"

"I believe the man should do the asking of his own free will, not be entrapped or prodded by his parents. Are you going to run crying to my mother?" He had to raise his voice over the noise of the dog.

"No, that would be unfair. I intruded between you and Camilla."

"Earlier, I thought I'd lost the bet when I noticed how close Astin stood, how he looked at you."

"He merely wanted to call me by my first name."

"As I overheard."

"The bet is still on, then?" She'd felt the seeds of passion in his kiss and recognized her own deep yearning. Surely, he realized they were intended for each other now. She hoped for a different answer than the one he gave.

Joshua answered coolly and with a slight edge of irritation. "Most assuredly. Why won't that wretched hound stop barking?"

"My fault, I'm afraid. He's the terrier your mother bought for the stables to keep down the vermin. I've been feeding him table scraps. I pity any creature that must live solely on rats. He hadn't even a name, so I call him Spot. I'm sure he thought I'd come to the gate to feed him."

"Well, here's Dear Harold to feed *you*."

Balancing a couple of plates, one atop another in one hand and two cups of punch in the other, Astin scanned the garden for Kate.

"Go first. I'll linger here. I would not be unfair either."

"Thank you."

Kate walked back to her suitor, wondering if he'd been able to see the trembling of the plume she wore in her hair as Josh kissed her, but no, he'd only just arrived. They found seats. Suddenly, she felt very dry, though she hadn't been not long ago. She drained her cup of sweet punch and forced down a few morsels, then asked him to excuse her. Badly in need of it, she hastened to the room set aside for the ladies to restore themselves. Even the cloying punch had not washed the taste of Joshua from her mouth— red wine and a rich cigar, no boy's kiss but a man's. She would remember it forever even if she never had another.

Instead of gaining a moment to gather herself, she walked in on a clump of wailing women.

"The back of my gown is stained with green and yellow. I must go home at once. Walk closed behind me, Tomasina," Matilda Everton cried.

"Oh, to Hades with your gown, Tilly. I have lost both Astin and Longleigh tonight. Joshua will not fall for that trick twice. Damn your mother for suggesting it." Tears cascaded down Camilla's face in such abundance she used two hankies to sop them.

"But you have so many to choose from. I would allow you Jason Longleigh since you are my dearest friend, even though I want him for myself." Tomasina patted Camilla's heaving shoulders.

"A third son! Never! At least Joshua has some chance of becoming the next Duke of Bellevue, and we would look so well together, his dark to my light. You!" Camilla noticed Kate trying to back quietly out the door. "You have ruined my life. First, you lure Astin with your snuff. Then, you witness me compromising myself with Longleigh and won't say a word."

"As I said, your secret is safe with me." She figured she could hold her own and better with Camilla in a catfight, but her rival had two allies, one taller and one heavier than she. Oh, for Pandora and Phemie to back her up. The Longleighs never flinched from battle, even the female members.

Camilla did not attack. Perhaps violence had been bred out of so fine a lady. Instead, she wiped her puffy, bloodshot eyes and mopped her swollen face. "A girl of your station and prospects would not understand. I must marry the best, while any member of the ton would do for you."

"I have heard many members of the ton make very foolish choices, running off to Gretna Green or marrying opera dancers," Kate said lightly.

"Besides, Astin has not proposed, nor have I decided if I would accept him. You still have a chance."

"What? You would reject the heir to the richest Duke in England."

"Possibly."

All three of the young women stared at her as if she were the two-headed calf at the county fair. Calculation entered Camilla's wide blue eyes. "Why, I believe we could be friends. If you would care to join my group, then Astin and Longleigh could see us side by side and compare. You can have whomever I decide against."

"Sporting of you, Lady Camilla. Allow me some time to consider your offer." Kate continued to back away until she found herself in the hall, and the door shut behind her. Once free, she fled back to Harold waiting as patiently as an old dog for its mistress.

~ * ~

Lady Rushmore passed Kate on the way. That imperial lady entered the retiring room. "There you are. Why isn't Joshua Longleigh begging your father for your hand?'

"She ruined our plan, that Katherine Morely. But I thought if I befriend her, I might keep a better eye on her."

Lady Rushmore, dressed in blood red, considered. "Yes, that would make it so much easier to be rid of this girl of whom Lady Flora is so very fond. Good, Camilla, very good."

Nine

Kate unfolded the thick sheet of paper embossed, white on white, with the Strictly coat-of-arms and addressed to her in care of Bellevue Hall. Pandora and Phemie craned to read over her shoulder, but the handwriting was the chicken scratch of a student who had not excelled at penmanship. Kate skimmed over the letter, pausing now and then to decipher a blotted word.

"It's from Camilla Sharpton, of course. She indicates she will be *pour prendre congé*, leaving for a short stay at her family's estate, Clifton-by-the-Sea. The pace of the season has overwhelmed her."

"It's April and the season not half over. Has she no stamina? If I were allowed out more, I'd certainly be able to keep up," Phemie claimed.

"She feels the sea air will restore the roses to her cheeks and knows I am in need of the same. She invites me to come along with her, Matilda, and Tomasina."

"I have to admire her for putting together an invitation both gracious and insulting," Pandora said. "But you cannot go. You will miss the next meeting of the Abolition Society."

"Oh, Panny. You know I wholeheartedly believe in ending slavery, but to be honest, I find those meetings as interesting as snuff. I should go and try to make peace with Camilla. Perhaps I should tell her of the wager and that I mean only to get a proposal from Harold, not to marry him."

"She should be able to figure that out for herself. Who would want to tie themselves for life to a boring snuff-taker?"

"A boring, rich, handsome snuff-taker," Phemie amended.

"Exactly. Any of those three would take Harold in a second and make him miserable for eternity. I almost feel I must protect him from them."

"What about you, Kate? You should not go alone into the fox's den even if invited. I will forgo the Abolition Society meeting and come with you," Pandora offered.

"Camilla has precluded that. She says she has but one seat left in the coach and regretfully Lady Pandora and Lady Euphemia Longleigh cannot be invited. We are to rest with no gentlemen in attendance, not even her father. She says we will laugh at the foibles of our suitors and mend our differences."

"She means to win you away from us. Next, you will be staying permanently with the Sharptons, not with us."

"Oh, Panny, she could never do that. No, I'll go and try to ease her mind concerning Harold without giving it all away. I will wish you there every day that passes."

"Watch your back is all I can say."

~ * ~

The duchess expressed a similar opinion before giving her consent, but Kate countered by saying they were only girls her own age, after all. She should not refuse an offer of their friendship. The large, black, crested coach arrived at the stated time, and the Strictly footman loaded Kate's small trunk suitable for a short stay in the country. Strictly's duchess got down long enough to pay her respects to the lady of Bellevue and assure her that Kate would be treated as their own daughter.

Kate's first feeling of unease came when she stooped to enter the carriage and found herself looking directly into the pale, cold blue eyes of Lady Rushmore. The three girls sat across, and they wedged her between the lofty, regal form of Priscilla Everton and the well-preserved face and figure of Camilla's mother, neither very warm or welcoming women. Lucretia

Sharpton did not bother to hide her annoyance at leaving the pleasures of the London season to restore her daughter's health, though Lady Rushmore said she did exactly the right thing. After all, their day was over, and the future rested with these young women.

A long day's travel with frequent stops for refreshment brought them to Clifton-by-the-Sea shortly after dark. The travelers partook of a cold supper and went to bed not too long after.

Shown to a smallish corner room, Kate found herself comfortable enough. An ample supply of coal in a scuttle sat available to ward off the damp and drafts. Curtains and bed hangings of glazed, flowered chintz brightened the rather plain walls and furnishings.

Alone with the sounds of the sea and a stiff wind prowling the grounds like a pack of vicious watchdogs, Kate missed the company of Pandora and Phemie. She heard the door to Camilla's chamber far down the hall open and close several times, releasing giggles into the hallway. Not comfortable enough with their tentative friendship to invite herself to join the group of young ladies, she finally slept.

A hot and hearty late breakfast and a walk along the chalky cliffs restored her confidence, even if she was constantly advised not to walk too near the edge lest it crumble or a gust of wind take her over the side. The path stayed well away from the verge, and the warnings seemed truly unnecessary for anyone but a small child or an idiot.

Camilla led them down a precarious path to the beach where they gathered shells, shed their shoes and stockings and dipped their bare toes into the chilly water. They returned blooming with health to the great, gray manor house which, from a distance, resembled a gargoyle wreathed with moss as it squatted in a walled garden behind a windbreak of gnarled trees. More pitted than poor Matilda's face, its façade stared with many glassy eyes at the sea. Kate could understand the duchess's reluctance to leave London. While she planned to enjoy her first introduction to the ocean, the environs were rather bleak and depressing, especially when the sun disappeared and the fog came up as it did that evening.

They dined and took a lie down after the meal. Kate, never one to rest long, soon went in search of her companions since none were in their chambers. She asked a maid for their whereabouts.

"In the attic, Miss. Is there anything else I might do for you?"

"No, I am quite fine and have all I need. Point the way, and I shall join the other ladies."

Kate entered a well-concealed door in the paneling and followed the sound of girls' chatter as she climbed the long, narrow stairs to another door at the top. As she let herself in, Matilda declared, "That hat is perfect for you, Milly," but they dropped the garments they held when they saw her standing there.

"What are you up to?" Kate asked. Did Tomasina redden and shift her eyes away? Hard to say in the ill-lit space.

"We thought we might play charades this evening and have come to search the boxes for costumes and props." Camilla whisked a moth-eaten black velvet cloak around her slender shoulders and put up the deep hood. Instantly, she became a sinister figure in the dim light let in by the dormer windows. "I am The Monk come to ensnare the beautiful Antonia with the help of the sorceress, Matilda," she said in a voice made deep and masculine, betraying a taste for the Gothic and a talent for acting all at once.

"Oh, Mama would never allow me to read that book," Tomasina complained. "Have you, Katherine?"

"Yes." She recalled several stormy evenings at Bellevue Hall in Panny's room lit with candles, each of the girls taking a turn at reading aloud the horrifying scenes of torture and rape in Mr. Lewis' masterpiece and not sleeping well afterwards. "Actually, it contains a great deal of political and religious commentary."

"I must have missed those parts," Camilla said as she threw off the cloak and became a beautiful and innocent young lady again. "We've spent enough time up here. I'll have the footmen bring the boxes down to the drawing room, and we will play our special version of the game after our supper."

~ * ~

The fog roiled past the long windows as if it were being stirred by a witch's broomstick. A large fire held back the dark and dampness of Clifton-by-the-Sea. The drawing room was far too large to be cozy, and the guests stayed clustered by the hearth.

Amid the after-supper tea and coffee services, Camilla's mother laid down an enormous tome entitled *Great Lives of Britain*. She directed the girls to open the book at any place and then act out the character found on that page, using the costumes piled behind an oriental screen at one end of the room.

Lady Rushmore offered to demonstrate for Kate how they played the game. She opened the book, made her selection and slammed it shut, went behind the screen, and rummaged through the discarded clothing. Not satisfied, she went out into the hallway. Moments later came the sound of metal crashing to the floor. She re-entered clad in a breastplate and an open helmet borrowed from a suit of armor displayed in an ornamental niche. Clutching a spear also belonging to the now dismantled man of metal, she marched before the other ladies with a murderous look in her eye that seemed to come quite naturally when she stared at Kate.

"Oh, oh, I know!" Tomasina squealed. "Joan of Arc."

"*Great Lives of Britain,* you ninny," Camilla prompted unkindly.

Lady Rushmore drew back an arm as if she were about to lash a slave or a horse and did a mock dash forward, making the women shriek.

"Queen Boadicea in her chariot," Kate guessed.

"Of course." Lady Rushmore shook her head at Tomasina. "You have earned the next turn, Miss Morely."

Kate rose, made her choice, and came out from behind the screen with the black cloak draped over her head and a bent paper crown in her hand. She peered out through a moth hole and seized a round bowl from a table since that seemed permissible. She sat the crown atop the bowl, tucked it under her arm, and wandered the room in a ghostly way.

"Mr. Irving's Headless Horseman," Tomasina guessed first again.

"*Great Lives of Britain,*" Camilla repeated testily.

"Anne Boleyn?" she tried again.

Kate shook her head beneath the very stuffy cloak. She went back behind the screen and found an old, plaid shawl in the bottom of the box. Laying it over one arm, she emerged once more.

"Mary, Queen of Scots," Lady Rushmore said promptly.

"Thank you." Kate shrugged out of the cloak. "It was stifling in there. I'm afraid I do not excel at acting."

"Really. I thought you were rather good at it," Camilla said. "Tilly, you go next since your mama has had her turn."

Matilda came out with an irrevocably stained, old bed sheet knotted on one shoulder and the paper crown on her head. She simply walked around the room.

"Julius Caesar, obviously," Tomasina said as Tilly shook her head.

"*Great Lives of Britain*," Camilla mentioned once more.

"The Emperor Claudius who conquered and civilized Britain," Kate ventured.

"Yes, right." Matilda quickly threw off the sheet and crown and sat down again. "Let Tommy show she can do better."

She could not. Tomasina put on the paper crown and a long, baggy blue gown. The ladies began wildly naming queens and even kings of England. "Oh, I need help," she appealed to her audience. None rushed to get her out of her predicament except Kate who stood nearest.

"Here, tell me."

Tomasina whispered the name, and Kate gave her a suggestion. She went to the tea service and poured from the hot water pot into a cup and back again, simply pure clear water.

"I have it. Eleanor of Aquitaine," Camilla said. "My turn."

With relief, Tomasina took her seat and turned the floor over to her best friend. Camilla took her time choosing the right props. She emerged in the velvet cloak thrown back over her shoulders and a large hat with a broken ostrich plume in the band. She strutted before them, stopped, bowed low as if a queen passed by, then ran ahead to throw her cape down on the Persian carpet. Doffing the hat and flinging it aside, she crowned herself with the paper tiara and walked regally across the cloak.

"Sir Walter Raleigh. Well done," Kate called out.

"You get all of them," Matilda sulked.

Unwilling to give up the center of attention, Camilla stated, "I have another not in the book." She retained the paper crown and mimed the taking of snuff, ending with a delicate sneeze.

"Queen Charlotte, Snuffy Charlotte," her mother guessed.

"Correct, and now another." Camilla tossed the crown away and stood there as a pretty young woman searching an imaginary reticule. She pretended to withdraw something and cupped her hand. She pinched the air, raised her fingertips to her nostrils and inhaled. Another sneeze. "Who am I now?"

"Ah, Miss Morely, Katherine," Tomasina said when the others did not reply.

The Duchess of Strictly was not amused. "We do not mock our guests,

Camilla. I understood you wanted this weekend to befriend Miss Morely. You must apologize to her."

"No need. I might as well confess I do not actually take snuff," Kate murmured.

"So I guessed, since you haven't brought any with you nor used it at all. You lied to win Viscount Astin away from me. I knew your fine eyes and lovely hair, your excellent figure, had nothing to do with it because mine are better!" Camilla accused.

"I did prevaricate, but you needn't fear. I won't be marrying him even if he offers. I have decided."

"How can I trust a liar?"

"Camilla!" her mother said sharply again. "Miss Morely has opened the door to the greatest match of the season for you. Thank her."

Camilla squeezed out the words as if she sucked on a slice of lemon from the tea tray. "Thank you, Katherine."

The duchess indicated the hour had gotten late and bedtime loomed. As they prepared to take their candles to light the way, Tomasina asked timidly, "Are we still going to—go on that picnic tomorrow?"

Camilla smirked. "Certainly. Once the fog clears off, we shall rove hill and dale like gypsies until we find the perfect spot to have our repast. I have apologized. Katherine and I are friends again. Nothing stands in our way of having a wonderful time."

"I am looking forward to it," Matilda said.

"You must take a footman and a few of the dogs," the duchess said.

"Oh, Mama. No one will bother us on Strictly land."

Lady Rushmore added, "Young ladies should experience some freedom while they can before entering the constrictions of marriage."

"Then at least carry a pot of goose grease to Old Burt's cottage for his chest ailment."

"We do plan to visit Old Burt and will leave him some of our provisions, too, I promise."

"Then you will need a good night's rest for all you have planned tomorrow."

"Yes, for all we have planned." Camilla smiled with angelic brightness above the flame of her candle.

Ten

The mist burned off by eleven, and the girls set out. Matilda lugged a very large hamper, and Tomasina a cloth-covered basket of fresh-baked loaves. They went inland away from the roar of the sea. Finding the wind cold, Kate gathered her cloak about her. Not unlike the one she'd worn for charades but far more practical, its deep blue wool became her, even if her eyes were not the color of the sky like Camilla's. The rest of the group wore the more fashionable short spencer jackets, and she was quite sure they grew cold as they walked farther from the house.

As they toiled up a long incline, the sun's rays grew hotter. Kate threw back her hood to embrace the warmth, but the others continued to protect their complexions within their deep bonnets. Below them, a deep ravine cut by a slender, riffled stream widened into an inlet. Far off, a whiff of smoke rose and vanished from the chimney of a small, stone cottage. Trees and brush clung to the sides of the declivity. Vague paths made by deer, goats, or the cottager crisscrossed the steep hillside.

"We are headed to the old keep for our picnic, but my mother has burdened me with a delivery of goose grease to Burt down there." Camilla sighed over the depth of her responsibility. "No sense in all of us delivering the stuff. Tomasina, you know the way to the tower. Guide Katherine there while Tilly and I visit Burt."

"Should I take the hamper?" Kate offered.

"No, no, it contains some old clothes for the caretaker. He's to watch the sea for French ships, but I'd guess he spends most of his time snoring by his fireside and taking bribes from smugglers."

"Smugglers? Should we be out here, then?" Tomasina said.

"They work by night and come by sea. I suspect smuggling is how the Dukes of Strictly made their fortunes. Not now of course, though there would be profit in bringing embargoed goods from France, good brandy and the like. Just take that path to its end. Tilly and I go this way." Camilla set off toward the cottage without looking back, and Matilda followed, still hefting the large hamper.

Tomasina beckoned Kate the other way. At first the path stayed wide enough for two to walk side by side, then it narrowed. Brush crowded the way and snatched with thorny branches at their clothes.

A good way along, plump Tomasina cried, "Drat, I'm winded and my feet hurt." She sank down on a stony outcrop. "The tower isn't much further. You go along. I'll wait for the others. Here, you can carry the basket."

"Shouldn't we stay together if there are smugglers about?"

"You heard Milly. They only come out at night. I'll be along once I catch my breath, but you might as well enjoy the view at the end of the path. This was a very poor idea, I think, but Camilla must always have her way." Tomasina stared at the toes of her aching feet.

"Very well."

More than glad to leave her whining companion behind, Kate continued on the path. To her delight, it widened and opened at a turret hanging above the sea and so cunningly built into the side of the cliff it seemed to be part of it. A great many people paid to erect follies like this, but she suspected the tower to be the real thing, a place to watch for enemies coming from the sea or a secluded prison for those who were caught. The ancient wooden door possessing a huge iron hasp and studded with bolts stood half ajar on massive, rusty hinges. She went inside and set down the basket. The round stone floor could seat four people easily for a pleasant picnic. Kate stood on tiptoes and gazed out through a small barred window. Several pierced the walls with the bars wide enough apart to allow arrows to rain down on attackers in the days before cannons. Now, the tower served only as a place for a gothic fantasy or a secluded lunch.

She heard the others coming, but their footsteps sounded heavier than women's dainty half-boots. They were not chatting and giggling as they had most of the morning. She half-turned to greet her new friends, but they fell upon her, three ruffians with bandanas hiding half their faces and large hats pulled low over their foreheads. Taken by surprise, Kate went down hard on the stones of the floor. Stunned, she failed to put up much of a fight until she heard the one holding her head say in a low, gruff voice, "Lie quiet now, girlie. We be taking a token to show we got ye held for ransom."

Her captor ripped her hair from its pins and yanked it around a fist. The cold metal of a blade skimmed across the top of her skull, and she felt her locks give way strand by strand as the bandit sawed. The tall man sitting astride her chest and pinning her arms growled, "Scar her cheeks and sop the blood in her cloak for proof." His own were pock-marked high on the cheekbones, and his light eyes glittered even in the shadow of his huge, floppy cap.

At Kate's feet, another assailant, soft and lumpish, wearing the brown homespun of a peasant, sat on her ankles. In the unchanged voice of a young boy, that one declared, "You said we would not hurt her."

"Hair grows back, you ninny. We'll not slice her, Matt."

Sensing a lack of resolve in the soft one, Kate drew her leg up suddenly and kicked out hard, catching the lad in a cushiony breast. He bounced backwards emitting a sharp cry. With her legs free, she began to fight in earnest and unbalanced the tall one who gripped her wrists in his big hands. With one fist freed, she bopped the man behind her hard as she could.

"Damnation, she's marked me! I should—I should…" The voice came out high and shrill. Kate's eyes rolled upward to see the knife that had shorn her hair raised high. The big one had control of her wrists again.

The lad scrambled to his feet and revealed a flash of violet eyes, but stayed that hand. "You promised. Let's go."

"Raise her up and hold her, Matt. Tom, take off her shoes."

That directive earned Tom a kick to the chin. The leader came and held Kate's legs until the shoes came off.

"Now hold her until we get to the door. Then, give her a shove and join us."

Her tall captor did as their leader said, but Kate made him pay with an elbow hard to the ribs. With an exclamation, he threw her against the far wall. As she sank to the floor again, the one who held her hank of hair plucked out a few strands and tossed the rest down. He kicked the mass of shining, brown locks aside with his boot.

"We have no need for the rest."

Before Kate could scramble after them, they were out the door and putting their weight against it as one fastened a huge padlock to the hasp. Charging against the barrier only did her more damage, adding a sore shoulder to her bumps and bruises. But if she had been quicker, she might have fought free.

The voice that had gone shrill deepened again. "Ye've got food for several days and this."

A small hatch opened in the base of the door. The leader toed a corked jug through it and other hands shoved a bucket through the opening. "Water and a pail for a necessary. Should anyone want to pay a ransom for a termagant like you, ye'll be released. Otherwise, ye'll die here. Come Tom and Matt. Let's leave her to rot 'cause no one will claim her."

Kate stared after the retreating figures through the small, barred window in the door. She started to call out, "I know who you are!" and then realized if she gave that away, they might never return for her.

Instead, she shouted, "The Longleighs will come for me. You shall see!"

Eleven

"We were superb!" Camilla Sharpton declared as she shucked off her peasant's clothes and heavy boots behind a stout bush and wriggled back into her gown and petticoats. Tomasina stepped forward to help her with ties and buttons. Matilda held her spencer. Both had yet to change their disguises. Camilla always went first. Now, she sat on a rock and stuck out her feet. Tilly knelt and replaced her half-boots as their ringleader dabbed her own cheek with a hankie.

"Tell me, Tommy, how badly did that bitch mark me?"

Tomasina leaned forward. "She broke the tender skin beneath your eye, and it will blacken. You'd better concoct some tale to explain it."

"A tale is no problem, but what if I should scar? For this blow she spends another seven days in the tower. I'd planned on only a week before I sent Old Burt to release her. Let her exist on bread and water even longer."

Matilda rubbed together those large, mannish hands she'd inherited from her mother. "Yes, we'll starve her down until her proud bosom is as flat as two pennies. Who will want a bald, flat-chested bride this season? Astin must reject her, and the Longleighs will turn aside."

Tomasina, taking her turn behind the bush, moaned. "Oh, I've a massive bruise on my left breast, and my chin is swelling. To think, we believed Katherine would cry and beg for her life."

"That would have been gratifying. She is an unnatural woman to be so fierce," Camilla pronounced.

"Mama says Katherine is practically a Longleigh, and they are a barbaric and murderous lot. Scratch their skin and they bleed red Indian. Lady Flora learned her fierceness from her husband, she says. All of society calls them and their close friends 'The Tribe'." Matilda paused in her exposé of the Longleighs to scratch under her armpit in a most unladylike way. "Do hurry, Tommy. I think these garments are louse-ridden. We should have stuck to our costumes from the attic and not borrowed more from Old Burt."

"The attic garments were too small to fit you, Tilly. Stop complaining. I had to wear his hat to cover my blonde hair, or she would have known us for certain. Thank goodness I have a true talent for acting, even if I rarely get to use it."

Tomasina came out from behind the bush to be helped into her own spencer that covered her bruise quite well. "But I shall not be able to wear any of my ball gowns without something stuffed in the neckline," she complained.

"Hurry up with your change, Tilly. We barely have time to eat before we start back for the seaside. We must pray for an early fog tonight. My, mayhem has given me an appetite." Camilla opened the hamper to take out the lunch and repack the costumes. She flicked aside the lock of hair she'd taken from Kate. "No real need to keep that. Merely a prop in our play."

After distributing bread, fruit, cheese, cold meats, and some chocolate biscuits from the depths of the hamper, Camilla worked out the cork from a pilfered bottle of wine with the tip of the knife. She held the green bottle high.

"A toast to our success! Katherine Morely is my rival no more." She drank from the narrow neck and passed the bottle to Matilda.

"To us!" Tilly gulped down several swallows and wiped her mouth with the back of her mannish hand. "I do feel like a true brigand."

Tomasina took a small sip. "Brigands are hung for kidnapping, you know."

"Stop fretting. You are ruining our triumph over Miss Morely. She will believe she has been captured and held for ransom by the smugglers. Burt will keep his eye on her and release her when I send him the key. Shattered by her captivity and physical condition, she'll not return to society for some time. By then, I will have decided between Astin and Longleigh, each so handsome and with such fine prospects, I wish I could have them both." Camilla blotted her lips with a napkin and tossed it into the hamper.

Still, Tomasina worried. "The Longleighs *will* come here, you can be sure. Katherine made no idle threat. Here I am with a chin swollen larger than Jason's and his is so very manly. I cannot face him."

"Better you don't. One languorous glance from him and you will spill the whole story. Come help me find a holly bush or some evergreens to block the path to the tower. No sense in inviting people to find her."

Camilla hacked off a small holly at its base and her cohorts ripped low branches from evergreen trees. They piled them in front of the path. Although overheated and scratched from their work, they were content with the results and merry from the wine. Camilla swung Kate's shoes from her fingertips.

"You see, we have only to plant one on the cliff and toss the other down on the rocks to misdirect any search for her. We shall hide until the fog begins to move onshore, then make our way close to the house. Our injuries will be explained by tripping over rocks and such in the darkness. We became separated from Kate, and alas, fear she took a header into the sea. We will be most distraught. Can you act distraught, Tommy?"

"I am already."

"Listen for a moment. I can hear her crying for help ever so slightly. 'Tis like the song of a delightful caged bird to me. Onward to the nether sea, my fellow brigands. Onward."

~ * ~

What a stupid thing to do, crying out for help because she thought she'd heard women's voices. Assuredly, she had. The same ones who had locked her in this keep. Now, she'd parched her throat screaming for help when she knew she had a limited supply of water. Kate sank down beside the basket that contained the bread and ate a small portion, took a few sips from the jug. During the scuffle, the basket had been overturned, some of the bread trodden upon, but she'd gathered up every morsel, not knowing how long they'd leave her there.

Clearly some planning had gone into her kidnapping since she'd carried her own prison bread into the tower. Only Camilla seemed bright enough for that—or Lady Rushmore. Well, the duchess had warned her, but she'd thought herself too clever to be caught. Just look at her now!

Kate ran her hands over her scalp. No blood, just a sorry stubble left on top and tufts around the back and ears. They'd done this out of sheer jealousy and malice because her hair *was* very lovely, even if not blonde. Was once very lovely, she corrected herself. She gathered it to make a pillow for the night, to make a hairpiece for later. A gust of wind skirled around the stone chamber, found a few loose strands, and carried them up to catch in the bars of the windows before returning to the sea.

Supposedly, Camilla had invited her to Clifton to make her a friend. Was this some sort of initiation rite? Men went in for that sort of thing: secret handshakes, hidden meeting places, strange ceremonies. Women had more sense than to dabble in such stuff, she'd always thought. No, this had the stink of vengeance upon it.

Did they really think she'd be fooled by big hats, bandannas, and men's clothing? Each had such distinctive eyes, and Matilda could not cover all her facial scars. When she'd kicked out her foot, it encountered no flat, male chest but the soft, sponginess of a woman's breast. Nor had they tried to rape her, a sure giveaway.

As for Camilla's acting abilities, certainly good enough for charades but hardly Shakespeare. Why, she could not settle on any one accent, now a pirate, now a shrieking eunuch, and the use of long words like "termagant," too. How would she explain the shiner to her mother or Kate's absence? The excuse would be well and cunningly thought out, for sure.

Camilla wanted only the best men for herself. Kate pitied anyone who did marry that bitch. So handsome and wealthy, yet not overly intelligent, Harold must be protected and warned against her. As for Joshua Longleigh, he should be able to see Camilla's slyness, but blinded as he was by her beauty and status, his brain remained addled. Regardless, her last words to those miscreant girls had been God's truth. The Longleighs would come for her. That family had skills and tenacity Camilla could not even begin to imagine. They would make her sorry.

The sun circled the tower windows at one point, glowing on a series of scratches in the wall near the door. Someone else had marked time here. Kate picked up one of her scattered hairpins and made a single mark on the opposite side. The golden rays slipped away like sand through her fingers. She licked her dry lips and took a drink from the jug.

The wind died, and its ghost, the fog, haunted her chamber. Kate drew her stocking feet up under the cloak and raised the hood to keep the unaccustomed chill from her naked neck. She laid her head on the bundle of hair and, exhausted by speculation, gave herself over to sleep.

Twelve

"Oh, my poor babies, my sweet young girls!" the Duchess of Strictly cried as she tried to keep her face impassive and thus less susceptible to wrinkles as she'd always taught her daughter.

With a piece of beefsteak pressed to her blackened eye, Camilla lay on her bed, Tomasina right beside her with a similar remedy applied to her chin. They looked and smelled like carrion, and her mother's exclamations helped very little.

Lady Rushmore directed a maid to tie the bandages around Matilda's rib cage more tightly. She gave the knot a smart tug when the servant could not get it done right. Tilly gasped, then scratched the back of her neck.

"How foolish of you to wander off and get caught by the fog. Who knows the fate of poor Miss Morely?" Lady Rushmore almost crooned.

She did. The fake abduction had been her idea. Camilla closed her good eye to shut out the sight of the woman. Lady Rushmore had given no hint that injury could possibly come to the perpetrators. Full of high spirits supplied by the wine, they'd started back to the coastline but when only halfway there, became aware of their throbbing wounds. Tilly complained of a stitch in her side sure to be a cracked rib and made the others heft the large hamper with its burden of clothes, soon to be abandoned behind a boulder. Then came the misery of waiting for the fog to approach after they had wedged one of Kate's shoes in a crack on the edge of the cliff, tossed the other over onto the rocks, and backed away.

They'd crouched in a dark area of the garden wall and waited for the search party to go out around the time they missed their supper, a fact Tomasina kept mentioning. Slipping closer to the gate, they feigned their rescue when the mist-diffused light of the lanterns held high by the servants came close. Still, no supper for them. Her goose of a mother had sent them straight up to bed to be treated as if they ran a high fever instead of having a few bumps and bruises. Clear soup was ordered up for them. The servants went out again in the thicker pea soup of the fog to swing their lamps and call for Kate.

Tomasina whispered that she wished she could eat the steak lying across her chin. Matilda scratched her head with both hands, and her mother's fingers descended like the claws of a raptor about to seize a mouse into the straw-colored field of her hair. Lady Rushmore cracked an insect between her fingernails.

"How did *my* daughter generate lice?" she asked sternly.

Matilda tried to stick out that retreating chin of hers. "The duchess asked us to take goose grease to that miserable old tenant. I am sure he had them in his cottage."

"No need to be so defensive. In the days of my youth, it was necessary to open our high coiffures once a week and root out the vermin. A paste of lard, quicksilver, and stavesacre laid on the scalp overnight will do the trick. We'd best treat all the girls to be safe. Go, bring the necessary ingredients," she directed the always inept maid. "I shall mix the cure myself."

"Fresh linens as well. Up, up," Lady Strickly commanded.

When the ingredients for the cure arrived, Lady Rushmore ground the herbs in a mortar with gusto. She blended crushed leaves with the lard and added a liberal dosage of mercury.

The remedy smeared on linen cloths and bound around the girls' heads like heathen turbans stank from the hog's grease. There might have been bacon cooking in the room as the three of them sat in their nightgowns close to the fire. Camilla's only satisfaction came from knowing Kate must be more miserable. Her mother began an interrogation of sorts.

"You did deliver the goose grease to Old Burt and then walked all the way back to the sea, a most ambitious ramble."

"Too ambitious, Mama. That is why we were caught by the fog. Poor Katherine walked behind us. She must have gone straight and toppled into the sea before we found the path home. Such a sad, cruel fate."

Tears came easily when one's beautiful hair was slathered with lard and quicksilver. Still, she rejoiced that they'd gone through with the plan. How she hated great, gray Clifton-by-the-Sea with its perpetual winds and filthy weather. All the trees about the place grew twisted, and flowers in the garden did not thrive. Now, Astin's place in the country, she'd heard, was a veritable Eden set amongst green, rolling hills and abloom with all sorts of exotic plants. Gentle deer and snowy white sheep grazed the area. Golden pheasants roamed the fields, and peacocks strutted the walks. Here, even the sheep were gray, their coats full of brambles. The birds were ordinary, and only gulls made raucous cries.

Bellevue Hall had a reputation for magnificence, too, but it lay far to the north, very isolated in winter. Though there was a good chance James Longleigh, the heir, would not survive his adventures, she had learned this very day that marriages and successions could be helped in the right direction with enough planning. Should she marry Joshua, James would surely come home for the wedding. How sad if he expired from indigestion at the celebratory feast.

With Kate out of the running, both Joshua Longleigh and Astin would be at her feet, a difficult choice—one so virile and handsome, the other so golden and pliable to a woman's wishes. Full of thoughts, Camilla barely heard her mother say, "Katherine might have taken shelter until morning. We will search again before sending word to Bellevue."

~ * ~

Come morning, the wind dispersed the fog and dispensed a three-day gale. The Devil seemed to be on their side. Though Camilla's mother fretted, naught could be done about a search for that common girl who had wandered off in the fog.

Instead, the young ladies chanced their health by washing their heads on a chill and rainy day. Camilla snapped at the maid who drew a fine-toothed comb through her golden locks in search of nits.

"You are pulling out my hair by the roots, you clumsy dolt. Look at that clump on the floor. I shall do my own combing. You are dismissed."

"I believe Mama's remedy might have been too strong," Matilda said. Her thin lips trembled as she regarded the wad of dark blonde curls caught in her own comb. "My hair is my best feature. Was my best feature."

Tomasina burst into tears as a dark hank came loose near her crown. Lady Rushmore arrived to chastise them all.

"Such pathetic, mewing little kittens, be grateful your hair will grow back louse-free, thanks to me. I know many ways to cover a temporary bald spot and disguise thinning hair. I wonder you had the courage to carry out your plans if this slight mishap makes you cry."

Tomasina bawled even harder. "We are being punished for our sin!"

"Bah, you are being treated for lice. This stormy weather favors you, but it might blow off by tomorrow, and the search will begin. Don't ruin everything by sniveling."

Those words of encouragement given, Lady Rushmore swept from the room. Her daughter commented as soon as the door shut behind her.

"I believe my mama enjoys seeing us so lowered. She is ever jealous of pretty young women. I suspect that is one reason she hates Lady Flora, because the duchess has kept so well in age."

"Do you think Lady Flora will come—and Jason and Joshua?" Tomasina asked in a tear-clogged voice.

"The whole family will descend once they get word. The Longleighs are very close." Camilla touched the cut under her eyes and squeezed the wad of fallen hair in her small, white fist. "And just look at us."

As Lady Rushmore predicted, the gale did peter out the next day. Under Lady Strictly's orders, a party of servants set out late in the day scouring the area along the sea where their young mistress said she and her friends had become lost. They returned with a half-boot found solidly wedged in a crack on the edge of the cliff and placed it in the duchess's hands. The young ladies identified it as belonging to Miss Morely as it was not quite as fine as theirs. The three wept with hands covering their eyes, Camilla hardest of all. A mounted messenger went to brave the muddy roads and carry the dire news to London.

Thirteen

Kate woke with one hip sore from lying on the stone floor all night. The wind splashed rain between the bars of the windows as if the god of the sea were sluicing the tower with giant buckets. She sat the basket of bread on top of her mass of shorn hair, unwilling to share any more of it with the breeze. Finding a dry spot, she sat with her back against the wall of the chamber. Surely, the girls planned to come for her today, but the weather would delay them. The gale might last several days, however. She must put her mind to practical matters like conserving her food and water.

Last evening, she'd had an unwelcome visitor. He'd nosed through the small trap door and snuffled his way to the bread basket, running right over her as if she were nothing more than a log in the way. How she'd wished she had a shoe to throw, but the rat, his red eyes resentful, did retreat when she sat up and waved her arms. After that incident, she'd cradled the bread under her cloak. The rain would discourage his company if it continued on into the night—and any rescue as well.

Water, evidently, would be no problem for the moment. She tore off a strip of petticoat and soaked the white cloth in the puddle forming under the windows. It spread out into a depression around the outer edge of the curved wall. Kate could imagine how that sunken circle came to be. Someone had paced away the days in this place. She might be doing that soon, too. For now, she sat in the center of the chamber like a washerwoman surrounded by her tubs, dipping the strip of petticoat into the rain water and wringing out the coil into the narrow neck of the water jug. Using the slop bucket would have made the task easier, but regretting the amount of water consumed already, she'd used it last evening and this morning. Sullied now, she could not use the container for anything else. Ah well, sopping water from the floor passed the time.

She ate only when her stomach cried out so loudly she swore it had a voice of its own. Saving the water in the jug, she scooped up handfuls from the puddle. Leaning over the ring of water, she marked the wall for the second day of her captivity. Other than that, she hadn't much to do except curl up in her cape in the center of the tower and sleep. Before lying down, she knelt in prayer thanking God for her hearty constitution, for the rain providing more water, and for the friendship of the Longleigh family who would certainly come for her.

By the scratches on the wall, Kate knew the gale lasted three days. The roads to and from London would be impassible and rescue delayed. She wondered what stories the girls had told to explain her absence. Lost while playing an innocent game, slipped over the cliff's edge, taken by smugglers? She had little else to do than make up stories of her own.

She gorged on water to fill her stomach, allowing herself only one piece of bread a day, but still her food dwindled down to the stale, squashed loaf bearing a boot print. The sun returned to dry up her moat and finally steal her puddle after another two days. She saved the water in the jug and drank only sparingly.

At least the ending of the storm brought her a diversion. A common sparrow looking to feather its nest perched between the bars of Kate's cage. The bird threw down a straw in favor of the few strands of hair still caught there. For the company, Kate placed a few more hairs on the bars hoping for its return. Industriously, the sparrow went back and forth, back and forth, building a home somewhere along the cliff.

A thought occurred. Birds were the messengers of the air. She'd heard of pigeons being used to carry letters and military orders. In fact, the Longleigh boys had attempted that once, but the ordinary pigeons merely flew away. Why not try a sparrow if the note were very light? She wanted it to return to carry her appeal for help. Tearing off another strip of petticoat—what a useful thing it was—she considered how she might write upon it. A hairpin, perhaps? Or a broken reed from the nearly empty and badly trampled bread basket? The reed snapped off, leaving a sharp, pointed end at its tip with a small hollow behind, not unlike the end of a quill or the nib of a pen.

And now for ink. Only one choice there. Driving the point of the reed into a vein at her wrist, Kate allowed the hollow space to fill with her blood. "Help," she wrote on the strip of cloth. She squeezed more blood from the wound into her makeshift pen and scratched out "In the." With the final dribbles before the puncture clotted, she got "tower" down on the thin piece of cloth. Hard to write so small on fabric that wanted to wrinkle at every stroke. The letters came out shaky and ill-formed, but legible, she thought. She poked a small hole in the cloth at one end.

Now to capture her messenger. Ripping off a wide swath of petticoat, oh, she would have cold legs tonight, Kate formed a net to throw over the sparrow. Carefully setting aside the remaining bread, she shook out the bottom of the basket onto the sill to scatter crumbs only big enough to feed a bird. She scattered more on the floor directly below and baited the window with extra strands of hair.

Carrying out each of her actions while the bird was absent so as not to startle it required patience. Patience, Uncle Bear had taught her, was required when hunting or hiding from an enemy. Patience and stillness. She had a talent for both.

How often had she run ahead to a divided path at Bellevue and taken a few steps forward on one branch, being sure to leave a footprint in a muddy place or disturb some moss? Then, she'd wriggle into the bushes and sit quiet as a woodcock for the boys to pass. The Longleigh sons were always in full cry like a pack of hounds and not very observant. After they ran off down the wrong trail, she'd double back to the house to be rewarded with a sweet by Uncle Bear and a berating by her mother for her torn and dirty frocks. Dear Auntie Flora would say, "Exercise is good for women as well as men."

Eventually, the boys had learned patience and stillness, too. Joshua would signal Jason to dash ahead, making as much noise as possible while he popped behind a tree. When she broke cover to run home, he'd leap upon her in a way that would have made her mother swoon. She'd liked it. Even then in the way of a child, she had loved Joshua Longleigh. Where was he now? Why hadn't he come searching with the family she'd always admired and adored?

No time for despair. Kate flattened herself by the window and waited. Out of the corner of her eye, she saw the sparrow alight and cock its head. To take more hair for its nest or to dine on crumbs? It pecked at her offering and finished it off. Beady black eyes considered the crumbs on the floor. The bird looked this way and that. Kate did not move. It fluttered down to the stones of the tower floor and began to feed.

When its tiny head turned away from her, she flung the cloth wide. The sparrow startled up, but she arched her body over the trap and held it down. Gradually, patiently, she moved her hands inward until the bird was caught in a small pocket. Gently, she cupped it in her hands and exposed only the fragile legs. The bird's clawed toes clenched up into a little fist. She worked the hole in the message strip carefully over the foot and released her captive. In a panic, the bird flew round and round the chamber at first, its little flag unfurling after it. Kate shooed it toward the window, and at last, it found its way out.

"Come again," she called after it, but the bird had more sense than to return to a lair where a predator waited. If only she'd had the same good instincts.

The rat returned that night, but Kate slept with the last portion of bread hugged close to her dwindling chest. When its whiskers touched her cheek, she awoke and batted it away fiercely. The vermin scuttled across the floor to the broken breadbasket, sniffed, and began to gnaw at the reeds still redolent with its former contents. She lay still, watching and thinking. If a bird could serve as a messenger, then why not a rat? When she had daylight again, she would write another message and set her trap for the nighttime visitor.

On her sixth day of captivity, Kate did exactly that. She prepared a slightly larger strip of cloth, poked a hole through one end and made another in her wrist. Did she imagine her blood ran slower because of her starvation? She'd eaten all but a morsel of bread this morning and that must be saved to lure the rat. Her message remained the same but slightly expanded: "Help me. In the tower below." She had no idea how far a rat might range for food but hoped it went seeking out of the ravine and into the fields. As for the basket, she twisted and worked off the handle already damaged by crushing and the teeth of the rodent so it would lie flat when she pushed it down.

After making her preparations, she had little else to do but pace round and round the tower following the groove left by another. This proved to be a poor idea as she became dizzy and light-headed. After emptying her lightly used slop bucket out one of the barred windows, her urine now dark as brown ale, she drank from the water jug and lay down to rest. After all, she would be up at night just like the rat.

By the time she woke, the sun had set on the other side of England. Kate stirred herself to place the basket on its side and put out the last bit of bread as bait. She wrapped in her cloak and sat as still as a part of the stone wall behind the trap. Hours passed in waiting. The moon advanced from one window to another as she sat on the hard, cold floor. A tiny squeak of the trap door sounded, and the rat entered. Rising up, it sniffed the air and looked toward where she usually lay. Finding nothing there, it advanced, skittering across the floor to the basket. How she wanted to snatch back the last of the bread as it began to nibble. Saliva pooled in her mouth. One could eat rat. Prisoners often did. But no, she needed this creature as a messenger.

Swiftly, she clamped the basket against the floor. The rat fought furiously. Its pink tail lashed out from under the edge. Holding the basket down with most of her body, Kate attempted to capture the scaly tail as elusive as a snake in the grass. Finally, she had it and slipped the message all the way up its length to where it rooted in the animal. Hoping the creature would not bite her when released, she cautiously raised the trap. It bolted for the small door leaving behind the bit of bread. Thankful, Kate raised it to her lips and ate.

On the seventh day, having no other choice with her energy waning, she sat with her back against the rock wall and rested.

Fourteen

"Oh, Milly, here they come! The Longleighs have arrived. Aren't they magnificent? Jason is with them."

Tomasina peeped out the window of the bed chamber where the three guilty parties had waited all morning. She fingered the crust on her chin and decided she must apply more powder. Better off than Camilla, she thought, as both paint and powder failed to cover all the damage around her eye. The small, crescent-shaped scab made by Kate's fist raised up on the perfect oval plane of her face, and the delicate eyelid remained slightly empurpled.

Matilda merely stood stiffly, her wound unnoticeable. "Mama said they would come on the seventh day, given the conditions of the roads. As for their magnificence, she is also correct in stating any one of them might cut your throat and take your scalp, even Lady Pandora and the duchess."

Still, en masse, they were a sight to behold. The Duke of Bellevue, that imposing man of the copper skin and iron gray hair, sat astride a black horse big enough to have served as a knight's charger. Next to him, Pandora Longleigh, her expression murderous, rode sidesaddle on a delicate mare, also black in color. Behind the pair, Joshua and Jason, tall in the saddle and dark-visaged, cantered along on matched bays. The impressive ducal coach and four brought up the rear. An ominous, oblong box rode on its roof—a coffin for Kate.

"Yes, even the duchess has come," Tomasina said with awe in her voice.

"They travel together like a tribe of wild Indians," a voice uttered behind them.

Lady Rushmore had entered so quietly while they stood at the window, none had heard.

"You have nothing to fear. Bold they might be, but the Longleighs have no head for guile and will suspect nothing as long as you stand by your story. If they should stumble across the girl while searching, she will know only that she was taken by three men who intended to ask for ransom. What became of them, who knows? So, steady your nerves and look them in the eye when they question you, especially that little viper, Lady Flora."

"Katherine is to stay another week in her prison for damaging me," Camilla said pettishly.

"It would be better if that did happen. The young woman is intelligent and might recognize the marks she gave you. Better you are all well-healed before she is released. Steel your nerves and ready yourselves to meet our guests." Lady Rushmore left as stealthily as she'd come, not a noise to mark her presence or her connivance.

Tomasina paused for a moment at the dressing table mirror to make sure her scab remained concealed and her tucker covered the yellow bruising on her chest. "I've been thinking. We locked Kate in the tower on a sunny afternoon, yet we claim we lost her in the fog. When she is released, won't she notice the difference in our stories?"

"If we'd followed Mama's first suggestion and simply shoved her off a cliff, we would not be in danger of exposure now. But some person lost their nerve and wouldn't have it—Tomasina." Matilda stood by the door ready to go as her looks could not be improved.

Camilla frowned, then quickly erased the line-forming expression from her face. "The fog story was necessary to lead any searchers astray and keep her release under our control. We are not murderers. We simply want this annoying girl to creep back to the country with her shorn head covered and not return to London this season. She will be in no condition to question our story by the time we let her go."

"But the Longleighs might," Tomasina fretted.

"Do not try to do the thinking for us, Tommy. You aren't up to it. At last resort, we can always say we feared the smugglers would come after us, too, if we ran for the house and tried to reveal their deed. So, we stayed hidden for our own sakes and then were caught in the fog. We made up the story about Kate's fall to cover our guilt over leaving her to the mercies of the kidnappers. We are only poor, frightened maidens." Camilla formed her pretty bowed lips into an oval of dismay and pretended to hold back tears with the batting of her eyelashes.

"Simple stories are always better," Matilda quoted her mother.

"Too late for that now," Tommy answered with a quiver in her voice.

~ * ~

The Duke of Bellevue, his diminutive wife on one side and his daughter, Euphemia, on the other, filled the gold velvet settee in the drawing room. Joshua Longleigh had chosen to stand behind them between his brother and sister who had also declined a seat. His hands, large and competent like his father's, gripped the carved rosewood back of their seat. Across the width of a low table bearing refreshments, the young women sat on a matching piece of furniture while Ladies Strictly and Rushmore perched on delicate chairs framing them on either side. Everyone was so exceedingly polite, as if they were about to play parlor games.

Joshua wanted to shout, "What have you done to Kate!" but of course, he let his father do the talking. As the duke slowly made his point that the Longleighs would conduct their own search of the coastline, Josh studied those three ornaments of the ballroom. Make that two as Matilda Everton would never be considered ornamental. She sat very stiffly, her face painted over her scars as usual, her pale blue eyes staring straight into the space over the duke's head and between his and Jason's shoulders. She showed no emotion at all over the loss of a supposed new friend.

Tomasina Murray's eyes avoided them all, now glancing at her shoe tips, now darting a look at Lady Rushmore. She showed less of her bosom than usual, that feature being one of her prides as she'd often hinted it exceeded Camilla's chest by far. Her chin seemed larger, more like her rotund mother's, and powdered more than usual. It bore a small dent he hadn't noticed before. He knew Jason fancied her in an off-hand sort of way, but felt his brother should beware of those shifting violet orbs.

As for Camilla, he'd never known her to use paint at all as her complexion was so very fine and porcelain. Now she sat as lacquered as some of his mother's friends in their pursuit of an eternal youth. Her expression remained as always: a slight smile on her bowed pink lips, cornflower blue eyes wide, innocent, and devoid of expression, very doll-like. Although her blonde curls were carefully arranged, they appeared dull and frizzled as if she had used the potion of a mad hairdresser and shared it with her friends, particularly Matilda.

"And so you see, since Katherine Morely was in our charge, we would like to make another search along your coast. Should we find her remains, we have carried along a lead coffin to return her to her parents at Greenway Grange," the duke stated.

The duchess added, "We have not yet informed her family while any hope remains. Her mother is making a slow recovery from a virulent fever, and this sad news might bring her down again."

"Poor Katherine," Camilla said. She dabbed at her eyes with a lace-edged hankie and not being used to paint, wiped a bit of it away. A yellow patch the color of mutton fat left too long in the larder appeared under her eye and drew attention to a small, raised crescent on her cheekbone.

Joshua recalled suffering a similar wound as a child when Kate had defied capture in their game and driven a fist into his face. The little scar had smoothed out as he grew, and even if it hadn't, he would have considered it manly so long as no one knew a girl had given it to him. He doubted if Camilla was pleased by this small disfigurement. She fluttered her lashes at him, and he felt faintly repelled by her attention for the very first time. How could she flirt when a girl of her own age lay dead somewhere? When Kate was no more?

"You know all three of us suffered injuries wandering in the fog," Camilla said as soon as she noticed the stain on her handkerchief. "God's will saved us from going over the cliff as well."

"I doubt God had any hand in this," the Duchess of Bellevue replied tartly. She glared at Lady Rushmore.

"My wife means that being more familiar with the surroundings, naturally you found your way home. We do appreciate the restoratives after our journey, but must make the most of the remaining daylight." The duke gestured toward the barely touched tiered plates of food. "Lady Flora and Euphemia will remain here and visit. Pandora insists on joining the search as Kate was her best friend, but I dread what she might see. Would you reconsider, child?"

"My stomach is as strong as any man's, Papa. I will do this service for Kate."

"Go along then, daughter. Phemie and I will sort things out here," the duchess said.

"Why would that be necessary?" Lady Rushmore asked as if offended.

"At the very least, we must see Kate's belongings are packed to return to her family. That was my meaning."

Lady Strictly answered. "We intend to return to London shortly. The girls need diversions from their sorrow and deserve their season despite this terrible incident. We could bring her box along with us." Slightly horrified with herself, Lady Strictly blathered on. "I meant her clothing and such, not the coffin. Oh, dear!"

"We will leave the coffin if we do not find her in case it is needed later." Having made this offer, the duke stood as did everyone else in the room. "If you will have a servant show us the place where the shoe was found, we will begin there."

"Of course. I will show Lady Flora to Miss Morely's chamber myself and assign a maid to assist with the packing."

The men and Pandora went to claim their mounts, and Lady Strictly led the way to the room where Kate had spent her last night at Clifton. The three girls ghosted after them, though Lady Rushmore remained behind tucking into the biscuits and tarts with surprising appetite. At the top of the stairs, the young ladies departed in the opposite direction to rest, they said. Evidently, Kate's chamber in a corner near the servants' stairs lay far from theirs. The duchess watched the three youthful forms open their doors and vanish from sight. Lady Strictly left, too, as soon as the maid arrived and received her orders to help with the packing.

The duchess gazed out over the walled garden meant to cut some of the wind from the sea. How it howled around this corner and blighted the plantings below. Lucretia Sharpton had traded her beauty for a grand title, Duchess of Strictly, and a forbidding estate. Personally, she felt Bellevue Hall to be most superior with its blue crags in the distance and its riotous burst of spring blooms.

The chamber itself was small, decent enough for lesser guests, and the furnishings of good quality. While not a luxurious space, Kate had certainly been comfortable in her last days—if she hadn't had nightmares brought on by the raging winds.

The duchess began to sort through a small bandbox of ribbons and inexpensive jewelry trying to recall if everything Kate owned remained there. Servants would pilfer if allowed in a situation like this. The maid opened the armoire and began removing Kate's neatly folded clothing. Phemie watched her pack the unmentionables and then a spencer jacket.

"She must have been wearing the blue cloak she so loved, Mama. That will keep her warm, but—but her feet will be so cold." Tears filled Phemie's large, dark eyes.

The duchess embraced her daughter. "There, there. I cannot help feeling Camilla's jealousy over the attention Astin paid Kate had something to do with her disappearance. I note she did not bring her snuffbox to keep up the pretense, unless someone took it."

"She left it behind," Phemie sniffed. "She intended to tell Camilla she would not accept Astin's proposal should he offer, so she would have no reason to harm Kate."

The maid looked up from her chore. "If I might speak, Your Grace?"

The duchess nodded ascent.

"Miss Morely was as nice a young lady as could be, not demanding like the others. I waited in the hall the night before her disappearance to carry away the tea and coffee service and the remains of the food after they had played their charades. Lady Camilla did not believe Miss Morely and accused her of lying to gain some man's affections. If it helps to know this, I am pleased, but I implore you not to tell our duchess I tattled on her daughter."

"I would not dream of betraying you and give you thanks."

~ * ~

The riders dismissed their guide and got down to examine the cleft in the rock where Kate's shoe had lodged.

"The edge is quite solid here. It certainly did not crumble beneath her," the duke declared. "It holds my weight very well."

"I cannot imagine Kate doing anything so absurd as wandering off a cliff even in the fog. She had the good sense to put her back to a tree or rock and wait until morning to move or be found. She wasn't silly and given to vapors like other girls." Joshua looked at the rocks a long way down. The surf surged around the toe of another half-boot wedged amongst them and unreachable.

"They pushed her over, I am sure," Pandora swore. "All because of that stupid, stupid wager. If you had married her as we all desired, none of this would have happened."

"Now Panny, accusations and hindsight do no good," her father scolded. "We are here to find Kate and bring her home."

"If she fell at this place, why is her body not below?" Jason asked.

"The sea might have claimed her, son. Often, it does not return its dead."

Joshua slammed a fist into his open hand. "Do not say it! We might find her still, injured below and unable to climb up. Jason and I will search to our left, and you to the right back toward Clifton. I think we should look beyond the house in the other direction, too, in case she was taken out to sea and fetched up on another beach. Stranger things have happened with tides and currents."

"Good plan." The duke hiked his daughter into her sidesaddle and remounted his own steed. He watched his sons start a careful progress away from them.

"Come, Panny. As the poet said, 'Hope springs eternal in the human breast,' but I suspect Joshua will suffer mightily if we do not find her. You need not chafe him about it."

Josh overheard as his father was not known for lowering his voice, no matter how gentle the reprimand. If only his sister were not right in her conclusions, but Pandora did have a good mind, often insightful. People might listen to her more often if she weren't so strident. Camilla had made remarks more than once about Kate's inferior breeding. While he did not agree with her, he had stayed silent. After all, hadn't he told the friend of his childhood, the girl who wrote to him at school causing his mates to tease him in their jealousy, very much the same thing, that she was not good enough for London?

Yet, suddenly, Camilla had wanted to befriend the young woman who had stolen Astin from her. As Panny might say, one solid push over the cliff and her rival was gone. No, the woman he sought as his wife surely had only sweetness on her lips and no evil in her soul. Yet, she had set that clumsy trap for him in the garden. Its very awkwardness spoke of guileless innocence. He hadn't liked her for it but understood Camilla might have been feeling some desperation after losing Astin. Her dry little gesture had not stirred him, not like Kate's kiss. Now Kate was lost to him. How fitting, how richly he deserved to suffer.

He and Jason searched on, finding nothing. They reunited with his father and Pandora for a quickly bolted and ill-appreciated dinner at Clifton. The duke announced their intention to continue on past the house as long as daylight held. Rapid glances shot from Camilla seated between the Longleigh brothers to Tomasina and Matilda seated opposite.

"Your way will be impeded by a jumble of boulders and a deep, impassible ravine, I'm afraid," Camilla offered suddenly.

"I would not venture into the ravine. It is quite treacherous," Lady Strictly cautioned.

"Yes, very treacherous," Lady Rushmore agreed.

"We shall be cautious," the duke assured her.

Declining the final offering of cheese and nuts, the search party resumed their labor. This way was shorter, and they did indeed come to a clump of boulders that blocked their way. The wind moaned through gaps in the rocks and made a sound like a woman keening.

"We could ride along the edge of the ravine and attempt to look down into it," Joshua suggested.

"A slim chance that, but we shall do it anyway," his father decided.

They set their heels to their horses and cantered away. Joshua pulled up suddenly and fell behind. "I swear I heard Kate's voice calling me just now."

The duke cocked his head to listen. The others did as well.

"Sorry, son. I hear only the wind. Sorry."

His guilt had shaped the very air into hope. He deserved his disappointment.

They continued on. Suddenly, a large flock of sparrows flushed from the clefts of the ravine directly in front of Pandora's spirited little mare. Her mount shied and reared, but she kept her seat despite being precariously mounted on what she called, "This blasted sidesaddle." Her father quickly grabbed her reins to make sure the horse steadied.

"I don't see why women cannot ride astride. We should be permitted a riding costume that allows us to do so," Pandora complained.

"Take that up with your mother. The Shawnee women rode like men when they had a mount. I wonder what disturbed the birds."

Jason's eyes followed the flock that wheeled and returned to their messy nests. "One of them had a cloth tied to its leg, but there, it's gone from view now."

"Probably the trick of some lad looking for amusement. I remember you boys trying to use the ordinary pigeons the cook kept for pies to carry messages. They merely joined a wild flock and did not return to their cages. Cook was quite upset with you. I had to pacify her with a new dovecote that could be locked against you."

"Kate knew of that escapade," Joshua said. "Perhaps..."

He saw his father and brother exchange pitying glances as if they knew everything said reminded him of her. He recalled her large brown eyes flecked with gold, and in those days, her dark hair worn in two thick braids down her back and tied on the ends with ribbons. And her spirit, her indomitable spirit. Surely, it had not gone from this earth.

"We should move along. Darkness will overtake us, and we do not know the terrain," his father said gently. "I wish we had found her, truly, I do."

~ * ~

Burt Cotter watched them go from the bush where he'd tripped and spooked the birds, damned twittering nuisances. The paths of the ravine remained treacherous even this many days after the deluge. First, he'd had to remove some wilted brush, then a small rock fall blocked the main path and forced him to clamber over it. His game leg twisted in a soft spot along the trail, and he'd come down hard, scattering the birds. He stayed down, too, when he heard the horses and the bits of conversation.

Someone looked for the lady in the tower, and here he was carrying her fresh water and stale bread. The blame would be put on Old Burt for sure, though he did only as Lady Camilla told him. Seemed mad, but then the nobility were as inbred as cattle with weak hindquarters. His grandpap had told some tales of the Dukes of Strictly and their ladies, a cruel lot those. One had starved his own daughter to death in that very tower because she refused to marry a man to his liking and wanted another. Well, this lady could wait another day for her vittles while he rested his sore leg. He had to be on the beach tonight carrying out his real duties to the duke, far more important than humoring Lady Camilla in some strange game.

Fifteen

Kate had new visitors that night, but not her old friend, the rat. That creature had learned its lesson and prudently stayed away. She should have learned not to waste her energy as well.

Late in the afternoon, she woke and could have sworn she heard the throb of hoof beats vibrating through the rocks at her back. Instantly, she'd gone to the windows and screamed herself hoarse calling out to Joshua first, and then all the other Longleighs, hoping, hoping they had come for her. The wind snatched her cries and threw them deep into the ravine instead of carrying them upwards. In the end, all she'd gotten for her trouble was a throat so dry she might have swallowed sand. She'd downed the last of her water and slumped back against the wall of her prison. The vibrations had gone away, maybe only a shifting of the rocks or an illusion after all.

When next she woke, the moon had come out. Far below, she thought she heard voices, voices speaking French. She could not make out the words, simply the difference in accent and cadence. What irony if she were freed by an invasion and then taken prisoner again. Still, she must try to gain their attention. First, she threw what little slops she had out the window, hoping they might see the glint of moisture by the light of the moon. A foolish hope, but at least she could use the bucket for a stepstool to raise her head to the openings.

Deep in the ravine where the stream met the ocean, six men drew a sturdy rowboat ashore on a spit of sand. In the distance a larger vessel waited out at sea. No soldiers these, but the smugglers Tomasina feared. They swiftly off-loaded their cargo of kegs. A large, shambling man with a limp handed over a purse. The captain of the crew counted out its contents into his hand, nodded, and turned back to the boat.

"Help me! Up here! Help me!" she called. Not a one looked up. She realized her voice came out as a dry croak, hardly to be heard beyond the tower.

Kate tried again. This time she cupped her lips with her hands and drew air deep into her lungs, pushing her diaphragm down, then allowing it to help her push out the words as opera singers did. "Help meee!"

Stepping off the bucket, she grated its handle against the bars trying to make as much noise as possible. Again, she used it as a stool to see if she'd been understood. Definitely, the smugglers had heard something. They scrambled for their boat and pushed off as if the king's own army were after them. The limping man shouted some insult and laughed. He began rolling the casks, full of brandy she supposed, one by one to a hiding place. He did look up once or twice, shaking his large, shaggy head as if telling her "no."

Taking her hands from the bars, Kate swayed off the bucket, so weak now, so tired and thirsty. She gathered her blue cloak about her and curled in the center of the tower to sleep some more. Toward dawn, the weather shifted again. Tendrils of fog drifted through the windows. The dampness settled in her bones. Dampness.

Kate rose and put out her tongue wishing she could suck the vapor from the air. Not from the air, but from where it condensed on the walls and dripped from the iron bars. She scaled the bucket again and sucked at the bars, taking in the droplets and the taste of rusted iron. She ran her tongue along the sill and over the walls themselves. Tonight, they carried a vague scent of mold she hadn't noticed when less thirsty. The very effort of sucking tired her. She had to pause and rest. Of course, she slept. Naturally, she dreamt.

The lady floated near her. Vague hands made of mist caressed Kate's cheeks.

"I heard your cries for help," she said. "I will do all I can to succor you."

This ghost did not dress in white as they were wont to do. Instead she wore a long, blue gown nearly the same color as Kate's cloak with wide sleeves like the ancient ladies in the tales of King Arthur. Thick braids of red-gold bound with ribbons hung over her shoulders. On her forehead rested some sort of diadem, not a crown, but more of an ornament. Only her eyes were hollow and her face colorless. Kate thought momentarily of Tomasina's inept portrayal of Eleanor of Aquitaine. This lady acted so much better, but of course the game of charades had conjured her.

"I will help you win the greatest prize," the specter continued.

"I no longer care about the wager or Harold Brumley, though he is nice enough, but how could you possibly know?"

"I was promised that no other woman would starve to death in this tower when I left this world for the next. None have until you. But you misunderstood me. The greatest prize is not a man. It is love. I died for love."

"Perhaps a foolish choice," Kate answered amazed she could be so flippant with a ghost.

The fog swirled as if the lady had shrugged her shoulders and disturbed its currents, but the figment did not move. "You do not love this Harold, but you would die for..."

The ghost's hollow eyes drifted upwards as if searching for a name. "Joshua."

"Ah, there's the rub as the Bard of Avon said. Can you tell me why a woman will always love a man who loves another?"

The fog shifted again as if the spirit's form shook with laughter. "He does not love another. I see this Joshua is simply too stubborn to be pushed into a marriage. He wants to make his own choice. Being a man, he fixed on the prettiest face and greatest fortune."

"As I thought, but I doubt I would be his second choice either."

"We shall see. I will make certain you have food and water tomorrow. After that, I am not so sure how far from here my powers will extend, but I shall try to bring your rescue."

"Certainly, I thank you for anything you might do."

Wonderful, she thanked her own illusion, the product of her delirium. Her mind had followed her body in wasting away. Yet, she enjoyed the lady's company as all lunatics must.

"Tell me, what became of the man you loved, my lady?"

"He died in battle not long after learning of my fate. A perfect knight, he came to join me in a blazing charge to glory. My father would have had me wed higher. But I said no, no, noooo."

The last no became the breath of the wind as it blew the fog away.

~ * ~

Hobbling feet made their way toward the tower and woke Kate from her stupor. "Help," she croaked, but her plea reached no farther than the padlocked door. Too weak to pull herself up, she crawled closer, intending to call out the small hatch at its base. The hatch opened. The broken toe of a boot nudged a basket of bread inside her chamber. She would have seized on it immediately if her throat were not so very dry. Hard and stale, the loaves had a hairy coating of black mold grown in its fresher days. She knew she would gnaw on it regardless.

A bucket of water came next. She put her lips to it and lapped like a dog immersing half her face. Fresh and cool, the liquid ranked with the finest wines ever tasted. The footsteps began to recede. Kate pulled herself up to the tiny window and viewed the heavy shoulders of a big man now bent with age. Greasy, gray hair sprouted from under a shapeless hat. His limp confirmed him as the man who had received the whiskey barrels.

"Please, don't go! Won't you release me for pity's sake?"

Without turning, he grumbled, "I have no key and did as I was told. You're to have naught but the bread they left and water. I don't do as they say, and I'll be put out me cottage. Sorry, Miss."

"Simply stay and talk to me, won't you? I've begun to hallucinate and need to cling to the words of a real person."

"Hallu—. What might that be? Is it catching?" The smugglers' receiver moved off a few more paces.

"No! Hallucinations occur when a person hasn't had enough food or drink. They see things that aren't there—and talk to them."

Finally, he turned. His face was no more pleasant or reassuring than his back. He'd done some fighting in his day that had flattened his nose and bent a large ear forward. A goodly number of his teeth had gone from combat or old age, and those that were left appeared in a smile surrounded by hoary stubble. Under a heavy brow, his small, dark eyes gleamed, reminding Kate of her friend, the rat.

"That's happened to me a time or two when I betook of bad spirits. Now, I drinks only the best, you might say." He moved closer to her prison.

"And if Lord Strictly discovers this?"

"It's Strictly gets the profits. I take mine in trade. That and the cottage. I'm to keep a lookout for Napoleon, too, ye see. I can tell the good Frogs from the bad. I'm to light a signal fire if the bad 'uns come ashore."

How wonderful to have conversation of any kind with anybody. "A very important job to be sure," Kate said, hoping to keep him talking.

"Aye, 'tis."

Another thought crossed her mind. "If you broke the lock open and released me, no one could hurt you because you know about the smuggling and would testify against them."

"If I told, his lordship would have me throat cut the same day I sang out. Besides, weren't him who put ye here. 'Twas that brat of his."

"I thought as much."

"Shouldn't have said. No, shouldn't have said. I was told to say three ruffians locked you away and threatened me life if I told. I kept you in food and water, remember."

Little food and some water. "Only once have you brought me anything. Will you come again?"

"Guess so. Fair Annet haunted me from my bed this dawn because I failed to bring your bread. Game leg, see. Climbing these trails ain't easy for me."

"Fair Annet?"

"Yes, the lady from long ago. She's not one o' those hallucinations, but a true spirit. She's appeared to the Cotter family many a time for many a year. Way back in great-grandpap's day during the Civil Wars, she told him to free a captive held right here where ye stay. The Duke of Strictly was given the care of one of the top Roundheads, you see. Right boring man, they say, always praying, no sport a'tall. Fair Annet haunted me forebear till he let the Puritan go. Worked out well for all. This mercy saved the Strictly estate, it did, when the Roundheads won. Course, the Sharptons turned again when the king returned."

As starved for company as she was for bread, Kate said, "Tell me more stories."

"I think you've had too much out o' me already, Miss. Just remember, I'm the one who brought you food."

"Will you bring more?"

"Bread and water, they said, only bread and water. Fair Annet says I must do better, but what does a poor tenant have to spare, I ask? 'Cause she needs nothing, she forgets the Cotters do not eat his lordship's game. Least ways, not very often, only a hare now and then. Maybe a deer what run off the cliff by accident like."

"Oh, for roast rabbit or a haunch of venison. I could eat the whole of it." Primed by the water, saliva welled up in Kate's mouth. She broke off a piece of bread, rubbed the mold off on her soiled dress, and began to eat.

"There ye go, now. That will keep ye for a while." The grizzled man turned to go.

"I beg you to come back if only to talk."

"Doubt if I got much choice, Miss. When Fair Annet wants her way, she's a right nag."

He limped off, leaving Kate in solitude again. So, she hadn't gone completely insane. A man who sometimes drank bad liquor had seen the ghost, too. Quite a testimonial. Fair Annet had promised to help and would keep her word as she had about the food and water. If only she could summon the Longleighs. Kate indulged in another long quaff of water to wash down the dry bread. Best to save the rest. Better to think of another plan for escape now that she had food again and felt a bit stronger.

What could she offer the old man in exchange for her escape? Her body? Would even he want it, unwashed for over a week, and considerably dwindled down. Amazing how quickly one thinned on a diet of bread and water. She should recommend it to Tomasina's mother. She ran her hands over her more prominent cheekbones and peered into the top of the gown hanging loosely on her frame. Not a bosom to be proud of now. With her hair gone, too, what did she have to offer any man? Gentlemen cared very little for intelligence and tenacity unless it came with a great deal of money.

A few tears rolled down her cheeks. She lapped them up for the salt. Her keeper was no gentleman. A bit of dirt and a sour smell would not put him off. She would try to seduce him, and when he broke the lock and entered, she would brain him with the empty pottery water jug and escape. If she still had the strength.

Sixteen

Joshua Longleigh helped himself to the generous breakfast buffet, though he had little appetite for it. He was the last dressed and down of his family. Even Pandora and Phemie had eaten already, but he gave as his excuse a poor night's sleep. His parents had shared a chamber as did his sisters, and he might have taken a bigger room with Jason, but instead, he'd asked to rest in Kate's place where her trunk sat latched and ready for removal. Had he really expected to sense her presence there?

First, the incessant wind whipping round the corner of the mansion had kept him sleepless. Then, a muffling fog crept across the garden and allowed him to doze until well past dawn. Even that rest had been disturbed by strange dreams, the last one before he woke of Kate. She was immured in a tower, and he stood at its base. She lowered thick braids of her gleaming, brown hair for him to climb. The braids had broken off in his hands when he made the attempt. He'd jerked up in bed and found his hands knotted as if holding a rope.

One must eat for the long ride home. His mother wished to be gone from Clifton as soon as possible before another storm might trap them. She'd given her orders the night before after the light supper and short stay in the drawing room afterward. The lead coffin would remain behind in case Kate's body was ever found. They would take her trunk and return it to the Morelys with news of her loss. Joshua picked out a piece of toast, a small sausage, a coddled egg. He failed to notice Camilla's entry until she spoke.

"Did you rest well in the corner room?" she asked.

"Not very. I'm unaccustomed to the sound of the winds. Bellevue Hall has some icy blasts in winter, but nothing as unrelenting as these breezes."

"Yes, I detest them, too. I hope to marry into a more pleasant clime."

She presented him with a charming smile. Her lips were still pink and perfect, her teeth white, her breath pleasant as she stood so closely. The painted face he found off-putting as he recalled Kate's freshness. Only a temporary disguise for Camilla, he knew, until she healed from her bruises. She wore a high-necked frock and long sleeves so there was no contrast of complexion. Her eyes remained innocently wide and blue, but now they seemed more like draperies hiding a dark interior.

Her golden curls were arranged rather stiffly and topped with a muslin cap frilled on the edges. A few ringlets escaped the covering. Camilla twisted one of them around her finger in a coquettish manner he found unbecoming at breakfast. The curl snapped off and left a small tuft beside her ear. Quickly, Camilla put her hands behind her back as if nothing odd had happened.

Being a gentleman, Joshua did not comment. Instead, he said, "I was troubled by strange dreams before waking. I saw Kate trapped in a tower. She lowered long braids to help me climb to her rescue, but they broke off."

Camilla must have blushed, but he could not tell under the paint. He hadn't meant to call attention to the lock of hair now residing on the carpet just beyond the edge of her skirt.

"An old fairy tale, is it not?" Camilla rushed to say. "Those German brothers, the Grimms, published it in a collection last year, I believe."

"Yes, Mama ordered a copy for our library. That must be where the image came from, but do tell me. Have you any towers on the estate?"

"None that I know of. Look, here come Tilly and Tomasina to join us. Tommy will be so sorry to have missed your brother. I believe she has developed a *tendre* for him."

The two friends ranged themselves on either side of Camilla like the Swiss Guard protecting the pope in Rome. They wore caps and costumes similar to their leader's outfit. Tomasina fingered the rough spot on her slightly swollen chin. He supposed these two did regard their friend as infallible and would agree with whatever Camilla said or ordered. No use asking them if they knew of any towers in the area. He acknowledged them with a greeting and took his breakfast to the table.

"Shall I pour you some coffee? Or would you rather have tea?" Camilla asked him in the most pleasant of domestic voices.

"Coffee, no need to dilute it with cream. Thank you."

She presented it with a flutter of hands and sat beside him. The other girls made their selections and took seats opposite.

"Lord Longleigh suffered a peculiar dream last evening," Camilla told her rapt audience.

"Really? Do tell us about it," Matilda said with little interest, but Camilla answered.

"He said he saw Miss Morely trapped in a tower. She put down her long braids to draw him up like a prince in a fairy tale, but they snapped off just like that." She made a small click with her thumb and forefinger.

Tomasina's violet eyes went wide. She gave a small gasp soon stopped up by a piece of buttered toast handed to her by Matilda.

"It's not so very horrifying, Tommy, though certainly all of us women value our hair. I believe the pigtails represent your childish attachment to Miss Morely, which is now severed for good. Sadly, you must go with your life." Camilla patted the top of Joshua's hand where it lay unmoving by his plate.

"My family greatly believes in the import of dreams, but I would say the tower was of more importance than the hair—which were not girlish pigtails, but the thick braids of a woman."

"We know nothing of any towers," Tomasina blurted out, nearly choking on her bread.

The Duchess of Bellevue walked into the room and gave the girl a sharp rap on the back to clear her throat. "There, all better. Joshua, do finish your meal. The coach is ready, and the horses have been brought round. Pay your respects to our hostess, and let us be on our way lest we be caught by the rain."

"Oh, the fog has lifted, and I see no clouds on the horizon," Camilla said. "You needn't hurry. In fact, if you stayed another day, we could travel to London together. That would be so lovely."

"We have a duty to perform. We must take Kate's belongings home and give the news of her loss to her family. We will pause in London only long enough to gather the rest of her belongings before traveling to Greenway Grange." The duchess fiddled her foot impatiently.

"Must all of you go on that mission?" Tomasina asked. "We will be attending Lady Proctor's ball later in the week and hoped to see you there." She turned to gaze past Lady Flora's shoulder to where Jason Longleigh stood ready to ride.

"We must all go. Now, Joshua."

He dabbed his lips with a napkin, nodded to the ladies, and followed his mother out the door.

~ * ~

The Longleighs made good time as they always did when on the march, thanks to the duke's discerning eye for good horses. Arriving shortly after dark, the duchess called for supper to be laid out before retiring to her chamber to wash off the dirt of travel. On her return, she passed the footmen bringing Kate's trunk into the house. A little brown and white spotted terrier dogged their heels and snuffled at the box as they moved along.

"Now how did that creature get into the house? We keep him to harry the rats in the stable, and that is where he belongs. Oh, Kate would always feed him scraps and ruin his appetite for vermin. He believes she's come home." The duchess put her hand to her eyes.

"Sorry, Your Grace. I'll see he is put out," Busby, the butler, replied as the footmen continued up the stairs.

"No, no, simply give me a moment." She stooped to pick up the dog and carried it into the dining room where cold meats had been set out for the evening meal. She selected a slice of mutton and allowed the terrier to gobble it down. He licked her cheek.

"Yes, I know. We all loved Kate. Now back to the stable with you." She handed the pup over to Busby, who looked as if he'd rather carry it by the scruff than cradle the beast as the duchess had done.

The family gathered around the table. Weary with travel and grief, they talked little.

"Tomorrow, we shall go to Greenway dressed in black to show our sorrow," the duchess announced. None objected.

"I still think Kate was pushed off that cliff," Pandora insisted.

"As do I," her mother said.

"You agree with me?"

"Yes, jealousy is a terrible affliction, and those girls suffer from it. Oh, Lady Camilla might have the finer looks, but Kate had substance. Men notice that sooner or later. Camilla was losing ground with Astin, and with a tutor such as Lady Rushmore to teach her devious ways, who knows what plan they devised to be rid of Kate."

Doggedly eating in silence, Joshua lifted his eyes from his plate and spoke. "I do not believe Kate is dead. She is held captive somewhere. I dreamt it last night."

Not one of the Longleighs disparaged this remark.

"Tell us," the duke said.

"I saw her entrapped in a tower. She cried out to me for help. We need to search again."

"We cannot delay telling her family the sad news anymore. But after, we will return to Clifton. Those girls do know something, if only we could get it out of them," the duchess replied.

"Let us leave Jason behind to attend Lady Proctor's ball. Of the three, Tomasina Murray is the weakest, and she favors him. Don't know why." He smiled wanly at his brother, a mere ghost of former teasing grins. "He might be able to winkle the truth out of her."

"Well, I have been working on *An Ode to Violet Eyes* and should be able to finish it before the party. If my modest talents can help bring Kate back to us, I would be happy to apply them to Tomasina—so long as I don't have to marry her to get the information. A beautiful young lady, but quite silly. Not like Kate at all. Ah, rhymes for eyes." Jason closed his own in an effort to court the muse.

"Flies," suggested Phemie.

"Lies," said Pandora.

"Precisely," said the duchess.

Seventeen

The completed ode tucked in his vest, Jason Longleigh moved through the crush at Lady Proctor's ball. Before he could reach the set of chairs where Camilla held court with her friends, Viscount Astin intercepted him.

Harold plucked at the black armband Jason wore and said, "It is true, then. Katherine Morely no longer walks this earth, the one woman who truly understood my passion—for snuff, that is. I would not have you think anything else."

"Chin up, old boy. Her body has not been found. We might yet hope."

"I delayed. I thought a young woman might want to enjoy the full of her season before settling down to marriage. I meant to offer for her and now it is too late." Astin flicked open his snuffbox du jour and inhaled a large charge to open his tear-swollen sinuses. Jason drew back from the power of the following sneeze.

"I must tell my brother what you intended."

"Why should he care?"

"Did I say brother? I meant my mother. She would be glad to know you held Kate in such high esteem and will pass along that sentiment to Mrs. Morely."

"Yes, I suppose knowing her daughter might one day have been a duchess will be of some comfort to her. Now, if I could only find some way to assuage my own grief."

"Lady Camilla remains unclaimed, as do her friends. Would you walk over there with me and say a word?"

"If I am able to get any words out in my sorrow." Astin blotted both his watery, blue eyes and his pink-tipped nose with one of his oversized handkerchiefs.

Jason led him through the clusters of people awaiting the start of the music. Astin's retinue trailed behind like the tail of a golden comet that came to a stop near the brightest star in the firmament, Lady Camilla Sharpton. She had adopted a new and original hair style with all the side locks drawn up on top and arranged in a pattern of crisscrosses more complicated than one of Joshua's neckcloths. The whole appeared to be glued together with some substance and heavily ornamented with silk flowers, ribbons, and plumes. Very old school, very last century, he felt, but what did he know of women's fashions. Both of her boon companions wore similar concoctions upon their heads. While the two blondes carried if off rather well, Tomasina's brunette locks seemed lusterless, sitting like an old hat above her pretty, round face. He rather missed the looser, more natural look.

Ah, well, work to do. He bowed before the group of young ladies directly in front of Tomasina and let Astin address and distract Lady Camilla.

"Oh, has your family returned from delivering the sad news to Greenway Grange?" Tomasina asked, fanning her bosom entirely covered in billowing tulle as if she were vastly overheated.

"They are due to return shortly to Bellevue House. I felt unwell before they left and stayed behind, but as you can see, I am fit again. My mother made it very clear, however, that we shall all cease socializing and observe a year of mourning for Katherine since we regarded her as part of our family. This might be my last chance to speak to a nonpareil."

Tomasina's little, bowed smile sagged. "You must wait in line to address Camilla."

"I spoke of you. I wished to deliver this unworthy poem before departing." Jason withdrew the paper from his waistcoat and struck a proper declamatory pose. "*An Ode to Violet Eyes,*" he announced over the noise of the gathering.

When he finished, Astin's cronies gave him some tepid applause. He thought he detected envy in Matilda's eyes and jealousy in Camilla's expression, but both ladies lavished him with praise. Tomasina sat speechless with one hand pressed to her heart. He offered his arm.

"Would you care to promenade before the first dance? Perhaps I could have that honor as well."

"The first four are taken, but do let me write you in for the fifth and sixth. Yes, to the promenade. My, yes." She fanned herself again before rising.

The crowd allowed for no straight direction, though they were never out of view of the watching eyes of Lady Rushmore and Tomasina's mother. They meandered like a babbling brook through rocky hills as Jason described it. Delicately, he began to fish in that stream.

"I did leave word of my whereabouts and know Mama will send for me immediately upon her arrival, but I had to have one last chance to speak with you and deliver my poem. Were it not for poor Kate's untimely demise, we might have enjoyed the entire season together."

"This is most unfair. Lady Pandora's season will be ruined as well."

"I doubt that Panny cares, but I do. I know you will be illustriously engaged by the end of June, my chance with you gone." He hung his head. Thinking of Kate's fate helped to etch his visage with regret.

Tomasina squeezed his arm. "We might still find Katherine alive very soon. It could be the smugglers who work out of Clifton's Cove found her wandering in the fog and abducted her."

"Really? Smugglers use the cove on Clifton's property, the one at the base of the ravine? Why haven't they asked for a ransom then?"

Tomasina stopped herself. He could imagine her shallow mind eddying with turmoil behind her extraordinary eyes.

"I've heard girls are sometimes taken and shipped to France. That is why we would never, never go near the ravine ourselves. But Katherine still might be found there held prisoner until a boat comes."

"But where would they keep her? Kate is very resourceful and often escaped us when we played games as children."

"I've heard it said an ancient, haunted keep exists in the ravine. Not that I've seen it. She could not escape from that. Possibly, a kindly tenant might find her and bring about her release. Then, you would not have to go into mourning nor skip the season."

Now those violet eyes seemed very pleased with the inventiveness of the mouth below them. How devious was the feminine mind! These proper young ladies had kidnapped Kate and held her in a tower exactly as Joshua dreamed. And why? Certainly because Kate had lured Astin from Camilla. Jason wanted to throw off the clinging weight of Tomasina's arm in disgust.

He was saved from doing so by the dramatic entrance of Pandora. She might have been one of the avenging Furies in her floating black garb and crepe-draped deep bonnet from which her dark eyes burned like a beast's in a lair. People parted before her, and Tomasina stepped back.

"Brother, the family awaits you in the coach. We stopped only briefly at home, and Mama would come get you at once. Oh, oh, my season is over because of Kate's tragic death."

He thought she overdid it a bit, but his sister had impeccable timing. "This lovely lady believes we might hope for her safe return yet."

"Really?" Pandora said, staring directly into Tomasina's unique eyes.

The girl shrank back even more. She looked frantically around, saw Camilla and Matilda coming toward her, and scurried to meet them halfway.

"Now you've scared her off with your fierceness, Panny. However, I do think I've learned all I can. Wait until you hear."

"Later. As planned, we did come here directly from Greenway Grange, and I am in great need of the ladies' retiring room. Go out to the coach and wait for me. Not a word until I join you."

Jason went off to reclaim his hat and walking stick, the one hiding a sword he was rarely without, and regroup with the family.

~ * ~

Pandora moved with unseemly haste to the retiring room and dashed for the commode chair behind the painted screen. She seemed to be holding in gallons. Other women entered while she did her business, and she paid them no mind until she recognized Camilla's voice, so much harsher than when that young lady spoke to the men who courted her.

"What did you tell him, you ninny?"

"Nothing. I merely suggested Katherine might not be dead. That perhaps smugglers held her somewhere in the ravine. That is our story, after all. She will be released soon."

"She hasn't served out her entire two weeks for marking me yet."

"Only a few days shy. Couldn't we send a message to let her go now? Then, Jason Longleigh can remain in London to court me."

"Yes, think only of yourself, Tommy," Camilla retorted.

Pandora quietly rearranged her clothes and prepared to walk out from behind the screen. Oh, they would go pale under their painted faces when they saw her. She'd like to snatch the plumes from their hair and trample them underfoot. Why not? Who would stop her?

She roared from behind the screen, "Treacherous bitches!" and charged forth to take some revenge for her friend. Grasping all three plumes anchored in Camilla's coiffure with a jeweled clip, Pandora tried to yank them free. Instead of coming out one by one, all the hair came away with the feathers and revealed a pink, bald pate fringed with broken, yellow strands.

Camilla screamed. The other two girls put their hands protectively over their own heads. Wigs. All of them were wearing wigs interwoven with their own thin hair. Horrified herself, Pandora started to toss the hairpiece to the floor, but then had another thought. She stalked from the retiring room holding it before her by the plumes like Anne Boleyn's head.

Gentlemen who had raced toward the sound of the scream milled in the hall, undecided if they should barge in and chance upsetting a lady's modesty or rush to the rescue. Lady Proctor, who was known to wear a wig herself, took one look at Pandora's trophy, hurried by and entered, followed by Ladies Strictly, Rushmore, and Harcourt. Some in the crowd recognized Camilla's extraordinary hairpiece and began to whisper. Pandora kept moving right out the door, down the torch-lit steps to the waiting Bellevue coach. The first splats of a rainstorm hit her bonnet as Jason reached down to help her inside.

She held up her trophy for all to see. "I believe I have just scalped an enemy in the best of Shawnee traditions. But even better, Kate lives!"

Eighteen

Kate collected water from the puddles forming under the windows and wrung out the rag over the bucket the old man had brought her, easier than trying to squeeze it into the jug. No gale, the farmers would call this a soaking rain. Whatever it was called, the weather had prevented her keeper from returning with more food. A couple of days ago, he'd come with a small covered pail of porridge sweetened with a few raisins and let her know how unhappy he was about the matter.

"They left me only bread to feed ye. Now I must use me own stocks. Who's going to repay me, I says, but Fair Annet continues to worry me like a hellhound."

How sweet that gruel tasted as she shoveled it into her mouth with her fingers. No food could be finer. Between mouthfuls, she'd asked the man to stay and talk.

"You're to be let go in two days and can do without company till then."

"I thought you had no key."

"Don't. Might be they thought Old Burt is too soft-hearted." He cackled at the idea. "Someone is to bring me a key on the appointed day."

"But you could smash the lock with a rock or a sledge before that if you wished. I would repay you."

"How's that?"

Quickly, she'd set her pail aside and wiped her mouth on her sleeve. She ran her fingers though her spiky hair and stood up, wobbling a bit. Turning her back to the small window in case he watched, she took the ball of her severed hair and stuffed it in her bosom to increase its size, then drew her gown tight over her shrunken breasts and came near the small window. The pottery jug sat just inside the door. If only she had the strength to raise and smash it down hard enough.

Knowing she looked as frowsy as the lowest prostitute on a London street, she offered, "I would give myself to you if you let me go."

"And if me withered dick still worked, I might take ye up on that. I've had worse looking and never no lady. Too old now. A warm cottage and regular meals means more than cunt to me these days, though I was a pisser in my youth."

"Tell me about it." If not freedom, then she'd settle for company.

"Oh, I couldn't do that, Miss. Wouldn't be right." A bit of red appeared on his unshaven cheeks and off he limped as fast as he could go.

She shouted after him, "Do you call this right—keeping me here, starving me?"

"Not me doing," he called back.

Drat that she'd eaten all the porridge in small portions all that day believing Old Burt would bring her more. Now, she'd gone two days with nothing as the rains fell, and she had only Fair Annet for company. The ghost was not as substantial as she appeared on foggy nights when she could shape the vapors to make her form, but she remained as chatty as ever.

"I am always here, whether you can see me or not, Kate. You must not despair. I was able to plant a dream in your beloved's mind that will start him thinking. Those lying, treacherous girls denied any tower existed on the estate, but in time, he will not be fooled."

"In time, I might be dead. I see you more and more often and talk to you constantly. That is not a good sign, I think. How is it I understand you so clearly if you are not simply a figment of my imagination. Shouldn't you be speaking Middle English?'

"Place your hand upon your lips and ask me again."

Kate did so. Her lips made no movement.

"As you see, we commune on a higher plane that surpasses understanding. I could be of very little help to anyone if I needed a translator."

"Granted," said Kate. "I'm glad I need make no effort to move my lips."

"Yes, rest. Conserve your strength. Tomorrow, I will harry Old Burt from his bed to bring you food."

"And if not, you and I shall haunt this tower together, I suppose." Kate let the rag sop in the puddle, and closed her eyes, too exhausted to do anything more today.

~ * ~

"Up, you lazy villein. A young woman starves because of you."

Fair Annet hovered at the foot of Old Burt's bed. She appeared faintly, but had gotten very much inside his head today. Might be the liquor. No matter how she scolded him, he was loath to leave his warm, snug cottage and go out in the damp to feed the lady in the tower. Just before the rains began, when his joints ached with the coming weather, the household steward arrived with fresh supplies, so he had plenty to share. He also had a key found in a packet the steward said bore his name, left by Lady Camilla before she returned to London and to be delivered this very day.

Although he could not read, he knew the meaning. He was to release the girl. But the rains had come and poured down for two days before moving inland to water London town and the fields beyond that city. He'd stayed abed waiting for a clear sky and the drying of the crumbling cliff-side paths, drinking up his portion of the smuggled brandy, and doing very little else. He would get no peace now with the ghost so determined.

Old Burt rose from his bed and took a long piss in his pot. He hoped this would ward Fair Annet off, but she merely faded away until he finished and returned again to nag him.

"Aw right. I can spare some bread and raisins, I supposes, but it's a waste as she gets her freedom today."

"How will she walk out of the ravine, weak as she is because of your negligence? You must see she eats, and then help her back to Clifton."

"That's a right long way with me game leg. I can't carry her, and ye don't see any fine steed in my stable, do ye?"

"Stop whining and fill a sack."

He did so reluctantly. With steps still unsteady from drink, he set out to climb the path from his cottage that intercepted the one leading to the tower. Oh, how his bad leg had stiffened from lack of use. He reached the apex and paused to rest, but Fair Annet would not have it. She tried to shove him along, but her pale, ghostly hands passed right through him, chilling his innards to the core.

"Now stop that! I cannot be rushed." Old Burt waved his arms and stamped his feet to regain circulation. One broken boot came down on the soft verge of the path. It crumbled under him, pitching him over the edge. He grabbed at bushes that broke away in his hands and plummeted downward. Until the very end of his fall, he thought he might survive, but he came up fast and sharp against the edge of a cask of brandy hidden at the base of the cliff. The crack of his neck was the last sound he heard as a mortal being.

Looking down at his corpse, Old Burt remarked to Fair Annet, "All me pain is gone just as they says."

"You've lived a sinful life, Burt. Your pain might just be at a beginning."

"Hey, I've helped you out, haven't I? Don't I get no credit for that?"

Fair Annet considered. "The best I can do is request that you haunt this cove for all eternity, but the decision is not up to me. In the meantime, you must wait below."

She glanced at a dark vortex forming in the sand of the cove. It widened, sucking in Burt's feet and whirling him round and round until his blackened soul disappeared like dirty water down a drain.

"Oh, dear. Now I must go tell Kate there will be no food today and no release."

The spirit wafted to the tower where she found Kate sucking water from the rag.

"Sustenance has been delayed. In my eagerness to help you, I pushed Old Burt too far, and he went over the cliff, food, key, and all."

"Key," Kate said.

"Yes. He was to release you. So sorry."

"I suppose I cannot kill a ghost with my own bare hands."

"Or in any other way. But good news. I sense the Longleighs are on their way to rescue you. You must simply hang on another day or two."

"And if I cannot?"

"Tell me, do you want Joshua to remember you as a shrunken, dirty corpse with cropped hair, or will you live to blossom again?"

That thought struck deep in her heart, Joshua, always meticulous in his dress and so conscious of his presentation he often bathed more than once a week, remembering her as stinking and shorn. She gathered her resolve.

"I will survive, thank you very much."

Nineteen

The Duke of Bellevue penned a perfunctory note to his peer, the Duke of Strictly, asking permission to search his estate again for Katherine Morely. He inquired about any towers on the property as well. Strictly returned a polite, cordial, and immediate reply. Of course, he granted them access and any other aid they might need. Such a tragedy, and though he did not see how a young lady might have survived all this time, he wished all to end happily. As for towers, the ravine held an old keep from darker days used to watch for enemies or incarcerate the same. A tenant by the name of Old Burt dwelled near the bottom and would certainly guide them there. Consider the paths treacherous after a storm. Take care.

The Longleighs would have gone without permission, but it was good to observe the social niceties as long as an answer came promptly and in their favor. The duke and his two sons set off immediately into the rain. The coach would follow when the roads proved passable again and bring the duchess, Pandora, and Phemie along as none of them wanted to be left out. Pandora sulked over not being allowed to ride with the men, but for once, her father had put his foot down firmly and denied her request. The duchess insisted they carry the rat terrier with them in a saddlebag as he might scent Kate out, so they took enough extra baggage in the duke's opinion.

The pooch rode along with his head stuck out and small tongue lolling, oblivious to the foul weather. The horses disliked the slop on the roads and had to be urged along. They did not reach Clifton on the first day, but stayed at an inn to dry out thoroughly overnight. Pressing onward in the morning through a lighter rain, they reached the manor by nightfall with Joshua cursing the weather that delayed them every step of the way. Presenting Strictly's letter gained them beds for the night and a hot and early breakfast in the brighter, sun-lit morning.

Given directions to Old Burt's place by the staff, the men set out cross-country. Halfway there, Joshua spotted a sodden mass of something brown half hidden by a rock. His heart twisted in his chest, but on closer view, it turned out to be only an old hamper stuffed with ragged clothes overturned by the winds. A peasant's loose trousers and shirt lay strewn across the grass and from a distance had resembled a woman's gown.

"I can't see this has anything to do with Kate, but put the dog down and let him have a sniff. Most likely the rains have washed all scent away," the duke suggested.

Having been stuck with hound transport, Jason lowered the terrier. The dog nosed the rags and finally lifted his leg to mark them, but showed no other interest. At a clap of the hands, he leapt up high enough to be caught by Jason and placed back in the saddlebag.

They rode on and finally reached the edge of the ravine. The sun sparkled on wet leaves, but the songbirds kept silent. Carrion birds circled overhead, making the smaller creatures wary.

"Something dead down there," Jason remarked without thinking.

"We must investigate. Dismount. That path into the ravine will not bear the weight of our horses. Joshua, attend them while your brother and I see what's what."

"I should go. Kate was so clever at escaping it might be her fallen as she fled." He knew his face had blanched at his brother's remark, all the blood being drawn back into his heart it seemed.

"That is why you should stay behind. You wouldn't want to see her as food for ravens and kites."

"This is my fault. I should go with…"

Jason pointed a finger toward a low bush where sparrows huddled. "Do you see? The bird with the cloth on its leg again. Let me see if I can catch it."

"A waste of time," Joshua grumbled, but his brother was gone, hat in one hand and a bit of bread pinched from their packed lunch in the other.

Jason spread out crumbs and squatted, seeming to turn to stone. First one bold sparrow, then another ventured from hiding. The bird with the strip of cloth bound to its leg finally made an approach. Jason waited until it was entirely engrossed in eating before he clapped his hat over it and held it close to his chest. The winged messenger battered frantically against his chest. He eased a hand inside and, capturing the sparrow in his fist, removed the cloth off the fragile leg and let his captive go.

"As I thought, a message. Unfortunately, the bird has shat upon it. But the last word is definitely TOWER. Can't make out the rest."

"Give it to me!" Joshua grabbed the strip. He stared at the one legible word. "This is Kate's hand, I know. She wrote to me constantly while I was at school and later in London. I rarely answered."

"I don't see how you can tell, shaky as it is and written in what? Blood?" his father said.

"I am certain. If only we had captured the bird before." Josh eyed the circling carrion crows. Did Kate lie below, her modest beauty being despoiled by big-beaked ravens and skin-necked vultures?

The dog grew restless, wriggled his way out of the bag, and dropped to the ground. He ran off sniffing along the path to the tenant's cottage and darted into a hole along the way. Snarling and squeaking ensued.

"Only good for ratting, as I thought. He's no bloodhound for certain," the duke said. "Let's start down. Josh, remain behind."

But a few steps along the way, the terrier backed from the hole dragging a rat nearly as big as he was and laid it at the duke's feet. "Ah, yes, good dog. Josh, give the animal some cold meat… to go with his kill. What's this? Another message?"

The duke knelt to remove the cloth from the tail of the vermin. Before he could rise again, Joshua had tied the horses to the branch of a stunted tree and made his way down the path. He flipped the ratter a chunk of ham from their provisions and reached out for the note.

"Let me see. It's half gnawed away. HELP, of course. Kate again, I know it. We are too late. We should have gone in here the last time." Josh closed his eyes and rested his head against the rock wall, scattering the small birds that roosted in its recesses. They drew his attention, and he saw the hair, weathered but still deep brown, lining a nest and keeping a clutch of small eggs warm. He pulled a few strands free.

"Kate again. The birds have gathered it from her body." He knocked his forehead harder against the side of the cliff and drew blood. He wanted to mourn as savages did by tearing his fine clothes and gashing his flesh. His father should understand, but did not.

"There, that does no good," the duke said. "I see you must come with us, for better or worse. No one will dare touch the horses, and I trust you have tied them tightly enough not to run off. Come along then."

Riding boots not being the best for walking on a slippery path that regularly shed rocks into the ravine, they made slow progress. The terrier abandoned his catch and ranged out ahead, joyous with the outing and so many new scents. The dog arrived first at the cottage sitting high enough to avoid flooding from the swollen stream, yet close enough to a narrow strip of beach.

"No sign of Burt who was to be our guide to the tower," the duke observed. A raven flew over, a gob of meat in its beak. "The carrion must rest over there."

"Don't call her that," Josh snapped.

"Could be a dead animal. No telling until we see."

Scattering the scavenger birds by their presence, they edged along the beach narrowed by the heavy rains to a clump of bushes that turned out to be nothing more than a screen for a stack of small barrels. Draped over them lay the eyeless corpse of a grizzled old man reeking in the sun. The dog sniffed busily, intrigued by the stench of rotten flesh.

"Burt, do you think?" asked Jason, pinching his nose shut. "And guarding a nice stash of French brandy. Does Strictly knows of this and Kate's abduction, too?"

"Considering I purchased a cask from him not too long ago, I'd say importing illegal brandy is a Strictly enterprise. But Kate, no, I doubt it. He rarely bothers with his wife and daughter and their concerns, terribly stuffy man. I wouldn't believe it of Lady Strictly either. She hasn't the imagination and seems to pour all her energies into marrying Camilla as high up as possible. No, this whole plot bears the mark of Lady Rushmore, a conniver if there ever was one." The duke stood his ground, too manly to show distaste for the body and its odor of decay.

"So now, we've lost our guide to the tower," Jason remarked. Quickly, he clamped his lips together as if holding back the urge to vomit.

Joshua raised his eyes upward following the gyre of birds waiting to attack the remains of Old Burt again. He offered a silent prayer thanking God it was not Kate who lay dead before them and asking for her deliverance. A flash of bright blue against the white of the cliff caught his eye and just beyond it, he saw the tower, so cunningly built into the rock it might have been a natural outcrop.

"Kate," he said. "She's up there. I swear she waved her favorite blue cloak at me."

In haste, Jason started back to the path. "Should I ride back to the manor and get us another guide?"

"Nonsense. I've taught you all to track and read signs. We'll find our way there ourselves," the duke stated.

"Kate! Kate!" Joshua shouted. "We are coming. Can you make some noise and lead us?" He waited for a response, but the only sound returned was the heavy flapping of wings from the annoyed ravens.

"I doubt she can hear you, son. Perhaps when we draw closer, we can try again." He rested a heavy arm on Joshua's shoulder and turned him from the sight of the dead man and the tower high above.

Exploring byways, they trudged up the path. Most proved to be dead ends or too narrow for a man to pass. Nearly at the top again, the terrier suddenly pricked its ears as if it heard a call they could not divine. The dog dashed a ways towards a thick holly bush and squeezed beneath it regardless of the prickling of the leaves.

"Dratted animal. Your mother will have my ears if I lose it. Come here, whatever your name is. What is the thing called?"

"Kate named it, but I've forgotten," Josh told his father. "How could I forget when its barking so annoyed me after we…"

"No need to say more, son." The duke strode toward the bush and bellowed, "Here, doggie. Come. What's this?" He stared at the holly as he approached, reached down as he arrived, and appeared to uproot the entire thing and toss it away. He kicked aside some evergreen boughs obstructing the way.

"I believe someone tried to obscure the way to the tower. If we hadn't focused on those damned birds and the dead rat, we would have noticed on the way down."

Before he'd finished speaking, Joshua rushed past. "Careful, son. Don't fall to your doom in your haste."

"Oh, he's doomed all right. Doomed to marriage, lost to love," Jason remarked, following behind.

"Shut your poet's mouth," Josh called back. "I have no time to beat you at the moment."

Indian file with Joshua in the lead, they moved toward their goal. They clambered over a small rock slide and kept going with Josh calling continuously, "Kate, Kate!"

No answer still, but up ahead, the dog barked energetically. Then, the path widened and the tower appeared before them. The terrier pushed through a small hatch in its padlocked door. Josh followed, wishing he could do the same, go to her immediately, but his way was blocked by the massive, bolted entry. Through the barred window, he saw Kate slumped against the wall, the blue cape wrapped around her, its hood raised over her head. The terrier licked her face.

Jason crowded up beside him. "*Full many a flow'r is born to blush unseen, And waste its sweetness on the desert air,*" he murmured.

Joshua shoved his brother aside. "Do not quote an elegy to me! She is not dead. Answer me, Kate. You are saved!"

She did not respond. He found a rock and began bashing at the lock. "Too late, too late," he said with every blow.

"Allow me." The duke drew a pistol from the deep pocket of his old-fashioned greatcoat. He checked the priming, took aim, arm out straight, and blasted the lock away. The smoke had not cleared before Joshua surged inside and cradled Kate in his arms.

"Speak to me now. Speak!"

The dog barked sharply.

"Not you, her!"

With eyes still closed, she said ever so softly, "Josh. I dream again."

"This is no dream. You are safe and will soon be home and well. I swear it. Our bet is off, do you hear me?"

She managed a faint nod. He lifted her up in his arms. The hood of her cloak fell back revealing her shorn head and sunken cheeks. For a moment, her brown eyes flickered open. All the sparks of gold had vanished from them. She plucked at the hood, trying to raise it again.

"Let it be. It doesn't matter."

Her lips moved, whispering.

"What do you say, Kate? I don't understand."

"You are right. I am no great prize."

Twenty

"Don't say that. Don't say it," Josh told her as he carried Kate from the tower. She was far too light. Her eyes closed again, and her head lolled against his shoulder.

The bronze of the duke's face darkened. "Someone shall pay for this."

"We must get her above and back to the house as soon as possible."

The duke led the way with no more talk, and Jason brought up the rear with the spotted dog yipping at his heels. They climbed out of the ravine and found their mounts still tied to the small tree, though the horses had nibbled away some of the leaves it could scarcely spare.

"Kate needs forage, too, and I have just the thing to sustain her for a while." Jason reached into the opposing saddle bag that he had balanced with a bottle of wine against the weight of the dog.

"Spirits? Are you sure? I have a canteen of water," his father said.

"Pour half of it out." Jason worked out the cork of the bottle and refilled the canteen. He held it to Kate's lips. "There you go."

She did not respond. Joshua chafed her hollow cheeks. "You must wake up, Kate, and drink."

With eyes still shut, she opened her lips, swallowed, and coughed, not expecting diluted wine.

"Can you eat?"

She shook her head.

"Try this." Jason tore off a part of the loaf he'd used to trap the sparrow and soaked it in the wine. Kate sucked the wet bread and got some of it down, then a bit more.

"Not too much now. There's always the danger it might come back up in cases like this," the duke prompted. "Let me take her. My horse is the largest."

"No. She'll ride with me." Joshua held her close to his chest, unwilling to relinquish his burden.

"As you would have it then. Jason, ride ahead fast as you can and ask the servants to prepare a bed and some light foods, beef tea, custard, whatever an invalid might be able to digest." The duke hiked his third son into the saddle and sent the horse off with a swat to the rump.

He helped Joshua onto his steed and handed Kate up to him. The terrier danced and barked around them. The duke snapped his fingers. "You are with me, I suppose. Up you go." He placed the dog on the saddle and found a rock to assist him in mounting. The terrier rode fearlessly in front of him as they turned back toward Clifton.

~ * ~

Even from a distance as they descended the hill, the riders could see the manor stirred like a termite mound broken open with a stick. Jason's horse stood tied out front. Close by, the Bellevue coach rested so coated in mud it might have been made of chocolate. The duchess and both her daughters had not gone inside, but waited for Kate's arrival. Servants dashed here and there, responding to orders.

As they came to a stop before the house, the duchess stepped forward. "What have they done to our Kate, those vicious girls?'

"Unexpected to see you here, but very glad, my darling," the duke said as he dismounted and placed the terrier on the ground.

"Did you really think the Longleigh women would remain behind waiting for the rain to end? We left shortly after you, but the coach was twice caught in mud holes and had to be pushed out."

The duke raised his arms to take Kate from Joshua and immediately headed for the stairs. The duchess ordered the housekeeper, "Put her in a warm, quiet chamber on the landward side, do you hear? We shall want bathing water sent up. Have Cook prepare an egg gruel at once."

She bustled after her husband and nearly tripped over the terrier who wound among the many feet in its way. "Phemie, see to the dog. Was he of any use to you?" she asked, as Joshua watched his father carry Kate off to a comfortable bed.

"Yes, he proved valuable in our search."

Phemie cuddled the animal. "Then he shall have the best scraps the kitchen can provide." She carried him away to get his reward.

Pandora scowled. "I'm glad I scalped Camilla Sharpton. You, Brother Joshua, have despicable taste in women." She followed her mother inside.

Of the family, Jason remained, giving out some orders for the care of the riding horses and the bespattered coach team. "I must say for a change I agree with Pandora. You shall have to find another bride."

"My thought exactly."

Joshua entered the house. The hubbub seemed to have followed Kate and his parents up the staircase and left the foyer in solitude. Having grown up in such a large, boisterous, and often eccentric family, he knew when the Longleighs took action, they also took over, and few stood in their way. But for the moment, he felt isolated and bereft of the slight weight of Kate lying in his arms. He seemed to be the only one who had no role to play in her life or the saving of it.

~ * ~

"We shall do for Kate as we would for one of our own and not leave her for the servants to attend. Pandora, remove her clothes, cover her with a sheet, and leave her close to the fire lest she catch a chill. Ah, the warm water arrives. Set it over there." The duchess, still in her plain gray traveling gown covered with a borrowed apron, bustled around the chamber like an army of maids, command and action being her natural element.

"What's this?" Pandora said as she lowered Kate's loose and filthy dress. "Good Lord, her hair. She saved it."

"Proving Kate has a sound and practical mind. We can have a wig made for her."

The room filled with the soothing scent of lavender soap as the duchess gently sponged over the old bruises and skeletal ribs of Kate Morely. Pandora cursed over her friend's condition and wished Camilla Sharpton and her followers to perdition without one word of correction from her mama. She held Kate's head over a basin while her mother soaped and rinsed the ravaged scalp. They dried her well with toweling and slipped one of Pandora's nightgowns over her head.

The duchess tenderly combed down the spikes of hair as if she were attending her own infant. "Once it dries, she must have a nightcap to keep her from catching cold. In her low condition, any illness could prove fatal."

The maid bearing the egg gruel arrived and assisted the two women in getting Kate to bed and well propped up with pillows. While their patient hadn't spoken, she did make their tasks easier by not fussing or attempting to walk by herself. Obediently, she opened her mouth to receive the food.

"Only half now and the rest in a few hours. One of us will sit with you round the clock, but for now, we must change our own clothes. We are somewhat damp from bathing you." The duchess rose to go.

"Like a babe, you care for me like a baby," Kate said, startling them all.

"Like a beloved child, yes. You revive. That is good to see." Trying to draw a smile from her patient, the duchess said, "Did you know that terrier we got to keep down the rats in the stable and which you so terribly spoiled found you?"

With a wan curving of the lips, Kate answered. "Good Spot. I would like to pet him and tell him thanks."

"Joshua carried you in his arms all the way home."

A frown replaced the slight smile. "I don't want him to see me this way."

"He has already seen you at your worst. He is out there pacing the hall as if you were about to give birth to his child. Won't you say a word to him?"

"Send him away. If I could not compare to Camilla Sharpton when well, I can hardly compete now."

"We know she played a part in your condition. I believe he has changed his mind about that vixen."

"That does not mean he wants me. Please, I cannot let him see me in my lowered state."

"As you wish."

She beckoned Pandora to come with her and slipped from the room. Both Joshua and the dog pounced as soon as the door opened. Bathed and beribboned by Phemie who sat near the door, the terrier was allowed access through a crack. The duchess waved Phemie inside as well. "Spot, here boy, up on the bed." The closing of the door cut off Kate's cry of delight.

Josh moved to follow, but his mother held him back with a hand to the chest. "You, she does not want to see."

"But I rescued her and carried her to the house in my arms," he answered, puzzled.

"Kate knows how much store you put in appearances. She is not at her best."

"Does she think me so shallow, so—?"

"So utterly stupid in your choice of women, yes. Make yourself of some use to her and carry the good news to Greenway Grange first thing in the morning. Take Jason with you. I hardly need young men underfoot when caring for the sick. Meet us at the London house once you complete your task."

The Duchess of Bellevue was not a woman to be disobeyed even by a distraught son. Joshua bowed his head, accepted his mission and his rejection by Kate. Traveling would give him time to sort out his thoughts, prepare his words, and make a case to convince Kate he no longer sought the season's greatest prize.

~ * ~

When Kate opened her eyes after napping, she found Phemie sitting nearby, engrossed in working on her stitchery, and Spot curled at her feet. Just beyond the dog, Fair Annet floated very faintly in strong sunlight at the foot of the bed.

"There, I have made Burt's death up to you. I deepened my manifestation until the men could see my blue gown even from the depth of the ravine. I summoned them to the tower and called to the little dog, too, in a voice only a hound might hear when they drew near."

"I am still very close to dying, am I not?" Kate answered her. She noticed Phemie did not hear, a sure sign she spoke only in her mind to the apparition.

"Yes, Kate. Your link to this world is very tenuous. You must will yourself better."

134

"Why should I do that? I might never recover what looks I had, but at least I can go to my grave clean and mourned by loved ones. If I live, Joshua will still spurn me and even Harold might roam to a more beautiful woman if he can find one that takes snuff."

"You give them little credit."

"After all, they are only men."

"Men are capable of great deeds. I know it. You are worthy of the greatest prize, Kate, and that prize is love. Fight for it. Hold out for it. Do not throw it away."

"Easily said, Fair Annet. Not so easily done, as you well know, having died for love yourself. Let me be!" Kate groaned, and this time Phemie heard.

"Mama," her little nurse called out. "Kate is awake. Shall I feed her again?"

She had only to refuse to eat, and all her sorrows would be over. Yet, when Phemie raised the pap boat to her lips, Kate opened her mouth and swallowed.

Twenty-one

Summoned to Bellevue House, London's most prominent Oxford-trained physician placed his ear to the opening of the long tube of the stethoscope pressed to Kate's chest as she lay in the canopied bed, its hangings pushed back for her examination. "Her heart is strong, the beat regular. Her pulse is normal." He straightened and lifted the instrument.

"The regimen of small but regular feedings of light foods for invalids is precisely what the patient needs, Your Grace. I have seen many a case of young women who starve themselves when crossed in love, and this is always the solution when they can be persuaded to eat."

Kate pushed the stethoscope to the side. "Love had nothing to do with this. I was incarcerated and left to starve by the most vile creatures on earth. I would be very grateful for something other than calf's foot jelly and chicken broth."

"Ah, the young recover so quickly, unlike us older folk," the physician remarked.

The duchess raised an eyebrow over his comment.

"I meant to say those who have a less stalwart constitution than your grace. As the patient feels so well, custard and beef tea might be added to her diet and rice or crackers put into her broth. Add stewed chicken if that goes well. If I might speak to your grace aside?"

The duchess nodded her assent. She and the bewigged physician moved to the far corner of the room.

"I noted in my examination that your ward was not molested. That is to say, she remains certifiably a virgin and a very fortunate young lady. Perhaps her captors planned to get a higher price because of this and so restrained themselves."

"Doctor, I believe they lacked the cock and balls to carry off a rape."

The physician took a turn in raising his brows, but he did not question the duchess's statement. He bowed, tugged his wig into place as he rose, and assured her in leaving that he would call again in a few days' time.

The duchess addressed her charge. "If you are well enough to complain about the food, I suspect you are strong enough to endure a visit from my hairdresser. He can be very tedious, but the results are well worth the time. I have asked him to come this afternoon."

Kate peered out from under the sleeping cap with the ruffled edge much like ones infants wore in the nursery. "I doubt I have enough hair left to deserve his attention."

"He can achieve marvels. Immediately upon our return to the city, I sent your locks to him to arrange into a hairpiece. If it does not do, we shall call in a wigmaker."

"Perhaps I should simply wear it short with a bandeau around my brow as the Empress Josephine once did. I will say short hair is amazingly light and airy."

"But men do so love it long." The duchess's mind wandered for a moment as if she were contemplating a moment with her husband.

Kate felt her cheeks fire with color. "I have no use for men right now and no wish to see any of them. Men got me into this predicament."

"So I have told Astin. Since our return to the city, he has called daily and asked after your health. The daffodils, the violets, the iris, and lilies are all from him." The duchess gestured to various vases sitting about the room.

"Not to mention delicate foods to tempt your appetite and the large box of medicinal snuff supposed to cure all woes."

"Dear Harold, he does believe that. As soon as I am able, I must confess my ruse to him. He will not want me then. Nor will anyone else." Her weakness overtook her for a moment and tears gathered.

"Stuff and nonsense! When you are up to it, we shall go out and look society in the eye. Those who made you suffer will pay. The duke was all for calling out Strictly as a matter of honor, but we both know he had nothing to do with the plot. This absolutely reeks of Lady Rushmore. Kidnappings are her forte. Such a pity women cannot duel. I know I could put her down with a ball between the eyes. No, our sex must resort to innuendo and gossip to get our revenge, and it can be quite as deadly."

"So, you know Matilda and Camilla were involved, Tomasina as well."

"Yes, Jason pried some of the truth from Tomasina who claimed smugglers had you in a tower. Pandora overheard more of their scheme. I did not want to press you about the matter when you were so ill."

"Smugglers indeed! The girls imprisoned me and did this." Kate put her hands to her head, then dropped them into her lap again. "I could have fought them off if there had not been three."

"That's the spirit."

"I would not have survived if it hadn't been for the old man who brought me more food, but then he stopped coming. Only Fair Annet kept me from slipping into death."

"Fair Annet?"

"Yes, the ghost of the tower." Kate watched the slightest hint of worry pass over the duchess's face and evaporate much as Fair Annet did in sunshine.

"The Longleighs have encountered stranger things, I suppose."

The clatter of booted men in the house interrupted their conversation. Deep voices and heavy footsteps sounded in the stairwell.

"I do not want to see Joshua!" Kate repeated as she had so many times.

"Of course. I will see to it."

~ * ~

The duchess left the sickroom and intercepted her sons on the stairs. Obviously, they had stopped at their lodgings to wash and change after their journey to Greenway Grange. Joshua, dressed in a bright blue jacket worn with an iridescent waistcoat, shone like a peacock's tail in full sunlight, and Jason had bits of immaculate lace about him. Their over-sized father accompanied them, and she supposed all three presumed to visit Kate without a second thought. She stopped them all with a wave of her small hands.

"Our invalid is not up to company at the moment, though the Queen's physician visited not long ago and says she is recovering very nicely. How did Mrs. Morely take the news of her daughter's resurrection?" the duchess asked Joshua.

"Joyously, and even more happily when I asked Mr. Morely if I could court his daughter, but then Jason…"

The duke slapped his second son on the back. "About time you came to your senses."

"Then Jason had to mention that Astin also had an interest in Kate and would make her a duchess someday. Her poor mother took to her bed with palpitations of the heart. It was all too much for her. Brother, you almost killed my future mother-in-law with elation. Besides, that bet is off. You heard me say so at the tower."

"Between you and Kate, perhaps. If you want to beg off, give me my fifty pounds. I am thinking of publishing a book of my verses with my winnings." Jason shot back the lace at his cuff and held out his hand for payment.

"Astin did not propose to her."

"But I had it from his own mouth that he wanted to and now probably will."

"Not if she accepts me first."

Jason dropped his hand. "Do let me know when that happens. Why should Kate have you when she can be a duchess like Mama?'

"Because she loves me and only me."

"Hmmm. Let's see. You told her she was not good enough for you, then accepted a wager making her prove she is, which almost resulted in her death. I think she might not be all that keen on you anymore."

"Step out in the garden, and I will show you how keen I am to break your poet's nose."

"Boys, boys, none of that." The duke parted his sons as he had so often during their childhood. "Joshua, remember soft words win a woman's heart."

"Yes," the duchess said with amusement in her voice. "I had so many of those when we courted."

"I should have used more and sooner," the duke admitted.

Jason held out his hand again. "Pay up, and I will write her a sonnet in your name."

Joshua slapped the hand away. "I will do my own courting, thank you."

"You will do nothing until Kate is ready to see you. My hairdresser comes to mend her looks this afternoon. Perhaps afterward, she will receive you. Until then, I suggest all of you go downstairs and find some way to amuse yourselves that does not involve violence. Am I understood?

"Yes, Mama."

~ * ~

Monsieur Laroquette, who claimed to have apprenticed under Marie Antoinette's own hairdresser, worked his magic. Still slim and spry, but given to the powder and patches of his youth, the man appeared ageless. He shaved his head and wore a peruke because he claimed he had no time to dally with his own hair.

Deftly, he snipped Kate's remaining locks to an even length, and then worked the curling iron on what was left. The smell of singed hair made his client wrinkle her nose and fear to look into the mirror. At last, that ordeal ended, not without a few minor burns which the hairdresser soothed with scented pomade. He opened a small, round box, withdrew a confection of braids, and placed his creation on the top of Kate's head. She recognized her own dark brown hair. It sat there like a heavy and awkward crown as the man affixed it with pins.

"Eh, voila!" he exclaimed and handed her the mirror.

"You are a genius, Monsieur Laroquette," said the duchess. "Kate, you have never looked better."

She considered her new coiffure. The braids sat very naturally in the nest of short, soft curls. Her nape felt naked and vulnerable, her head top heavy. "I think it might fall off."

"No, no, no. I assure you. I will show your maid how to affix it every day. My clients do not suffer from the embarrassment of slipping hairpieces. If Lady Strictly had called me first, her daughter would not have suffered such embarrassment at Lady Proctor's ball and been forced to leave the retiring room with her head wrapped in a shawl. I believe you were out of town, Your Grace, but did you hear of it?"

"Oh, yes, I heard." To cheer Kate, she had shown her Camilla's hairpiece, still befeathered, prior to the hairdresser's arrival.

"Now, of course, her mama wants me to work miracles when clearly the scalp has been damaged by a pernicious treatment. Who knows if it will grow back? But I do what I can for Lady Camilla and those other girls. We have an epidemic of sick hair, it seems. You are fortunate to be the victim of only a very bad cut. Did you suffer a fever and have the doctor remove it to affect a cure, Miss Morely?"

She hardly knew how to answer, but the duchess did it for her.

"No, some vicious, jealous young women attacked her and cut it off, Monsieur. I believe poor health, worry, and perhaps even guilt over wrongdoing might cause hair to fall out. Is that not so?"

"I think you are correct, Your Grace. Those ladies robbed Miss Morely of a treasure," the hairdresser said as he patted the shining braids. "But these riches will return full and lush as ever. As for myself, I do not think I would care to assist those who had done such a thing to a beautiful head of hair." Laroquette removed the sheet that protected Kate's dressing gown, packed away his sharp scissors and curling iron, and took his leave with the knowledge that he would be generously rewarded for agreeing with the duchess.

"There goes the finest hairdresser in London, possibly all of England, and he will never do the hair of Camilla Sharpton and her friends again. And that, Kate, is how women get revenge."

Kate's smile banished the gauntness of her face. How she did love the Longleighs.

"Now, do you feel well enough to dress and come downstairs for a bit? No more than a half hour. I know sitting for Monsieur Laroquette fatigued you."

The door cracked open, and Phemie and Pandora asked if they might enter.

"Pandora, make yourself useful and select a frock for Kate to wear downstairs," the duchess ordered.

Pandora rummaged in the tall wardrobe. "You missed the most stimulating meeting of the Abolition Society, true accounts of the condition of the slaves on sugar plantations. I cannot wait until you are recovered enough to attend with me." She shook out a green and white striped day dress with a flounce on the bottom and a broad ribbon to tie under the bosom. "Will this do? We can tighten the bow to make up for your lost inches."

"A good choice. Let's get it on her. Be careful of the hair," the duchess cautioned.

Like a bride being adorned by her maidens, Kate dropped her dressing gown, raised her arms, and let the frock flow over her. The duchess tied the bow snugly.

"How well you look, Kate!" Phemie exclaimed.

Kate regarded the stranger in the mirror again. Who was this wan creature whose thin face made her brown eyes appear so huge under an intricate coiffure? Certainly not the fresh country girl fully confident she could win the greatest prize. Joshua had been right in one respect. Unprepared for the intrigues of London society, she had paid the price.

A loud knock sounded on the door of the townhouse. The butler would see to it, but Kate asked, "Who could that be?"

"Astin, of course. As I said, he comes every day. Won't you see him for a moment and relieve his mind?" the duchess asked.

"Will Joshua be downstairs?"

"My dear, since the boys are grown, I rarely know where they are."

Pandora and Phemie exchanged glances. Another Longleigh conspiracy afoot, Kate guessed.

"I will go down for a short time."

She snapped her fingers, and Spot crawled out from under the bed where he had gone to earth, offended by the medicinal scent of the physician, the perfume of the hairdresser, and the presence of the girl who had given him a bath. Somehow, the small dog's devotion gave her comfort and confidence. Spot adored her, no matter what her appearance.

~ * ~

"How confoundedly long does it take to dress a woman's hair?" Joshua asked as he paced the drawing room.

"A question I have often asked myself and never received more than an exasperated sigh for an answer," the duke said, rattling his newspaper as he turned a page. "My old acquaintance, Shooting Star, Tecumseh, makes war against the Americans. I fear for him."

"I've seen you waste an hour trying to coax a single curl onto your forehead from that straight mane of yours. Women find my long and natural look just as attractive, I must say. But poor Kate, what was done to her." Jason shook his head as he read the latest of Lord Byron's poems.

"I do not care. Hair grows back."

"I am sure Camilla Sharpton is saying exactly the same and wondering why you no longer slaver at her feet. To think those girls did the deed themselves, according to Mama. I wouldn't have thought they had the strength or the intelligence to pull that off."

"Women often hide both in order to be more appealing to men. I can't say that of your mother, of course. For all her small size, she can inflict some damage because she puts all her heart into it. As for intelligence, I've long known she is sharper than me." The duke helped himself to the coffee set out for callers.

Word had gotten round about Kate's rescue and her fragile state, so most simply left their cards and good wishes at the door. "No sense in wasting a good brew," he remarked as he added sweetening and cream.

Busby entered with a card on a small, silver tray. "Viscount Astin wishes to know if you are at home."

"Are we?" the duke asked his sons. They shrugged. "I'm usually at my club this time of day. Ask the duchess, Busby."

But a moment later, Astin entered with a huge spray of lilacs on one arm and Kate on the other. Joshua jumped up in chagrin, not in greeting, but as the duke and Jason also rose in the presence of the ladies who trailed the couple, his annoyance went unnoticed.

"Won't you sit here, Kate?" Josh asked, gesturing to a solitary but well-padded chair.

"The settee will be fine." She sat, and Astin immediately filled the space next to her.

"For you." The viscount proffered the bouquet of honey-scented flowers.

"I believe you've bought out Covent Garden this week, Astin," Joshua remarked wryly.

"I would if doing so might speed Kate's recovery."

Kate bestowed the softest and loveliest of smiles upon the golden boy, the prize catch of the season. Joshua gritted his teeth and searched his mind for some delicate compliment. Kate had always been so hardy, so sensible, and never in need of flattery.

"A sweet for the sweet," he said, offering her a dish of bonbons.

Did her big, brown eyes roll, and her beautiful lips pucker with amusement?

"Too rich," his mama said. "Let me give those flowers to the maid to put in a vase before they wilt."

Unburdened of the bouquet, Kate considered the display of refreshments. "I should love to have a single chocolate biscuit."

Astin's pale, long-fingered hand shot out toward the plate holding the desired treat. Joshua slammed his own on top. The chocolate cookie crumbled, leaving two broken halves. Each man grabbed a piece and held it out to her. Phemie giggled, and Pandora waited to see what Kate would do. She took both. They watched her closely to see which half she would eat first. She nibbled on one, then the other so quickly they could not be sure which she preferred.

"Some tea would be wonderful," Kate said.

"I will pour," the duchess intervened. "I prefer not to have my china broken."

Kate accepted the beverage and sipped slowly. Astin focused on Joshua.

"I say, Longleigh, how goes your courtship of Lady Camilla?"

"I no longer seek her affection." Now he had Kate's total attention. She gazed at him, not Astin, with her lovely brown eyes. Take that, you snuff-sniffing, curricle-driving, bouquet-bringing nincompoop whom I could pummel into pudding at Gentleman Jackson's if you would fight me, he thought.

Unaware of Joshua's harsh opinion, the viscount asked, "Because her beauty has been marred by a small scar and an unfortunate loss of hair?"

Kate startled. The teacup shook in her hand. Only the family knew of her own condition.

"No, because I find she lacks the character I would desire in a wife. Her hair, though once beyond compare, is a superficial thing." He addressed Astin but kept his eyes on Kate.

She finished her tea with a gulp. "If you will excuse me, I am in need of rest."

She stood and all the men stood with her.

"Yes, I must be on my way. Allow me to escort you to the staircase." Astin held out an arm, and Kate rested her hand upon it. "Tomorrow, if the weather is fine, perhaps we might sit in the garden," he suggested.

"I would enjoy some sunshine."

Joshua trailed them like the possessive dog who pattered along behind as well. Astin parted from them at the bottom of the stairs and was shown out by Busby. Kate began to ascend.

"Take my arm lest you fall in your weakened state," Joshua offered.

"The banister will do just as well."

"No, I must insist for your welfare."

She did not like being coddled. His concern had brought the golden sparks back into her eyes. Thank heaven. He'd feared they were gone forever.

"Very well."

He captured her arm, and they walked sedately upward and across the landing to the door of her chamber. He lingered in the entry.

"Kate, I was to deliver a message from your mother."

"The duchess said the double shocks of my disappearance and return has sent her to her bed again, but she is expected to recover swiftly."

"Yes, but she bade me to give you a kiss from her."

"My mother? She has never been overly affectionate."

So she suspected him of lying, a small lie for a good cause, his cause. "She rejoiced to have you back among the living."

"Do it then." Kate offered him a hollow cheek.

Joshua laid his lips lightly upon it. She turned to enter her room. He must do more to make her his. He pressed his mouth to the vulnerable nape of her neck, warming the spot that felt so cold and naked. She did not move away. He kissed her again and again along the sensitive length of her neck and would have followed her inside if the dog had not squeezed by them, begun barking, and broken the trance. Kate quickly shut the door in his face.

Joshua turned to see the gathering of Longleighs at the foot of the stairs, his performance on the landing viewed by them all and possibly by some of the servants. He paused a moment to conquer his arousal, all too obvious in very tight pants, before going downstairs to join his family.

"Now that's the winning ticket. What the Longleighs lack in soft words, they make up for in action," the duke declared.

"You will marry the girl now," the duchess stated, "since you are no longer twelve and fifteen."

"I intend to, if only Kate will have me."

Twenty-two

That blasted Astin showed up again on the morrow to whisk Kate away for a ride in his curricle. They should have stayed in the garden, and Joshua had been prepared to sit with them the entire time. Seeing her son's predicament, and perhaps enjoying his discomfiture, the wily duchess gave permission for only a short spin in the park and held the viscount in conversation long enough for Joshua to rush to the mews and bring his horse around. Jason followed along on his own mount for the amusement value, he claimed. They joined Astin's entourage riding behind the sporty, two-wheeled vehicle and matched two-horse team, catching most of the dust in the rear.

With her hair covered by a deep, high-crowned straw bonnet that also shadowed her face, Kate sat very straight beside Astin. With the viscount's hands busy handling the ribbons, he at least could offer her no snuff. Arriving at the park, they whipped past a bench where Camilla, Tomasina, and Matilda sat like pastel water lilies atop a green pond while their mamas croaked behind them, a convocation of frogs. She did not turn her head to acknowledge the wave of their fingers. Joshua answered with a curt nod. Jason pulled up, dismounted, and lingered a while in conversation, rejoining the group upon their return. He fell into place beside his brother. They dropped to the rear of the cortege to speak to each other.

"How can you bear to be near those women when you know what they did to Kate?" Josh asked his brother. "Whenever I see them now, I get a bad taste in my mouth as if I've eaten a pretty, frosted cake and found spoiled meat to be the filling."

"I was spying in the enemy camp. They asked after Kate's health and twittered on and on about her ordeal at the hands of smugglers, so they are sticking tight to their tale. When I said the perpetrators must be caught and hung, Tomasina swooned into my arms, Matilda fanned so hard I thought she would break the end pieces, and Camilla went white in all the places not covered by her paint. Their mamas berated me for speaking of such harsh matters before innocent young ladies. Innocent—I scoff at that. Camilla hinted Kate might have been ruined by her captors."

"I should ride back there and..."

"No need. Tomasina said if something like that happened to her, she would retire at once to the country and never show her face again. I assured them the finest physician in London had called, and all is well with a complete recovery imminent. I shall tell Mama who will crush that rumor firmly beneath her little heel." Jason bowed from his saddle with a flourish toward the subject of one of his poems but continued to ride beside his sibling.

"As annoying as I sometimes find you, brother, I do thank you for this."

"Tell me, when will you offer for Kate? It seems Astin is getting the jump."

"I thought to wait until she fully recovered, but I can see I must act more quickly. Today, I shall do it today as soon as we return and rid ourselves of Astin."

Jason gave his brother an astounded look. "What, the cool-headed, aspiring barrister is acting in the heat of romantic passion. I have lived to see the day!"

"Not at all. Kate does not dote on flowery words. I will state my case plainly, and being a sensible girl, she will accept."

Jason shook his head. "You might excel me in learning the law, but you know nothing of women. Still, I wish you luck." In a gesture reminiscent of their father, he freed a hand to clap Joshua on the back. "And now, I am off to the park again to pay my respects to some long-neglected widows."

Not much after, the curricle stopped before Bellevue House. Astin handed Kate down and escorted her to the door. Joshua caught only a glimpse of her face before riding around to the stables. Though still too thin, she had regained that pleasing flush to her cheeks during the outing. More fresh air would be good for her, and under that pretext, he would ask her to walk in the garden and pop the question.

He handed his horse over to the groom and brushed himself off. Not prepared to ride this morning when Astin arrived with the curricle, he had gone along in a rush wearing the same deep green jacket and striped waistcoat as the day he and Kate had made the wager. Surely, she wouldn't notice or hold that against him, not Kate. He raced through the garden to catch her before she made for her chamber and shut him out again. Fortunately, or unfortunately, Astin had lingered to urge Kate to take a pinch of snuff to clear her head after the outing. She was still going through the motions when he approached, but now she thanked the viscount and sent him on his way. Kate moved toward the stairs.

"I see the fresh air agreed with you. Would you like to sit in the garden awhile?"

"No, thank you. I am quite fatigued."

"Come, Kate. We've barely spoken a word together since I rescued you."

"With the help of your father, brother, and a very brave little dog," she reminded him tartly.

"Yes, the dog. He deserves an outing, too. Call him for a romp in the garden." A barrister must be a quick thinker, and he certainly had that in his favor.

"Here, Spot! Come."

The terrier raced from wherever he had been snoozing so fast that he skittered on the marble floor and bunched a small carpet at the foot of the stairs in his haste. The three of them moved toward the garden door and descended the steps. Kate ignored his offer of an arm. In fact, she kept the bonnet, newly removed and dangling from its ribbons at her elbow, between them.

Spot ran hopefully to the gate leading to the mews where the juicy rats lived. Kate summoned him again, and he came reluctantly. "If you go back to the stables, Phemie will only bathe you again," she explained, giving the ratter a good stroking before sending him off to snuffle in the flower beds and mark the corners of the yard.

Josh found himself wishing she might touch him in the same way. He could easily imagine her hands caressing his hair as they kissed after his proposal. He envisioned those same capable fingers roving his body on their wedding night. The dog would be put outside the bedroom. They took a seat on a bench in the shade along the wall.

"Well, you wanted to talk," Kate reminded him with heavy sigh.

"Yes, very much." For all his silvery tongue in a courtroom, words failed him now. What to say? "As you may recall, our wager is off. I no longer seek the hand of Lady Camilla."

"A wise decision, considering her nature."

"Of course, I could have lived well on her dowry, but now I must succeed as a barrister before I can truly support a wife and family."

Kate considered those words and went off in entirely the wrong direction. "Then you should not be sitting here with me, but be off working on your career. You have the intelligence and ability to do very well for yourself. I might suggest adopting a more somber mode of dress. The barristers on whom your acceptance depends will take you more seriously."

"Thank you for that advice, but—"

"Consider your waistcoat. I detest it."

"I think it's very smart. However, I do not want to talk about fashion with you."

"Because I am only a country girl who has no taste?" The dog came to curl at her feet, and she patted it rather roughly again.

"No, because you are the country girl I should marry. I have come to see what my family desires and your family will be happy to accept, is right for both of us." He drew her hand away from the dog and gave it a squeeze.

That pretty flush on Kate's cheeks grew brighter. The golden glints in her eyes sparked. For a moment, he was glad to see both. Then, she shook off his hand, stood abruptly, and spoke.

"Too bad because that country girl no longer exists. She has become a wiser woman through suffering and knows she is worthy of no less than the greatest prize, no matter what her background or dowry. A good and ancient lady told me so."

"Mama? My own mother told you to accept Astin if he offers?" The hurt of her rejection and his mother's betrayal went deep inside him and twisted in the wound.

"Not the duchess. Fair Annet."

"The ghost of the tower you mentioned to Mama. I am being turned away on the say of a haunt."

"I see the duchess shares all I tell her with you, but yes, a spirit who knows more about what to prize than you do."

"You will take Astin for his title, his wealth, and his appearance, and yet you mocked me for seeking the same with Camilla?"

"Harold has not proposed, and so your question is moot."

"He will. Jason told me Astin means to offer."

"I will accept only the greatest prize. When you know what that is, speak to me again. Come, Spot."

Kate turned and marched away. The dog paused long enough to wet Joshua's boots.

~ * ~

She went directly to her chamber. Being out with Astin and dealing with Joshua had given her a headache. Perhaps she should take some medicinal snuff. Kate laughed at the thought. No, she only wanted to lie down and forget she had just turned down a proposal from the man she'd always loved. That was not to be.

Pandora and Phemie swarmed into the room. "We watched from a window and could not tell if Josh proposed. He only took your hand and did not go down on one knee as he should," the younger sister exclaimed.

"Yes, he should grovel," Pandora agreed. "But did he ask?"

"He did."

"Then why aren't we celebrating? Phemie, go tell Mama and Papa."

"Stay, Euphemia. I turned him down."

Even the man-despising Pandora seemed shocked. "But you want him. You claim to love him. Why, I am not sure, but regardless, you would be our sister. We shall have such jolly times together once you are wed. We can work together to end slavery and gain rights for women." She peeped out the window. "Go back and tell him you accept. He is still in the garden wiping his boots with some green leaves."

Must she explain? Apparently. "He offered for me because our families desire our union, he said. He felt that the wise course since his debacle with Camilla."

Phemie understood immediately. "He offered no words of love?"

"None. I do deserve better."

Pandora needed to argue. "I know he is my brother, but obtuse like all men. Still, most marriages of the ton are based on little else but the best bargain. Marry him anyway and make his life hell. That is how it usually turns out, and you will still have us as life-long companions."

"I could never make his life hell. I care too much for him. If Joshua has no passion for me, he would soon turn to a mistress. That, I could not endure. I want a marriage like that of the duke and duchess."

"Oh, la!" said Pandora. "Our parents hold up too high a standard of affection. Everyone cannot be like them, running off to the bed chamber in the middle of the day, and 'darling' and 'my dearing' every other word. It merely embarrasses their offspring. Joshua is simply a cooler sort."

"No, she must hold out." Phemie came down thoroughly on Kate's side. "I hope to have a loving union like Mama and Papa."

"Well, I hope to have none at all," Pandora countered.

"Please, please, enough! I do love you, but until Joshua can say the same to me, there will be no marriage."

Twenty-three

"We shall all be hung or at the very least deported to Australia." Tomasina threw herself on to the chaise longue in Camilla's chamber and put a hand over her violet eyes, slightly dislodging her hairpiece. "The Longleighs know. That awful Pandora told them. What are we to do?"

"I tried to imply Katherine had been ravaged as Mama suggested. Only men could do that, but it appears the Duchess of Bellevue has already squelched the idea with her summoning of the Queen's physician," Matilda said. She threw her long arms up as if surrendering to the King's justice.

"Perhaps if we came forward and explained that we only intended a merry prank, and Old Burt was to bring her food and water and then release her in a timely manner, all would be forgiven. Consider we had no part in his death or the foul weather that kept him from tending to her," Tomasina whimpered.

"I doubt we would receive any mercy. The Longleighs are a vindictive lot, Mama says, especially Lady Flora." Matilda crossed her arms under her flat bosom.

"It's because of Lady Flora we cannot get a decent hairdresser anymore." Camilla peered into the looking glass and primped the sides of her coiffure. Her curls appeared stiff and unnatural—which they were. The bald spot had continued to grow until she resembled a dotard with long hair growing only at the sides. She'd had to order a larger wig and stuff the remains of her locks beneath it.

At least the bruise had faded, leaving only that small, annoying scar. She could leave off the paint at last, but the use of it had left her skin with a sickly hue. People were beginning to say she suffered from consumption or an even worse illness. Had Lady Flora started that rumor, too? She had no proof, but her suitors were cutting away to court less tainted lovelies. How difficult it was continue smiling and speaking mildly when she wanted to curse and rant over what had befallen her.

"Camilla Sharpton does not surrender. We must come up with another plan to save ourselves."

"That will be difficult. Earn the enmity of one Longleigh and all will hate you. They are thick as thieves," Matilda remarked.

"Yes, family is all to them," Tomasina agreed without removing her hands from her tear-swollen eyes.

"Then, one of us must become family and beyond prosecution. That person can then plead for the rest of us. Joshua is not likely to fall for our little garden ruse again. In fact, he avoids me now. But Jason is a weak link."

"I could not think of marrying my cousin, and one of those eccentric Longleighs at that. Still, Jason is very handsome. I suppose I could make the sacrifice if he can be lured," Matilda declared, exactly as if she had a chance of marrying anyone.

"People often marry their cousins, but Jason has shown he favors Tomasina. He does not shun us like the rest of them."

Tomasina sat up and wiped her lovely eyes. "I would be willing to have him to save us all." She straightened her hair by removing and replacing a hairpin. "Do you think my hair will grow back by our wedding night?"

"You think too far ahead, Tommy. At the next social occasion, when Jason appears and we are all together, you must lead him to a dark spot under some pretext. Do not wait for him make a move, but press your lips to his in an ardent kiss. Offer him a touch of your bosom, and when he succumbs to lust, scream and tear your gown. We will come running. If he refuses to do right by you, the Longleighs and all they say will be discredited. If he marries you, we will be safe. Our future rests on your shoulders, Tommy."

"Yes, yes! I will allow him to do all that to me! For our sakes, of course."

Tomasina stuck out her plump bosom and firmed the chin that had acquired a rather attractive permanent dent from Kate's kick. The slightly bluish tone of her complexion brought on by the face paint actually made her eyes seem more brilliant, and her brunette hair had suffered less damage than that of the fairer girls.

Camilla felt a slight pang of jealousy, an emotion so new she took a moment to recognize it for what it was. She had never been envious of any woman before since she reigned as the nonpareil. Oh, she hated Katherine Morely, but still felt superior to that girl in most ways. Now, she was to take second place to Tomasina. How horrible not to be the prettiest, most desirable woman in the room. How did Matilda bear it?

She swallowed such a great amount of pride, she almost choked on it. "We have our plan, then. Tommy must save us all."

Twenty-four

"Kate insults your waistcoat, turns you down, and vows to accept Astin. Yet here you are dressed in black and white like a penguin or a preacher. She has plucked your peacock plumage and trodden it underfoot, but you are still trying to please her. I find this vastly amusing."

Jason settled back onto the squabs spilling stuffing into the elderly hackney coach they had rented to get to Lady Buxton's soiree from their lodgings. Josh had ceased haunting Bellevue House since Kate's refusal. He applied himself to his studies, sold off some of his finery, and replaced the garb with mostly black garments as if he were in mourning for the loss of her.

"I find Kate was right. Since I adopted somber dress, the barristers are taking more serious note of me. I expect to pass the bar very shortly now, leaving you to eat with the other law students. If for some reason Astin should not propose to her, I will at least have a profession to offer."

"I still say you should have let me write out a pretty speech for you. No wonder you failed."

Jason tried to be tolerant, but his brother simply wasn't any fun to be around. He'd only succeeded in getting him away from his books and cases by mentioning that Kate would attend Lady Buxton's soiree briefly. Showing the colors, their mother had called it. Now that Kate had regained her strength, they must appear in public to tout her health after her terrible ordeal. She was to look everyone in the eye, especially those horrid girls, and reply to any who asked that she had fully recovered.

The Buxton place was a warren of small rooms with no proper ballroom and so there would be listening music in one room, cards in another, a display of art and curios in a third, food in the dining room, and plenty of nooks and crannies to entertain a certain widow he had been cultivating. The brothers got down a block from their destination to avoid the crush of carriages and walked the rest of the way side by side as they often did, tall hats cocked, walking sticks swinging. At the entry, Joshua pressed ahead to begin a relentless search for Kate. Jason followed good-naturedly. After all, he had to discover Lady Tartte's whereabouts as well. He hoped she continued to live up to her name, or rather her late husband's name.

Avoiding the queue up to the buffet in the dining room, they climbed the stairs and had immediate success in the crowded drawing room. Kate sat with her back to them, but was easily recognizable. Boldly, she had chosen not to wear her hairpiece. A golden brow band holding a single plume nestled in her thick, short curls. The feather waved like a brave flag in battle as she turned her head this way and that, answering questions. Lady Flora and the duke stood nearby, her color guard. The duchess gave her second son an encouraging nod as he passed.

Joshua took up a post on one side of the fireplace where Kate could not help but notice him. Jason placed a hand on the back of Lady Tartte's chair, not touching the attractive widow, but letting her know he had arrived by the spill of lace at his sleeve. His prospective inamorata leaned forward, engrossed in the conversation and gave him an excellent view of her very ripe breasts. Kate's own bosom was making a nice recovery, but Joshua gazed at nothing but her eyes and the movement of her lips as she spoke.

"I existed mostly on rainwater blown into my prison by the coastal storms. At one point, I considered trapping and eating a rat raw. Such is the nature of extreme hunger."

Several listeners stopped stuffing themselves with refreshments, either out of squeamishness or a general indigestion of the stomach brought on by her description. She went on to tell the tale of capturing the rat and using it as a messenger to bear a note written in her own blood. Her audience remained rapt.

"But as the rat was not discovered until the same day as my rescue, this did me no good. I would have fared better if I had feasted upon it."

The low table before Kate held many small plates heaped with delicacies as if everyone in the room wanted to make up for her time of starvation. Astin had claimed the place beside her on the settee and offered her now a tart of peach preserves and then a pinch of snuff, both of which she waved away. Pandora perched on her other side as if guarding Kate's left flank from the enemy.

"If only you could have fought free during the initial struggle and been spared such terrible suffering!" Lady Tartte exclaimed.

"I did try to combat my kidnappers, but could not overcome so many. However, I left my mark on them all."

Kate's eyes sought, not Joshua, but the group of young women huddled together at the opposite end of the fireplace like chickens when a hawk flies overhead. Tomasina Murray, wearing a becoming violet and lace gown that matched her eyes, fingered her chin. Matilda Everton sucked in her breath. Only Lady Camilla, all dressed in white, did not flinch.

"One I hit one in the eye, and another received a kick to the chin. I might have broken a rib of another. Still, they cut off my hair, locked me away with scant food and water, and did not return."

"But you were rescued from the tower by three valiant lords and a charming pup, I've heard. Here is one of them now," Lady Tartte concluded, as if trying to rush the end of the story because she had other things to do this evening.

The widow reached back, patted Jason's hand, and locked her fingers with his for a moment. A few eyebrows raised. Lady Flora glared at her third son.

"There is little romantic about starving to death or licking the walls for moisture," Kate said a little too sharply. "I believe I was sustained by a heavenly spirit who appeared to me in a vision and would not allow me to surrender to my misery. She was a lady who lived in ancient times and had suffered the same fate because she could not have the man she loved." Her wide, brown eyes flashed toward Joshua and quickly turned away.

An awkward silence followed. The duke ended that with his basso voice.

"The Shawnee put great stock in visions. In my thirteenth year, I fasted for four days and nights to discover my guardian spirit. On the fourth night, the bear came."

The older members of society, who had heard this tale many times, began to break off from the group and seek other amusements, but the curious young stayed on, including the loyal Pandora. Kate finally accepted refreshments from Astin and spoke no more. Lady Tartte rose and gave her seat to another.

The widow announced rather loudly that she would seek out the music room. Jason Longleigh watched the red bow mounted just above her derriere on her black gown sway from view and trailed after her.

~ * ~

The three young women by the fireplace turned their huddle inward making a circle much like the witches in *Macbeth*. The head witch spoke in a whisper, her words easily covered by the duke's deep voice and the stir of guests moving about the room.

"Now is our chance to snare Jason Longleigh. You know his reputation with older women. He will seek out a dark place to be with Lady Tartte. Tilly, intercept her and engage her in conversation. Ask for advice. These old crones love to tell us what to do."

"I'd hardly call Lady Tartte a crone. I would give much to have her bosom. Perhaps I could ask her how to improve mine."

"A good idea. Tommy, follow after Longleigh and slip inside when he goes to ground. You can be sure the place will be dark. Allow him liberties, then scream and tear your clothes. I will not be far away and shall help raise the alarm. Go!"

Both her minions rushed away as quickly as if they had an urgent need to use the necessary. Camilla came behind them at a more leisurely pace. They surpassed Jason Longleigh, who sniffed on the trail of Lady Tartte and caught up with her at the base of the stairs leading to the bed chambers. She might have been going to the retiring room, but the girls knew better. They gathered around the widow and prevented her from moving forward. Jason continued up the stairs, and Lady Tartte gave him a slight nod as if to say she would be along shortly.

"Might I ask you a very personal question?" Matilda enquired so sincerely. "I have always admired your figure and would so like to enhance mine, especially about the bosom. Have you any secrets you might share?'

Although Lady Tartte seemed somewhat startled, she also appeared pleased. "You must understand, dear child, I have been blessed by nature. The bearing of children also has something to do with my current endowment. Padding and ruffles everyone knows about, but I can recommend certain creams that will plump the bosom. Some say lifting books just so will help." She held out her arms out at her side, then pressed her palms together in front of her substantial breasts. "This helps to firm the arms as one ages."

Camilla and Tomasina left them in conversation, linked arms as if they were chained together, and stalked after Jason. As they pretended to enter the retiring room set aside for ladies at the head of the stairs, they spied him listening at one of the bed chamber doors, shaking his head, and continuing down the hall to find a room not already occupied. Dropping his handkerchief before a door as a guide, he turned the knob and entered an empty chamber. Tomasina dashed after him, leaving Camilla waiting to sound the alarm.

Entering the dark room, Tommy squealed when strong arms encircled her from behind.

"Who is this? A buxom young lass come to offer herself to her lord and master?"

Jason nuzzled her neck, and Tomasina giggled. What delightful games older women played with men. His hands moved from her waist to her breasts, cupping and massaging each plump cushion while he continued to nibble at her neck and the line of her jaw. Breathless, she had no air to scream as he worked inside the bodice of her gown. In fact, she leaned hard against his chest for support when her legs grew wobbly with the pleasure. Why not allow him the ultimate gift if they were to marry anyway? Impatient foot taps sounded in the hall. She recognized them as Camilla's when that young lady was in a snit over something and about to call her a ninny.

Reluctantly, Tomasina inhaled and let out a scream that thrust her breasts even harder into Jason's hands. She tore a sleeve at the seam and raked a lacy ruffle and a clump of artificial violets from her bodice. With her arms flailing, Jason failed to extract his hands from her bosom before the door swung open and light from the hanging lamps illuminating the corridor showed all to Lady Camilla who shrieked in an amazingly strong high soprano voice. Ladies flocked from the retiring room. Men dashed up the stairs, some bearing small pocket weapons or unsheathed sword canes.

~ * ~

Before the shouting began, Kate sent Astin off to fetch a beverage and then retired to a quiet seat away from the firelight and the center of attention. Seeing his chance, Joshua moved to stand beside her.

She acknowledged his presence by saying, "You must think me completely dotty to mention the lady of the tower in public, but I give credit where it is due. Whether angel or ghost, she would not let me die and promised me help."

Kate braced her shoulders as if waiting for his scorn or laughter.

"I believe your angel might have sent me a dream," Josh admitted quietly, hoping she would not rise and move away from him. "You've heard my father's tale of his vision quest many times, but I've never had such an experience. Mama absolutely forbade him from starving us for four days as a manhood rite. I wish now I had undergone that initiation so I might better understand your ordeal."

"I would not inflict it on you either, but do tell me about your dream."

"You were trapped in a tower, and I stood at its base. As in the old fairy tale, you let down your hair, glorious thick braids of dark brown, but they snapped off in my hands."

Self-consciously, Kate patted her short curls. "Yes."

"The style becomes you." He wanted to add a "my dearest" but had no right.

"Do you think so? Pandora says she would cut off her hair in a minute if it weren't so straight, but then she would resemble Jason."

"Let's not talk of Jason. He is off dallying somewhere as usual. I wanted to say when I could not reach you in that tower, when I thought I'd lost you forever, I felt such deep, cold despair I am unable to describe it. A blackness engulfed me and..."

Two cups in his hands, Astin wove across the drawing room, skirting clumps of guests. He would interrupt them in a minute. Proprieties and public places be damned. Joshua bent to kiss her, to claim her for his own. But the screaming started. Kate stood suddenly, nearly bashing his aristocratic nose.

Across the space, one cup was knocked from Astin's hand as the crowd surged for the door. The other upended onto a superb waistcoat embroidered with songbirds like the ones on Kate's snuffbox. Unhappy with the plain vest he wore, Joshua had admired it earlier. More's the pity because Kate rushed forward, hankie extended, to dab his rival.

How did he know the shouting must involve the Longleighs? Because it always did. Sometimes, he wished he'd been born into another family.

Twenty-five

No help for it. Joshua pushed past Kate and the dripping Astin and headed for the source of the uproar. Since there was to be no dancing, he had retained his walking stick, the one with sword inside the shaft. Wisely, he chose not to unsheathe it. Enough armaments were being brandished to assure someone would be accidently nicked or shot. Thanks to his height, he could see the tableau unfolding on the upper landing.

A girl in a violet gown wept on Lady Strictly's bosom. Jason, red in the face, waved his arms in denial of some heinous act. Of course, his mother stood in the thick of business, and his father glowered nearby. He half expected to hear the Longleigh battle cry, but the duke looked more troubled than belligerent. Call to battle or not, he needed to be with his family to help sort out another of Jason's scrapes. His brother's romantic notions often ended in disaster, though ever since diving naked into a holly bush from the boudoir window of a married woman, Jason had confined himself to widows.

Joshua sidled through the people crowding the staircase and found himself stuck behind two slow moving hippopotami in the form of Lord and Lady Harcourt, Tomasina's parents summoned from their places at the card tables. Their chubby eldest son made slightly better progress toward his sister's side.

Close enough now, Josh could hear Tomasina sobbing out, "He grabbed me as I walked past the bed chamber, pulled me inside, tore my clothes, and—and…"

What a ridiculous accusation. Jason had far more finesse with women and needn't force himself on any of them. His brother denied all by saying, "She followed me, and I mistook her for another." He looked desperately at Lady Tartte who pursed her rouged lips and glanced away.

"I kept my eyes on those girls. They entrapped my son," his mother shrilled.

Lady Rushmore, towering over her, answered, "I do not know why these people are allowed in polite society. Wherever the Longleighs go, there is chaos." She attempted to stare the duchess down from her greater height and failed.

Lady Tartte fluttered a fan before her hot face and replied, "Because these affairs would be deadly dull without them."

The Murray family entered the scene, and Joshua squeezed by them to stand beside his brother. Below, he noticed Kate and Astin bobbing in the sea of guests. Kate's worried face turned upward as if she yearned to sprout wings and fly to their assistance. Instead, Astin offered some snuff to calm her. How could she care so much for his outrageous family—and no longer care for him?

Lord Harcourt, purple and heaving, managed to wheeze out the words, "I shall expect you to offer for my daughter tomorrow, or my son will meet you on the field of honor."

The Harcourt heir's face went from an overheated scarlet to pale in a second. Everyone knew Jason Longleigh excelled with a sword, could more than hold his own at fisticuffs, and seldom missed a shot despite his poetical notions. Even the females of the Longleigh species were rumored to be armed, and Joshua knew this to be the truth. At the moment, Pandora, who stood staunchly beside her mother, looked as if she would kill Tomasina with the glint in her eyes like a latter-day Medusa. For all their wild ways, he felt proud of his family at this moment, how they held together defending his brother.

The Duke of Bellevue's voice boomed out. "No need for violence. My son will be at your house tomorrow."

"What! Don't you see it's a plot?" his duchess said, grasping his arm.

"The Longleighs are honorable men. My son will do what any honorable man should do under the circumstances. Make way!" The duke took his wife's arm and led her down the crowded stairs. People flattened themselves against the railings to let them pass. Pandora followed with her brothers, a solid, straight-backed cohort, defying the stares of the enemy. They gestured Kate into their ranks as they moved to the exit to summon their coach and abandon the fray.

Once out of the clatter and confusion of carriages, Lady Flora spoke up, "I cannot stomach the thought of Jason marrying one of the girls who so injured Kate. That is their scheme, you see. We cannot retaliate against them if they are family." The duchess wrung her hands in unaccustomed dismay.

The duke heaved a sigh so great their vehicle shook. "Do not fret, my dearest, we shall go directly to the docks and have Jason put aboard the first ship to Canada. Even with the war on, I trust our British merchant marines to get him there safely. After arrival, you might consider offering to fight alongside the Shawnee against the Yankees, son."

"But you said…What about the Longleigh honor? Can't I simply poke or shoot a few holes in the Harcourt heir and be done with it? I will try not to kill him and make matters worse," Jason said with the faintest hint of pleading.

"That's what I would do if I were a man, fight a duel or go to war with Indians," Pandora claimed from her seat opposite his.

"You should have stayed away from Tomasina instead of encouraging that violet-eyed vixen," Joshua told his brother.

"I was trying to infiltrate their group and find Kate, thank you very much. Afterward, I felt I must keep an eye on them in case they schemed again."

"Only this time their scheme involved you, brother."

"I appreciate all that you did to help me, Jason. I believe I see another way out for you." Kate spoke reasonably and without their heated passion. All the Longleighs paused to listen.

"If Jason offers for Tomasina and she refuses him, then honor has been served without violence or exile."

"But the ploy is to have Tomasina marry him. Why would she refuse?" the duchess asked, lowering her own excitable voice.

"Because Jason will have been disowned by his family and have utterly nothing to bring to the marriage. He might suggest they take Tommy's dowry and set off for Australia to raise sheep or go to live in Canada and trap beavers. Better yet, to live among the Shawnee as you once did, Uncle Bear and Auntie Flora. I doubt any of those ideas will appeal to Tomasina, who prefers fetes and furbelows."

"I do love this girl. She should be a Longleigh. We need her good sense. In fact, after a certain display of affection we all witnessed, we should be on our way to the cathedral tomorrow instead of delivering Jason to the Murrays," the duchess said pointedly.

Joshua stiffened his shoulders and stared at the space between Kate and Pandora. "I have proposed and been refused. She holds out for the greatest prize."

The duchess considered the young couple avoiding each other's eyes. "The greatest prize, but of course she must have that. Kate deserves it."

Twenty-six

Sinking back into the overstuffed cushions of his coach the next morning, the Duke of Bellevue stayed deep in the shadows. With the shades drawn over the windows, he might have been concealing his grief on his way to his son's funeral. Not so. Jason sat next to him alive and well, if extremely nervous. As they approached Lord Harcourt's home, he took the young man's hand in his large grip and shook it firmly.

"Remember, your grandfather dabbled in acting and once disguised himself to play King Lear. I suppose you come by these poetical notions honestly. Use that talent for all it is worth today. You rehearsed very well last night."

"Thank you, Papa. I will do my best."

Jason had managed to keep his hand steady, but was sure his father had noticed the sweating palm and simply did not remark upon it. The coach rocked to a stop. They waited a moment for the footman to get down and knock upon the imposing black door. As the entry opened, Jason plastered a jaunty grin on his face and fairly bounded down the carriage steps and up the short flight to the house.

"Get my baggage, Elliot," he directed the footman.

The man's face took on the most lugubrious expression. Each of the servants had been given a chance to play a minor part in the drama by repeating a specially crafted line. Elliot had proved to be the most talented, possibly because of his already long face and hound dog eyes.

"Might I say, your lordship, how sorry I am we are losing you?'

All the while the Harcourt butler stood at attention holding the door open. Beyond the servant, Lord and Lady Harcourt waited to receive him.

"Never fear, my good man. I believe I have landed on a very soft cushion in more ways than one. Just pile my boxes in the foyer."

Hauling a huge trunk between them, two more footmen struggled up the steps. Elliot brought along a small but obviously heavy chest. More boxes followed. As soon as the mountain of luggage had been disgorged into the Harcourt manse, the coachman roused the black horses and turned the carriage smartly into the noon traffic. All over London, bells marked the hour.

"And therefore never send to know for whom the bell tolls; it tolls for thee" thought Jason, silently quoting his favorite line from John Donne. The manic smile still glued to his face, he stepped forward to bow before Lord Harcourt. "I beg of you, lead me to your beauteous daughter so I may prostrate myself before her delicate feet."

Harcourt frowned deeply into his heavy jowls at the flowery language and gestured to the luggage. "I know you came to offer for my daughter, but what is the meaning of all this?"

"As you might know, the duke has a very high sense of honor. In disgust, he disowned me last evening, told me to pack my belongings and go. He has forbidden my brother to share lodgings with me as well. So, here I am where I mean to stay. I have brought my library of poetry, which I shall be happy to share, not to mention the unpublished manuscript of my verse. Still looking for a benefactor to foot the bill. Papa does not care for rhyme. Do you?"

"I cannot say I am overly fond of it."

"I adore a well-written sonnet," Lady Harcourt claimed, all her chins aquiver. "But to the matter at hand. Our daughter awaits you in the drawing room, upstairs and to the right."

Jason mounted the steps, thirteen, as many as a well-built gallows. His feet grew cold inside his boots. Lord and Lady Harcourt trundled after him.

No way to escape without rolling them both down the stairs like two giant kegs. His escort followed to the open door of the drawing room but remained outside.

Tomasina posed in a gilded chair too spindly to hold either of her parents, yet as he approached, he noticed for the first time how she might become like them—that slight doubling under the dent in her chin, the ample bosom not overripe as yet, the soft shoulders so well padded. Unlike Kate, she'd never starved a day in her life.

But she was well turned out for the occasion in a becoming white gown sprigged with small, purple flowers and a charming cameo on a lavender background tied round her neck on a black velvet cord. With her stiff, dark hairpiece firmly in place, more natural brunette curls cascaded beside her face. As he neared, he scented violets and thought the theme too overdone. Thinking of which, he bowed deeply and with a flourish.

"Lady Tomasina, as you know I have come to ask for your hand in marriage, but first I must confess a minor impediment."

"Oh?" said Tomasina, clasping her plump hands tightly in her lap.

"My father has disowned me and so as a third son, I no longer have even my allowance to depend upon or the support of my family in pursuit of a barrister's career. I've never really warmed to the law, so just as well." He flicked his fingers as if disposing of something nasty. "How great is your dowry? How much shall we have to live upon if we wed?

"F-five-thousand pounds," she answered, dismay showing all over her round face.

"I thought it would be more, but then you have a sister before you and one behind and that must reduce the pot. No matter. Five-thousand pounds will suffice for our future—especially if we go abroad to live."

"Abroad? But where?"

"I thought Canada where I might buy a commission and fight the Americans while you remain behind in the safety of the garrison, of course. Occasionally, the forts are overrun and the women...No, we won't speak of that."

"I do not believe I would like Canada."

"With Napoleon on the loose, Europe is impossible. These wars have robbed me of my Grand Tour. Australia, then. We take ship, crossing by land over the Suez and then on into the Red Sea and the Indian Ocean. Why the trip is so lengthy, we might have our first child by the time we arrive! Then, our little family will purchase a sheep farm with your dowry, and we shall live on lamb and mutton all our days. Adventure, how I crave it!"

"But Australia is filled with convicts. It is a rough and violent place. Few ever return from there." How wide those violet eyes became.

"I am doughty enough to protect you, but should I fall to another man's weapon or succumb to the venomous snakes or the toothy crocodiles, you need not worry. I hear the colony suffers a great shortage of women, and men will fight to have you almost immediately. I relish the challenge! But to business, dearest Tomasina."

He dropped into the classic pose of the supplicant, kneeling at her feet, and pried one knotted hand from the other in order to squeeze her round, white fingers. "Will you be my wife?"

She jerked her hand away and waved frantically to her parents who blocked the door with their bulk. "Mama, Papa, I lied. I did follow him into that room and tore my own dress. I do not want to marry a Longleigh. They are as frightening as everyone says."

Jason captured a fluttering hand and held it as he would a fat, floundering fish. "My love, you have not answered me directly."

"No, no, a thousand times, no!"

How trite. He prevented himself from rolling his eyes in disdain and adopted an air of great sorrow. "You refuse me?"

"I do. Go away. Go to Canada or Australia, but do not take me with you." Tomasina covered her most beautiful feature and began to cry.

Before he could rise, two of Lord Harcourt's footmen raised him under the arms and dragged him back into the hall.

"Be gone with you and find a hackney coach to haul your belongings," Harcourt raged.

"But where shall I go? I thought I would be living with you until the marriage and publishing my poetry with your financial assistance. I haven't the price of transportation on me." He turned his pockets out to show the truth of it.

"You may go to hell, young man, and I'll gladly pay the way for that. What my daughter saw in you to make her perjure herself, I will never understand.

A handsome face, a glib tongue is all a young girl notices. I thank God you revealed your feckless nature before it became too late. Have this scoundrel's baggage put out on the street and summon him a hired coach," Harcourt directed his butler.

The footmen walked the rejected suitor down the stairs and to the door. None too gentle in ejecting him, Jason stumbled and landed on his hands and knees on the sidewalk. His belongings came tumbling after. No matter. Mostly, the trunks contained worthless rags and rocks. He'd been quite confident of his acting ability, or so he told himself now.

Twenty-seven

Jason got down from the hired coach and gave his mother's direction for the return of the luggage. He bade the driver to wait for a moment for his payment and bounded up the two steps of the dark and narrow lodging he leased with his brother near the Courts of Law. He found Joshua, as was usual lately, working on a brief in the chamber right of the entry that served as a study and meeting place for any willing to use the services of an untried lawyer.

"I am free of Tomasina Murray!" he announced. "She confessed to lying about our encounter in front of her parents. Still, I was a trifle stung that she did not desire me enough to pack her bags and run off to Australia. I find proposals to be most stressful, even false ones. Never would I want to go through that again. You have my condolences on having actually asked Kate and failed."

"Thank you," Josh replied drily.

"Oh, I've the forgotten coachman. Have you enough to pay him? I didn't want Lord Harcourt to think I had a penny on me and so went without a cent."

Joshua reached into a drawer of his desk and withdrew their petty cash box. He gave him adequate coins pay the driver and send the boxes on to Bellevue House and went back to his work. Jason returned to settle himself in the client's chair and babble some more.

"As I talked to Tomasina, the idea of going to Canada began to appeal. I am sure Papa would buy me a commission as a lieutenant to go forth and fight the Americans."

"And Mama would say again she has no sons to spare, and her tears would end the whole matter. You had best spend more time on your law studies—as I am trying to do right this very minute. I am preparing a case for a notable barrister, and if I impress him, my crossing of the bar is assured."

"If we both become barristers, we can no longer share our chambers, and I do enjoy living above a man who keeps a valet."

"I've let the man go. My simpler mode of dress needs no assistance."

"What? Did Kate put you up to it?"

"She did say my allowance would go further without keeping the man."

"Yet she will marry Astin and have a hundred servants. What am I to do when I need assistance getting into my evening wear?"

Joshua pounded his fists on the desk and made him jump. "I suppose we could help each other. Please, I need to finish this brief. It could mean my future. Becoming a barrister might not be the greatest prize of all, but it is a very good one that would allow me to support a family. I will lay that accomplishment at Kate's feet."

"Have we anything to eat? Lady Harcourt offered me not so much as a crumb, and I find proposing has made me peckish. Of course, I couldn't get down any breakfast this morning."

"Might be some cheese and crackers in the pantry," Joshua said, applying himself to his work again.

"One thing is for certain. If you married Kate, we'd have some food in this place."

"If you would stop bothering me, I might be able to bring that about."

"I plan to take dinner at Bellevue House. What about you?"

"I will dine with the law students again and hope the barristers invite me to their side of the bar."

"Good luck with that, brother dear. I'll have the better meal and the pleasure of announcing I am done with Tomasina."

"They will know that when your baggage returns."

"Then I go to a victor's feast!"

"If I give you the fare, will you leave now?"

"But of course." How stuffy his brother had become!

Paying for his peace and quiet, Joshua doled out the money.

~ * ~

Joshua delivered his completed work to Sir Richard Crumm, King's Counsel, shortly before the seating for the afternoon meal. The esteemed barrister, his stern face etched with deep crevices, skimmed the pages, and then tucked the brief under his arm as they walked side by side to the dining hall. He left Joshua at the barrier that separated the aspiring law students from the best barristers in London.

As usual, the meal served in the lower part of the room could only be called mediocre. Day-old bread and inferior ale accompanied some sort of gray stew, by its strong taste, mutton. The same cheese served yesterday was good enough for today as were the apples beginning to wrinkle from long storage. Regardless, Joshua tore his roll, dipped his spoon, and tried not to imagine what a fine dinner his mother would provide.

Up on the dais, Sir Richard thumbed Joshua's work. A dollop of rich, brown gravy dropped from a bite of chop onto the paper. The barrister rubbed it off with a fingertip. Imaging his ink smearing, Joshua winced. Fresh and crusty, the barrister's bread showered crumbs on the pages of the brief. Sir Richard passed the papers to a colleague who added a wine stain, and so it went down the table until a servant at the end returned the bedraggled manuscript to his mentor. The man rose, moved to the railing, and summoned Joshua with a crooked finger, most likely to request he make a clean copy.

At the bar, Sir Richard cleared his throat. "Good work, young man. I might even say brilliant. Been reading the law for three years, have you?'

"Yes, Sir Richard."

Josh prayed the barrister would not recall he'd dawdled at Oxford studying elocution and debate before coming up to London where fashion and frivolity diverted him from earnest study for the good part of that first season. He'd sobered in attitude if not in dress his second year and done excellent work the third, but Kate's advice about changing his appearance had earned him Crumm's attention.

"One of the Duke of Bellevue's many sons, correct?"

"I am pleased to claim him as my father."

"Would you care to join me and my fellow barristers for pudding?" Sir Richard opened the gate in the bar.

"I have—I have passed the bar?"

"Not yet. Do not dawdle. The dish grows cold."

Joshua moved to the other side of the barrier. By the time he took a seat before a portion of pudding, steaming, studded with raisins, and swimming in hard sauce, his fellow students had risen to applaud. The various barristers congratulated him and offered advice on where to buy his robes and find a wig with a good fit. Certainly, the pudding was excellent, but he barely tasted it. How he wished Jason or his father had been there to witness the moment when he passed the bar. Now, he had a true prize to offer Kate. All women wanted a man with a solid career, one that offered a good living and a chance of great prestige if he eventually became a judge. When he told her how her advice had advanced his cause, she would fly into his arms and agree to be his.

Joshua left the dining hall with some decorum, accepting good wishes and absorbing envious glances along the way. He appeared to be returning to his chambers, but once around a corner, he increased his stride and rushed in the direction of Bellevue House. Along the way, he found a hackney to take him even more swiftly. Bursting into the townhouse without a knock and startling their butler, he hoped to catch the family still at dinner and headed directly for the dining room. Only Jason and his father remained, both of them enjoying a glass of port.

"Ah, Joshua, won't you join us? The ladies have gone to their tea. You know what would go well with this excellent wine? Some of those Spanish cigars you carry. We could take our drinks outside and enjoy both in the garden," the duke, well-fed and mellow, invited.

"I'm sorry, but I have none on me."

"A shame. You did hear of your brother's escape from Lady Tomasina, I suppose."

"Yes, at length."

"And now we make our next move. We must have justice for Kate."

"Do you plan to take the women to court? I might know a barrister who could assist us."

"I don't think we need go that far and make a public spectacle of it."

"He would work for free. Papa, I have passed the bar!"

Josh braced himself for the back pounding and the bear hug and was not disappointed. Jason joined in the congratulations and, the port forgotten, the men moved the celebration to the drawing room where the ladies waited. His mother stood on her tiptoes to kiss his cheek and all the while he looked over her head and sought the approval of Kate who hung back from the family group. He could tell she was happy for him by the glow of her cheeks and that lovely smile. He gently extricated himself from the hugs of his sisters and went to take her hand.

"What, no kiss from Kate?"

"Of course, you must have one."

She placed her hands around his neck and lowered his face to hers. The kiss landed lightly on his cheek and was gone. It reminded him of the one Camilla had given him in the garden that had left him with no desire for more and of the embrace he'd shared with Kate afterwards, so much more satisfying. Where had her passion flown? The family watched them avidly. Naturally, she would not do more in front of them.

"Walk with me in the garden, Kate. Let me tell you how it came about."

"Surely we would all like to hear the details," she answered.

"We will hear them later. Go along." The duchess made shooing motions with her hands.

He offered his arm, and Kate did not hesitate to take it. The trouble with this city garden, it offered no privacy, and night had not yet fallen. Even as they settled on the same bench where he had proposed before, he could see the all Longleighs with their noses pressed to the window glass like urchins before a sweet shop. He'd grown up with nine siblings and little privacy. Even with that number reduced to three by marriage and careers, he was still to have none at a crucial moment in his life. At least, the little dog did not tag along this time to show its displeasure on his boots. On with it then.

He took her hand in his. When she looked down, he raised her chin with a finger.

"Kate, I took your advice to dress more somberly and was noticed by Sir Richard Crumm, a very influential barrister who lauded my work to the others. Without your counsel, I would never have been invited to dine on the other side of the bar. This is my greatest achievement, the greatest prize I can offer you. I will work very hard and aspire to become a judge. Would you consent to be the wife of a new made barrister?"

Kate exhaled as if she'd been holding her breath. Instead of elation at getting what he supposed she had wanted for a very long time, he saw only a mild sorrow in her eyes. Her answer would be "no," but he knew not the why or the wherefore.

"You can do better by me." She removed her hand and stood.

He shot from the bench and exclaimed, "What, what! Do you want me to murder my brother, James, so I may offer you a title and a great fortune like Astin? I do not understand."

"That is precisely the problem."

She turned and walked away again just as she had the last time, and he was no more the wiser over how he had offended and failed again. As she entered the house, the Longleigh women clustered about her and bore her away. Only the duke and Jason remained by the time he followed.

Jason gave him a brotherly pat on the back. "Third time is the charm."

"Papa, what does Kate want?"

"Damned if I know. I asked your mother, but she said it would be a betrayal of her sex to tell. Let's put our minds to less obscure matters and consider how to deal with Lady Camilla and her conspirators. Perhaps Kate wants to be sure you no longer take their side."

~ * ~

She couldn't help herself. She wept. Lady Flora held her close and Spot came out from under the bed in her chamber to dance at her feet and lick her hand as a comfort.

"There, there, Kate. I admire your courage in rejecting my son again. He was so very wrong to spurn the wisdom of his elders by not proposing to you before the season began. We gave him every chance in the garden that day and on the long journey south. Still, I know one thing about Joshua, he can be very stubborn, very determined—first not to have you, and now to want you again. He will ask once more."

"But what if he doesn't? What if I have bruised his self-worth so badly, he turns back to Camilla despite what she has done?"

"He would never!" the duchess assured her.

"Well, there is always Astin," Pandora commented, slightly bored with the aftermath of another proposal.

Kate sat on the edge of her bed and dried her tears. Phemie put an arm around her. "When he finally says those words of love, this will all be worth it."

Panny snorted in a way that drew her mother's disapproval. But perhaps she was right, Kate thought. Astin was a decent man, the best catch of the season. All would envy her as the next Duchess of Martindale. She'd come to know Harold's mild nature, his only passion for snuff. Why, he wanted to stay in the country and attempt to raise his own tobacco in England's unsuitable climate. His conversation often dwelt on glass houses and varieties that might take to being raised in them.

Her life as his wife would be very pleasant, her every command answered, any amusement she wanted provided. If they did not come up to London very often, that would be fine with him and her. She doubted Harold would demand very much in the bed chamber either. She found his aloofness toward women to be the mask for a shy nature. He would get an heir because his father demanded it, just as he had endured fencing lessons and fisticuffs to please the man. An only child, he had none of the Longleighs' competitive nature. If she accepted him, and she knew Astin came closer and closer to that moment, theirs would be a tepid marriage. Would it be better to accept a man for whom she had a gentle fondness and so would never hurt her, but instead forgo the possibility that Joshua would ever love her deeply?

At the last soiree, she thought Josh had come close to understanding what she needed from him, not the seduction he'd attempted in the hallway, but emotion true and deep. Jason's escapade had interrupted that moment. Since then, Joshua had turned to his studies and stayed away, not willing to reveal himself again, thinking of her as just another woman who wants a man with a good income. After today's failure, she felt she must consider the possibility of accepting Astin, but she could not say so to the duchess or the girls she loved like sisters.

She patted Phemie's hand and said, "Yes, all will work out as it should."

Twenty-eight

The letters written in the duke's own inelegant hand went out the following day. They appeared on the outside to be a cordial invitation to an intimate social gathering to be held the next evening at Bellevue House. The contents were another matter. The duke demanded the appearance of the Duke and Duchess of Strictly and their daughter, Camilla, the Earl of Rushmore, his wife and daughter, and the Earl and Countess of Harcourt with Lady Tomasina to discuss the matter of Katherine Morely's kidnapping.

Outraged by the tone of the missive, most of them came nonetheless. Only Lady Flora's despised brother, Roderick, did not arrive. Rumor had it that he had sunken so far into dissipation he no longer had command of his faculties. Lady Rushmore ruled the manor in his stead. She sat, iron stiff, beside her daughter in the drawing room well lit with many candles and arranged so that Kate and the Longleighs faced their adversaries. From their ranks, Jason and Phemie were missing, one being supposedly disowned, and the other considered too young to participate. One brooded in his room, and the other sulked upstairs.

Introductions being unnecessary, the duke did, however, announce his second son's new status as a barrister. As requested, Joshua wore a hastily acquired barrister's wig and judicial robe to give the proceedings an air of legality and stern purpose.

Camilla widened her blue eyes at her former suitor and cooed, "How official you look. What a triumph for you."

"Thank you." He acknowledged her compliment with only a nod. How could she have done such a thing to Kate? His distaste for her sat bitter on his tongue.

The duke at his most impressive, immense as an animal that has ruffled its black fur to appear even larger, paced to the cleared center of the space. He addressed his guests.

"Miss Morely has identified her captors."

Tomasina released a small gasp. The other ladies sat steadfastly still.

"Good. Give me their names and I shall have them hunted down and hung," Lord Strictly, sitting straight and stiff, said. "Then we can be on our way."

"The matter is not so easily handled. We have known their identity for some time, but in deference to Miss Morely's weakened condition, we waited until she felt up to facing her adversaries. She recognized them by their builds and the color of their eyes—sky blue, ice blue, and an extraordinary violet—and marked each one as she fought for her life. One now bears a scar under the eye, another has a dent in the chin, and the third, perhaps a broken rib."

Tomasina covered her face with her hands and began to snivel. Lord Harcourt rose slowly from his chair like a tun of ale being lifted by a winch. "Are you accusing my daughter and these other young ladies?"

"Precisely."

Camilla's eyes flashed. "She was taken by three smugglers. I've heard her tell her pathetic tale to one and all."

The duke beckoned to his son. "Joshua, if you please."

He came to stand beside his father in the ring of light cast by a hanging lamp. His dark eyes gazed hotly on Camilla, the woman he had considered a nonpareil.

"I have taken down Miss Morely's account of her abduction. Prior to this, we asked that she not divulge the number of her attackers nor describe them, and you have just confirmed them as being three from your own knowledge. Furthermore, Lady Pandora Longleigh overheard these young women admit they had knowledge of the kidnapping in the retiring room at Lady Proctor's ball. Lady Camilla stated she had 'sentenced' Katherine Morely to two weeks in the tower. Recall if you please, the word of a Longleigh of either sex is never disputed."

Pandora smiled maliciously at Camilla and said, "And then I took your scalp."

Camilla held her place though her hands had begun to tremble. Her mother spoke up. "How can you accuse these delicate blossoms, sheltered all their lives, of such awful actions? Why, my daughter is the nonpareil of the season, the most refined and gently nurtured of them all. She could never contrive such a plot, nor carry it out."

"She might have had the help of an older, more worldly woman, one who delights in such schemes," the duchess replied with her eyes turned to Lady Rushmore.

Her remark brought an outburst from Camilla, who stood and stamped her foot in a most indelicate way. "Why do you all assume I haven't the intellect to do my own plotting? Simply because I have been taught to sit quietly with my hands folded and make inane conversation does not mean I have no ideas of my own. Yes, I helped to contrive the plan to punish Katherine for taking Astin away from me. But she is a liar, too. She has never taken snuff."

Joshua surveyed the shocked faces of the parents, all but Lady Rushmore, ever impassive. "Lying about taking snuff or wearing a hairpiece or other personal matters is not punishable by law. The sentence for aggravated kidnapping in which a person's life is placed in jeopardy is death."

Tomasina's whimpers became full-blown sobs. "We did not mean for matters to go so far. Old Burt was to see to her care and release her before you began your second search. He neglected his duties."

"Yes, by dying. How inexcusable of him," Joshua answered drily.

"I pleaded with Camilla to let her go early. Lady Pandora must have heard that, too. Surely, it counts for some lenience." Tomasina raised her tear-filled violet eyes to his, darkly burning.

"Your sex may save you from the rope," Joshua intoned like the judge he aspired to become.

For the first time, Matilda Everton showed some emotion. A long, show shudder shook her gangling body. Lady Rushmore scowled at her weakness.

"Thank you, Joshua. Our only concern is for Kate, that she need not endure another ordeal in the courtroom. I believe we can come to a quiet and just punishment among ourselves. What do you say, gentlemen?" Lady Flora spoke, unable to stay silent any longer.

"They have no real evidence, only hearsay, and the Strictly word is as good as theirs, Papa," Camilla insisted.

"Not anymore. You have claimed this deed before too many witnesses, and I am ashamed to be one of them," her father said, shaking his gray head sadly. "What is to be their punishment?"

"In lieu of hanging, deportation. Australia is in need of women." Joshua pronounced the sentence.

"Not there! Not where snakes and crocodiles swarm the earth!" Tomasina's face showed true terror.

"Then, Canada for you since you asked to have Kate freed," the duke answered.

"Among the wild Indians?"

"In some ways, the Indians are more civilized than the three of you," he concluded. "We will give you some time to arrange for their passage and, perhaps, a suitable match in foreign lands. They are never to return."

"Humph, fair enough for getting caught," said Lady Rushmore, her cold eyes unblinking. "Australia might provide Tilly's only chance to wed. She's a strong girl if nothing more."

"I will prove that," Matilda said firmly.

"If we are agreed, you may go." The duke gestured to the door, but Joshua held up his hand to stay them.

"Kate, have we punished them sufficiently for what was done to you? I am more than willing to bring these charges to the authorities."

Sitting quietly under orders not to talk by the new barrister, she finally spoke. "Since I survived, I am content."

"I'd rather see them all hang," muttered Pandora close by her side. "A good thing they did not tamper with me."

Still defiant, Camilla shot back, "Nor will any man!"

Joshua intervened. "Ladies, we are adjourned."

The company filed out. The men and Lady Rushmore kept their faces strictly controlled. The Duchess of Strictly and Lady Harcourt wept, already mourning the loss of their perfect daughters. Of the guilty girls, only Tomasina hung her head.

"That went rather well. Good job, son. I'd hate to come before you if you served on the bench. Let me send Busby to the cellar for a bottle of champagne to toast our victory."

As they waited, milling and congratulating each other, Joshua moved close to Kate. "*Now*, have I delivered you the greatest prize? Justice."

"No." That was her answer, succinct and final, but her brown eyes shone soft as velvet with not a bit of hardness in them. "But you did very well by me."

Instead of letting his anger rise and go away ranting, he sat beside her and gazed into those eyes. "I beg you to tell me what it is. I will get it, and lay it at your feet."

"I believe you already possess the greatest prize and have only to offer it to me."

"What is this, some quest like Sir Gawain's search for what women want most? As a new barrister, I have no time for romantic nonsense like Jason."

Kate touched his cheek despite the extreme interest of his family. "A pity. I believe I will go and rest now."

She was the first to leave the celebration. Lady Flora sadly shook her head and gave her son a look that said she did not know how she had raised so dense a son. He had failed to win Kate again.

Twenty-nine

His own comment about Sir Gawain triggered the dream, certainly. After Kate left the little party, he had no desire for champagne or more congratulations and took himself off to his lodgings. The thought of sleeping under the same roof as the woman who had once clearly adored him and now played cat and mouse games hurt rather cruelly as if she caught him and let him go over and over like a naughty feline.

Naturally, Jason remained behind where the wine flowed freely and every bed had a feather tick. Just as well. He was not in the mood for Jason's banter—though probably his brother could explain what he had that Kate wanted. He would ask in the morning after arranging for a sign announcing his new status as a barrister and perhaps lurking about the Courts of Law hoping to snag a case. He would need to order new cards. That should fill his day before he went to dinner at Bellevue House, now that he no longer had to eat with the other law students.

But sleep came hard. What did Kate want? He polished off an inferior bottle of wine in his quest for rest. Of course, that led to a bad dream, though not too terrible a one.

Transported to medieval times, his own mind cast him in the role of a fop, judging by his shoes with pointed and curled toes, his parti-colored hose, and a lavishly embroidered tunic almost too short for decency. Why it barely covered his buttocks and privates, though his parts were manly enough to be very competitive. His straight, black hair, however—had someone clapped a bowl over it and shaved up the sides? As for the cap with the feather in it, it laid so flat someone the size of Lady Harcourt must have sat upon it. Why wasn't he attired like a knight, valiant and capable of rescuing fair maidens, the way Kate believed him to be until very lately.

Yet, Kate seemed pleased enough with his appearance to be watching him from her high-backed chair on the dais. Restored to its former glory and held in place with a circlet of gold and gems, her rich brown hair flowed loose and thick down her back. He wanted to bury his face in it and smell its perfume. The man next to Kate frowned and covered her hand with his. Astin, as golden as ever. Harold offered his companion a pinch of snuff from a small bag. An anachronism! That proved he dreamt.

"Why do you scowl so, Lord Longleigh," his dance partner asked because, yes, he did dance in a skipping, hopping sort of rigamarole that ended with a clapping of hands held high.

She, too, was lovely with her red-gold braids and eyes of misty gray. Fair Annet, the name came to him immediately.

"I do not know what Katherine wants and fear she will marry Lord Astin."

"Why, she wants your heart."

"Cut from my chest and lain on a platter in revenge for jilting her?"

For a moment, Fair Annet's face resembled his mother's when she was most disgusted with him. "No, Lord Longleigh. Your symbolic heart. She wants your undying love."

"She has that. When she vanished, I began to understand how much I loved her, and what a fool I had been not to offer for her sooner."

"Now you understand." Fair Annet offered him a dazzling smile as if she were presenting a reward of sweetmeats to a prize student. "Something you already have, but have not offered to her."

"But we've known each other forever. I assumed she understood. Even as a boy I admired her, how clever she was, how she did not cry when she fell down or got captured by the boys. Of course, I could not admit that to my brothers. Kate has always been so very sensible. I did not think she needed sentimental words, too."

Fair Annet tweaked his cheek. "You must offer her what you feel because love is the greatest prize."

"That's it? That's all?"

Exasperated, Fair Annet raised her hands in the air for a final clap and evaporated, taking the dream with her. The product of bad wine or no, she had given him the answer.

Joshua sat up in his sleep-tossed covers. How many hours to dawn? How many more before he could decently appear at Bellevue House and propose to Kate? Too many. All this time she had not wanted the security of being a barrister's wife or the punishment of her enemies, but only the declaration of his love. Today, he would give her the greatest prize. So simple, so easy he should have thought of it before.

Thirty

Joshua Longleigh took the steps up to his parents' townhouse two at a time with his long stride and entered before Busby could open the door. He found his mother, dressed to go out, descending the interior stairs and called out, "Where is Kate?"

"What? No good morning for your mother." She came up beside him and offered her cheek. He bent and brushed it lightly.

"Good day, Mama. Now where is Kate?"

"Gone off in Astin's curricle again. She is looking so well. I believe these outings do her good. The roses return to her complexion."

"She's gone out with him alone?"

"Hardly. He always has those toadies with him hoping for a free meal or a pinch of expensive snuff. Jason has been lying about here since we opened the house. I sent him along as well. And Pandora, she becomes as unmanageable as a high-strung horse when she hasn't had enough exercise."

"Fine. When will they return?"

"Why, I have no idea." The duchess cocked her head and scanned her son with her large, gray eyes, eerily like Fair Annet's misty orbs. "Something has changed. I can see it in your face, Joshua."

"Mama, I know what Kate wants. The greatest prize is love, and I can give her that."

"Of course, you can. I am proud you finally found the answer."

"I had help—not that you have given me any."

"After setting Kate aside so callously for that poisonous Camilla, you did not deserve it. Who gave you the solution?"

"I'm embarrassed to say Fair Annet came to me in a dream. You and she have a great deal in common."

"Really? I consider that a compliment. Your father will be pleased. He sets great store by dreams. When will you ask Kate again?"

"As soon as she returns."

"Do wait until I am present. I have a round of visits to make, and the duke is attending to some business. We will want to watch. You can keep company with Phemie until then as she has no desire to be bored by her elders, or so she said this morning." The duchess checked the set of her hat in the hallway mirror and whisked out the door to the carriage that had just come round.

The house, usually bustling with Longleighs, fell silent. The tall clock on the landing ticked off the minutes until Kate would be his. Until then, he could pace, or seek out Phemie for a game of chess. He found his youngest sister writing letters to school friends in the small, sunny sitting room overlooking the garden. They set up the board and played until she had taken four games. Usually, their skills matched, but today her sharp, young mind overcame his time and again.

"Distracted, brother?" she asked.

"Yes. I mean to offer for Kate again. Love is the answer."

"Isn't it always? I hope to be swept away by love someday myself."

Joshua pointed a finger at her. "You are far too logical for that. That's why you can beat me at chess."

"Am not!" She stuck out her tongue at him.

"And so very lady-like, too."

The duke returned with several newspapers tucked under his arm and joined them. The duchess completed her visits and called for some restorative tea for all. Still no Kate. Finally, the noise of many horses and the rumble of the curricle on the cobbles sounded from the mews. She came laughing through the rear gate with Astin by her side. Joshua went to the window at once and the other Longleighs joined him. How vibrant she looked, restored to her old self, a fetching bonnet covering her short curls.

They watched as Astin put all his weight against the gate and shot the bolt to keep the others out. On the other side, Jason protested loudly enough to be heard in the sitting room and the little, spotted dog barked in protest. Ignoring all, Astin escorted Kate to exactly the same bench where Joshua had proposed. He dropped to his knees, soiling a very fine pair of buckskin britches in the garden loam. Kate protested and patted the seat beside her. She took Harold's hands in hers and spoke to him most earnestly.

Pandora, holding her riding skirts up, dashed into the sitting room to join her family. "I was still mounted and came around the front as quickly as I could. Do crack a window, and we might overhear."

The duke did so very quietly, but Kate's face was turned away from the house. She spoke quietly, and they could not make out a word from either party.

~ * ~

"Dear Harold, there is no need to kneel." Kate raised Astin to sit beside her.

"Thank you. My valet will be upset enough over what I've done to my outfit. I like that about you, Kate. You don't care for the grand gesture, but prefer more plain ways. You share my enthusiasm and are ever kind. I think we would do well together."

"I need to confess." When she saw the alarm on her suitor's face, she immediately rushed on with what she had to say. "No, nothing too terrible, but still in all, a lie. I have no real taste for snuff, Harold. I used that lovely blend you gave me to scent my room. The aroma soon faded."

"As it would if not properly stored. I believe I've known for some time that you were prevaricating on this matter. Yet as we went along, I sensed you liked me for more than my money or my title."

"That is true, but still I used you to make Joshua Longleigh see that I could attract the greatest prize of the season, Harold Brumley, Viscount Astin."

Astin's face screwed up. "Him again! First, he stands between me and Lady Camilla, and now you! What is it Longleigh men do to make them so attractive to women?"

"I believe they were born with that power. It is difficult to duplicate. But, I've come to regard you fondly as a friend."

His sigh nearly burst the buttons of his tight jacket. "I suppose Lady Camilla will still have me. We do look splendid together."

"Not her, Harold, never her. Her beauty masks a truly devious mind. Besides, I know for a fact due to a part she played in my kidnapping she will be marrying abroad. Wait a season and look elsewhere like my cousin, Sir Guy. He tells me he is going let the rotten apples lie and wait for a new crop."

"Good advice, I suppose. Ah, Kate, I shall miss your companionship."

"I will still receive my good friend and give him a dance now and then."

"I doubt if Joshua Longleigh will tolerate that. I wish you a world of happiness."

They rose together and went to the gate. She went up on tiptoes, brushed his cheek with her lips in farewell, and squeezed his hand before he opened the latch.

There, she'd had her chance to be Duchess of Martindale and had tossed it away when the time came, hoping for a single word of love from Joshua. Exactly how foolish could she be? Josh would never be able to return her passion.

Harold passed through the gate, and Jason Longleigh and the terrier tumbled into the garden. With a nod to them, Viscount Astin, the greatest catch of the season, mounted his curricle, whipped up his horses, and drove off. Those of his sycophants who had dismounted scurried to find a block to get back in the saddle and ride after him.

"What was that all about? Did I win my wager with Joshua?" Jason pressed.

"I suppose you did."

"Ha! Wait until I tell them."

He gestured to the window where the Longleighs stood. The Tribe they were often called, not just for their dark visages, but for their solidarity. She wanted to stand among them now, a part of the family. Had she erred in holding out for the greatest prize?

Thirty-one

Jason flew up the garden stairs, entered the house, and soared into the sitting room, his palm extended toward Joshua. "Astin has proposed to Kate. I imagine he is traveling forth to ask her parents' blessing right now, and why would they refuse? My fifty pounds, if you please."

"No!"

"Reneging on a bet? What of the Longleigh honor? I can print a small volume of my poetry with that blunt."

"Bugger your blunt. Kate has always been mine!"

Jason dropped his hand rather than having it slapped down and took a step back, but Pandora stepped into his place. "You tossed her away several months ago. She may marry whomever she pleases. I'd like my money as well. The Abolition Society is raising funds."

"They are always raising funds, and yet still we have slavery. Wouldn't you rather invest in timeless verse?" Jason suggested.

"No, no, and no! He cannot have Kate." Joshua sliced through his family group by widening his arms and stepping forward.

"That's it, son. Go get her," the duke urged.

"So romantic," murmured Phemie.

"Nothing about this will be romantic, Phemie, but I will stop her from marrying Astin."

His mother, who had a better idea of what might take place, called out, "Be gentle!" as he surged through the garden door.

Kate still stood near the gate, her back turned to him, the feisty terrier at her feet. One hand rested on the latch as if she contemplated going after her fiancé and calling him back for a fuller, more intimate kiss. That would not happen.

The dog barked as he neared and caught her attention. She turned to see Joshua bearing down on her like a steamboat about to run aground. She'd always thought his dark eyes contained the glow of banked embers, but now something had set them alight. He seized her by the shoulders and shook her slightly.

"You cannot marry Astin."

"But, Joshua…"

"I have no title, no great fortune to offer, but you do have my heart and all my love."

"Josh, I…"

"Do not protest. I am going to make you mine. I shall try not to be rough, but do not think you can fight me. Afterwards, you must tell Astin you have been ruined by another man and cannot wed him."

He swept her off her feet and held her close as he kicked the gate and jumped open the latch. They traveled across the cobbles to the stable where the coach and riding horses were kept. Entering the barn, he shouted to the grooms and stable boys, "Be gone and pull the door shut behind you!" They scattered like the vermin in the straw, but the terrier, undistracted, still followed, yapping.

Her bonnet fallen backwards, Kate nestled against his chest above the furious beating of his heart, the heart he had given her at last. Joshua did not notice her total compliance. He looked desperately around for a place to lay with her. The terrier launched itself into the air and latched on to his pant leg. He shook the creature off, but still in the nature of terriers, the beast did not give up.

"Down, Spot, down!" Kate cried. "Don't try to stop him!"

She feared for her pet. Did she think him such a brute that he would hurt a small dog? How he must terrify her when he had been so cool since that day in the garden at Bellevue Hall and plied her with such tepid proposals these past weeks. No help for it, he must take her up to the loft to get rid of the dog. The ladder was stout enough but narrow, not an easy task. He held her on his straining biceps as he used his hands to climb, finally tumbling her over the edge into the mounds of fresh hay and straw kept there for the stock.

~ * ~

At any time, she could have shifted her weight and sent them both tumbling to the ground. Now as he came over the top, she might have kicked him in the face and sent him crashing down. The thought did not seem to occur to him, though he knew her to be a fighter. His reason, it seemed, had fled to another part of his anatomy.

"Do not be afraid," he told her as earnestly as Astin had proposed.

Afraid? She'd waited for this day, for this moment when Josh would lose all coldness and take her with ardor. Of course, she had assumed they would be in a featherbed on their wedding night, but this would do. The featherbed could wait.

Men. This rising star of a barrister had taken so long to figure out the meaning of the greatest gift, and then had needed help. She'd had a dream of sitting on a dais with Astin, her hair all grown out again, watching Joshua dance with Fair Annet. The lady had given him the answer, and thanks be to heaven she did, or he might never have understood.

He tossed aside her bonnet and began a clumsy unfastening of the many buttons on her tight spencer jacket. She almost wanted to help, but no, let him work for it. At last, he got the garment open and plunged his hands deep into her bodice, drawing out her breasts and kissing each one, suckling her nipples until they hardened in his mouth. She closed her eyes and let out a small gasp. That might have prompted him to move his kisses upward to her lips. She waited for their ascent, and the kisses came as blazing hot as that light in his eyes. If he'd bothered to remove the spencer entirely instead of shoving it half down, she would have raised her arms to stroke that straight, black hair of his. At last, at last, the boy who had given her his breath was hers.

~ * ~

The kisses went deep, a hot twining of tongues. She did not try to close herself against him. He wondered at that. She responded like a woman who knew her lover thoroughly. Had Astin gotten to her? But no, someone in the Longleigh family, most principally himself, would have shot the man if so. He cast the thought aside. No matter, no matter, he was making her his alone.

In preparing Kate, he'd over-prepared himself and had to school himself to slow down. He raised himself off her chest, away from her lips, and found the parting difficult. Fighting through her petticoats and undergarments, he found the opening to her most private parts: the nest of dark curls, the throbbing bud, the wet orifice. Had he done enough to ready her for deflowering? He stroked with one finger, then two.

Kate took a great breath of air and released it as a heavy sigh. Her legs shifted restlessly. Her back bowed. She half-raised, trying to escape her jacket. Once her hands were free, she'd most likely try to fight him off. He must take drastic measures and distract her to the utmost.

"This is not unnatural. Women love it," he announced and dove into that froth of skirts and linens.

"Anything, anything!" she responded. "I feel about to burst apart into a thousand colored sparks like the fireworks over Vauxhall Gardens."

Intent on increasing her pleasure, he barely heard her odd reply. His tongue laved against that pink pearl in her cleft. She stiffened and cried out. "Ready at last," he thought knowing he could not have held out much longer. Rising up to unbutton his pants, he released his shaft so urgent and engorged it would have freed itself if it had fingers instead of just a head. Better to make it quick. He penetrated to the hilt. She did not scream in pain as he thought a virgin might, but if he'd done his job well, she should not suffer. Above all, he did not want to cause her pain ever again in her life. The thought made him pause, arched above her body and her face with its closed eyes and open mouth panting for air.

Her legs curled across his thighs, and her small boot gave him a kick as she might a stubborn mount. Encouraged, he moved faster, lost track of what he should be doing, and simply did. He made Kate his in a most explosive way. Resting his head on her naked breasts and still breathing hard as a

Derby winner, he apologized. "I'm sorry. I saw no other way to keep you from Astin."

"I'm not at all sorry. I refused him—as I tried to tell you."

Did she smile, his clever Kate? He rolled aside and hastily buttoned himself. A flood of embarrassment over his uncontrolled impetuosity overcame him, and he looked away.

"Joshua, you gave me your love, the greatest prize. It's all I've ever wanted. No need to be ashamed. I am not." Still trapped in that jacket, she managed to lay a small, comforting hand at the base of his spine.

Kate pushed herself up and attempted to straighten her spencer. He did it for her, first tenderly pulling up her gown and smoothing it over her breasts. She gave a little shiver as he did so. Certainly, they would have a good married life like the duke and duchess. He was their son after all, and now he had shown it.

He tried to button the coat, got it crooked because his hands still shook from losing control. She did it herself. He ran his fingers tenderly through her short curls, ridding her hair of bits of straw. She pulled his face closer for a kiss that went long, hot, and deep. Assuredly, Astin had never gotten one like this.

When they finished, she said, "We must stop before I have the urge to do all of this again."

"Really?" he answered, so proud of himself. He replaced her bonnet and tied its ribbons as well as any man.

One at a time, they made their way down the ladder, Joshua going first in case she slipped. Spot yapped. Had he been doing that the whole time? Neither had heard him. Joshua threw open the stable doors and addressed the hands who idled in the mews, telling bawdy tales of the gentry and enjoying a pipe away from the hay and straw. "Carry on," their lordship said, and so they did with another tale to add to their repertoire.

Expecting to be mobbed by Longleighs, they made their way through the garden to the house, but found only Lady Flora in the sitting room. She wrote on thick squares of paper at the small escritoire.

Joshua cleared his throat to get her attention. "Ahem, Kate and I are engaged to be married."

The duchess looked at them blandly, no surprise showing on her face. "Yes, we figured as much. Your papa has gone to see about the special license. Jason waits to reclaim his horse. He is to carry the announcement to the Morelys. The nuptials will be in two weeks, time enough to gather Justinian from school and your older sisters from hither and yon for a simple ceremony and a wedding breakfast unless Kate wants something more lavish."

"Not at all. I want only Joshua and to be part of this magnificent family."

"Very well, then. Pandora and Phemie wait upstairs to greet you as their sister. Do you know, Joshua, if you hadn't been so stubborn, this could have taken place two months ago without so much of the theatrical about it."

"But," said Kate. "Then it wouldn't have been a real Longleigh courtship."

"True enough," the duchess answered.

Thirty-two

May, what a glorious month to be wed! Trees blossomed in the park and wherever else they found space enough to grow in the crowded city of London. Joshua and his bride were blessed with a sunny day and no lack of well-wishing guests, most of them Longleighs. Joshua's older sisters—Thalia, Iris, Clio and Calliope—their husbands and children old enough to behave decently in church thronged the cathedral. Justinian, the baby of the family and just entering young manhood, sat pleased with himself among the adults. James, absent as ever, would get word of the union eventually and breathe a sigh of relief that his brother now had the responsibility to provide an heir.

Overwhelmed by Longleighs, the Morely family—mother, father, brother and sister-in-law—seemed to cower in the front pew as if they rested on an island about to be hit by a tidal wave. Mrs. Morely repeated to every person of the duke's large family who paid their respects that she was entirely sensible of the great honor being paid to her daughter. Kate wished her mother would stop, but Joshua countered by saying, "No, the honor is mine. I have won the greatest prize."

The bride wore a bonnet trimmed with silk roses to cover her shorn hair, not that the duke and duchess or Kate cared. Nor did Josh. As they told her, her short curls represented the overcoming of a great ordeal and so were a badge of honor. Mrs. Morely, shocked at her daughter's appearance, had demanded the covering. Still, the hat did go nicely with a gown of polished cotton in a cabbage rose pattern and a snug bodice of green that showed off the bride's restored figure. Like the trees of London, she bloomed again.

Joshua surely thought so as he gazed into her eyes, the golden glimmers like sunlight on dark water today. She said her name, Katherine Elizabeth Morely, and repeated her vows. He rejoiced at her delighted smile when the priest asked him to state his full name, Joshua William Big Paw Longleigh, and would have placed another wager that his bride had never realized the Indian name he used in childish games was his legally as well. All the Longleigh offspring possessed an official Shawnee designation well buried in their Christian names. He would have to think of one for Kate now that she had become a member of their tribe.

Thank heaven for the brevity of the Anglican nuptial service when unaccompanied by communion. The duke, never happy in church and more of a heathen than most men knew, had put his foot down about that. "Let them get on with the best part of married life," he'd said with a naughty glint in his black eyes as he argued with his wife about the length of the service. They'd gone to their bed chamber to settle the matter in private. To their son's delight, the duchess had capitulated.

As Joshua kissed his new wife, though the priest had not indicated he could do so, he thought of how often his parents' outsized affection for one another had embarrassed him. Now, he had hopes of the same kind of love, thanks to Kate who would have the sense not to be quite so publicly extravagant as his elders. When Mrs. Morely exclaimed, "Oh, my!" he realized the embrace had gone on too long and reluctantly raised his lips.

A change in the light shining through a stained-glass window portraying the annunciation to the Virgin Mary by the angel Gabriel caused him to raise his eyes from his bride's radiant face. For a moment the angel sported red-gold braids, wore deep blue raiment, and a glowing smile. He turned Kate toward the sight. "She's here," he whispered.

"Fair Annet has come to bless our marriage and wish us well."

"How do I thank her for giving me the answer that won your heart?"

"Merely think it. She will understand."

He did. The spirit nodded regally and faded, leaving the jewel tones of the glass as they had been.

Supposing the couple exchanged endearments, the duke and duchess beamed. Jason and Pandora, untouched as yet by deep, passionate love, smirked before signing as their witnesses. Both had collected on their bets. The rest of the Longleighs applauded them out of church and into the first of the many carriages waiting to take bridal couple and the rest of the horde back to Bellevue House for the wedding breakfast. Much as the duke detested feeding what he called the parasites of society, he did enjoy feasting with his large family. Champagne would flow, Josh knew, and the meal would go on and on.

And so it did, with endless toasts made by the duke, sons-in-law, and even Justinian, plus Jason's hastily composed but very lengthy wedding ode with far too many references to the god, Hymen. Kate kept smiling throughout, but Joshua felt his patience wearing thin. Because of his new ranking as a barrister and the need to establish himself, not to mention support a family, they would have no wedding trip, simply a week alone in the Temple Inn house while Jason stayed out of the way with his parents.

A gift from the duke and duchess awaited them there—a bed nearly as lavish as their own filled most of the sleeping chamber. Their present was far more insightful than Harold Brumley's large, chased silver communal snuffbox with the initials "L" and "M" engraved on the lid. His sisters had outfitted the bed with the finest of new linens, and he'd overheard a rumor that the feather tick might be strewn with rose petals. Kate would enjoy that. He imagined the silky petals giving off their rich scent as they crushed them beneath their naked bodies. The thought made him even more restless and distracted and very glad of the tablecloth that covered his lap.

Kate had to say the words twice before he heard. "I believe we can go now without offending."

"Truly!" Josh exclaimed as he watched Kate's eyes take on an entirely different kind of glitter as she gazed at him.

~ * ~

Her husband, Joshua Longleigh—how handsome he looked in a black jacket and trousers not quite as tight as before. He had added a quilted gold waistcoat and a fairly complicated neckcloth tied by himself. Kate suspected that beneath his somber barrister's robes, he would always harbor a small bit of the dandy. At the moment, however, she wanted only to take those clothes off of him at leisure. Surprisingly, the duchess had enforced their strict separation after the engagement. Unorthodox or not, she did still have young daughters at home and must set an example of propriety.

"Many an old biddy will remark on the haste of your marriage and count upon their fingers until your first child is born. Let us not give the ladies more to talk about," she'd said.

Still, Kate would not put it beyond Lady Flora to enforce such a rule simply to build their desire. If so, the ploy worked. The deed had been done well enough the first time, but now she wanted more. She kept smiling as she accepted her teary-eyed mother's kiss and her father's embrace, the duke's bear hug, and the duchess's jubilant pressing of her hands as she said, "Now you are a Longleigh at last."

Kate felt she truly was, always had been in spirit. As soon as the carriage door closed behind them, she grabbed Joshua's lapels and drew him closer for a long, deep kiss that ignited her flames and his candle. She had thoroughly ruined the tie of his neckcloth by the time they arrived at their home. He made her wait while he unlocked the door and returned to carry her over the threshold, kick the door shut behind them, and head directly for the first-floor room at the rear where their marriage bed waited. Yes, rose petals sprinkled the linens.

"My turn, my turn," she said as they fell back on the mattress and made the bed ropes sigh. Her turn now to fumble with too many buttons and layers: waistcoats and under waistcoats, the many turns of his cravat, the tight jacket, and blasted boots. At last, she had him naked, his entire length illuminated by a ray of sunshine that had found its way across the tiny, unkempt rear garden and through their still uncurtained window. She scanned the muted bronze skin that showed his Shawnee ancestry from top to toe, the length and strength of his limbs, the vigor of his manhood that seemed to be cocking in her direction and beckoning her. She moved her eyes up to the self-satisfied smile on Joshua's face as he leaned back, allowing her to look.

She would show him she could be as bold as any Longleigh. She placed her lips on his organ, planning to play a merry tune, but he drew her up quickly.

"Don't, if you want this to last, my darling." His white grin only grew broader.

No wonder. Somehow, he'd managed to unfasten the buttons on the back of her bodice and in pulling her up, both breasts fell free. She'd been vaguely aware of losing her bonnet and the lace cap beneath it, of toeing off her slippers, and feeling the tapes of her petticoat give way, but not this.

He cupped them in his hands. "Even more beautiful in full sunlight. I don't think I will be dining with the barristers too often when I might feed on these." He took them in his mouth one by one and suckled, but his hands kept working and soon her gown and undergarments fell aside, leaving only her stockings tied up prettily with red ribbons.

"Leave them," he said. "They won't get in the way."

They did not, not even when she begged him to do what he'd done before down there between her legs in the loft. The heat built again until it burst into that blaze of sparks throughout her body. She opened her eyes and saw the same fireworks in his. This time in no haste, he prolonged their pleasure until the sun moved away from their bed, and they lay exhausted in each other's arms.

"Now I truly am a Longleigh, brazenly making love in the afternoon," Kate told her husband.

"Yes, after the wedding feast, I am fairly sure my parents and married siblings all felt in need of a rest. Who knows how many more Longleighs will be conceived today?"

"Perhaps the heir to Bellevue."

"No need to hurry on that. But I think I must bestow your Indian name. We all have them. Yours shall be Wild Rose for a simple beauty I overlooked, for your hardiness in adversity, and for your unexpected and greatly appreciated wildness in bed."

Kate gently pinched his cheek for the last part of that statement and placed her lips on the small, red spot she'd made. Joshua drew her tight.

"Now, my greatest prize, I think we should sleep and begin anew tomorrow."

Epilogue

Bellevue Hall, North England, March, 1814

A long chill prevented the North Country from blooming, but kept the frozen roads passable. Soon, the Longleighs would remove to London again for the Season, Phemie's first and Pandora's second. The ladies of the family sat near the sitting room windows to take advantage of the cold, sparkling light for their sewing, though this required them to be wrapped in warm shawls and place their feet on hot bricks as they were so far from the fire.

Pandora pulled out her stitches because she'd left a gap in the lace edging of a handkerchief, one of many being prepared for Phemie's debut. "I don't see why sister needs such a pile of these things. A dozen did quite well for me."

"I went through two dozen a week when I feigned taking snuff and besmirched them all with hidden gobs of the stuff." Kate finished a satin-stitched leaf, made her knot, and snipped her thread with a small silver scissors. Spot looked up adoringly from where he lazed at her feet and got his ears scratched for his effort.

"She must have extras to drop for her suitors to claim and wear next to their hearts," Lady Flora said light-heartedly.

"Oh, Mama, that will hardly be the case." Phemie's dusky cheeks pinked as she worked her initials into a corner of her hankie.

"Phemie, you are not only pretty, but sweet and so very intelligent. Young men will want to carry you off." Her mother completed a row of tiny stitches hemming a square of fragile lawn.

"Let them try that with me, and I shall use Papa's stiletto on them!"

"Panny, that attitude is exactly why you had no offers last season." Her mother sighed.

"I for one am more than ready to leave for London. I miss Joshua so. Go rest in the country, the Queen's physician says. Restore the balance of your humors after your ordeal. Then you should be able to conceive. How can I get with child so far from my husband? I should be sewing baby clothes, not hankies." Nearly as frustrated as Pandora, Kate threw her handiwork into her lap.

"Oh, there are ways women have used before if Josh cannot do the job," Pandora said archly. "Why should this be considered all your fault?"

"Not another word from you!" The duchess pointed both her needle and her steely gaze at her most difficult daughter.

"I think while we are near the border, you should send to Edinburgh for a Scottish doctor. They do not believe in the humors, but rather in the study of anatomy and the use of observation to diagnose and affect a cure." Phemie showed off her acute interest in science again.

"Kate and Joshua married last May, and that is not so long a time ago. No need to rush and call in more physicians. After all, I have four sons. One of them will get an heir for Bellevue. Kate, you are under no demands from me. I believe feeling you must produce a son immediately is part of the problem." The duchess resumed her work.

"Thank you for being so patient. I am well aware that you conceived an heir for Bellevue on your wedding night."

"In a Shawnee wigwam in the middle of a great forest after she'd been captured by Indians. Yes, that puts no pressure on the rest of us," Pandora said, having heard the tale so many times.

"Well, one cannot be sure of the exact date, but I do believe so," her mother answered a trifle smugly. "Still, no need to hurry. My advice is to enjoy each other. While I adore all my children, once they come, there is little time for anything else." She dared Pandora with her eyes to deny her affection. For once, the girl stayed silent. "Oh good, here comes Busby with the post."

The butler laid the silver tray holding the mail on a table by the duchess's elbow. He observed the empty cups of tea they had used to warm their hands and their insides. "Shall I have another pot prepared, Your Grace?" he asked.

"That would be lovely, Busby. Ah, what do we have here? A lengthy letter from Lady Tartte—how dare she! We can only hope this means she is done dallying with Jason. Hmmm, she begs us to return to London swiftly as society is so terribly boring without the Longleighs. Perhaps Jason is done with her, and she thinks he has come home to hide."

"I believe he is still in Bath seeking a patron for his book of poetry as Joshua said in his letter a few days ago. Really, Uncle Bear should provide the funds," Kate said.

"As you well know, the duke will not put out money for something he considers worthless. Investments in inventions or real estate, yes. Poetry, no. Unlike his own father, he is no great lover of literature." The duchess skimmed the pages sent by Lady Tartte. "*She* surely did not scrimp on paper or postage."

"Do read it to us, Mama," Phemie asked, her face animated by the prospect of London gossip.

"I shall read aloud those parts fit for the ears of young ladies. Older women can be rather salty at times."

"Do tell." Pandora raised her black eyebrows, but not high enough to draw her mother's wrath.

"Here is a passage that will interest all of you."

"I have mentioned how dull the season is thus far, but one mysterious incident from last year has provided a thrilling tale. You recall how three of the most promising flowers of society were suddenly sent abroad last spring. Well, make that two and Matilda

Everton. Rampant speculation had it that these young ladies engaged in unholy, satanic rituals with some of our most notorious rakes and were so thoroughly compromised they needed to be foisted off on unknowing husbands in foreign lands."

"Serves them right!" Pandora interrupted.

"Hush. Go on, Mama," said Phemie, eagerly leaning forward to hear more.

"I suspect, my dear duchess, you could tell us the truth of the matter, but will not. Tomasina Murray immediately took ship for Canada to wed a cousin serving as a captain with the 49th under General Vincent at Ft. George on the Niagara. Lady Harcourt claims they were childhood sweethearts, but we all know her daughter preferred J.L. This cousin had recently inquired after her second daughter's availability. My guess is he sought a woman with enough of a dowry to raise his rank, but not to hear her say it."

"Just what Tomasina dreaded, living on a frontier caught up in war," Kate mentioned.

"Again, I say good." Pandora balled up the lace she'd ripped from the hankie.

"No sooner had Lady Tomasina arrived at the fort, but American forces began a bombardment from across the river. Most of the buildings within the palisades were destroyed, leaving only the casements where the women and children huddled. General Vincent sallied forth to engage the enemy who so pressed him. He was forced to evacuate the fort and leave it to the Americans. Unfortunately, he left the dependents behind in the rubble. An American officer taken with Tomasina's violet eyes and total helplessness, sent her on to his family in Boston, fortunate because the cousin died in battle. Sometime during the winter, this officer managed to get home, marry her, and start a nursery. No matter what these Americans say, they are still attracted by an English title and a fat dowry.

Kate kept her face lowered and formed another leaf with her thread. "She was the softest of the three. I am happy for her."

"There is more." The duchess turned over the sheet of paper so densely written upon.

"If you find that story amazing, allow me to tell you the fate of homely Matilda Everton. A general garrisoned in Australia lost his wife to a fever and was left with five children. He sought a hardy wife to come to the colony and care for his family, a free governess, if you ask my opinion. Lady Rushmore could not get the girl on the ship fast enough, not that Tilly had any prospects at home. The wedding took place in July. Let us never say our military men shirk duty. Their child is to be born this month. Whatever would we do without our armed forces when we have a daughter to be rid of, I ask?

"Away from her mother and with a babe to love, she might improve," Kate offered generously. "Any word of Camilla?"

"None. Lady Tartte says her ship disappeared at sea on the way to Australia. Whether taken by pirates or sunken, no one knows. Lady Strictly is still prostrate over losing her nonpareil and remains at Clifton-by-the-Sea. She has no plans to come to town this season."

"It was not her doing. I pity her."

"Kate, you are far too kind." Pandora, always awkward with a needle, began laboriously reattaching the lace. "Aren't you wroth that those creatures are to have children, but not you?"

Her mother glared at her comment. Kate, however, answered steadfastly.

"No. I learned in the tower that the greatest prize is love. Joshua has given me that. I wish it for them, too. But most especially, I want you and Phemie to find love this coming season."

Meet Lynn Shurr

Lynn Shurr grew up in Pennsylvania Dutch country but left to wander the world shortly after getting a degree in English literature. After living in several states and Europe, she picked up a degree in librarianship. Her first reference job brought her to the Cajun Country of Louisiana. Eventually, she became director of a library system. For her, the old saying, "Once you've tasted bayou water, you will always remain here," came true. She raised three children near the banks of the Bayou Teche and lives there still with her astronomer husband where she writes, paints, and studies history.

Other Works From The Pen Of

Lynn Shurr

Lady Flora's Rescue: ***Book One of the Longleigh Chronicles***. - Lady Flora follows the man she loves into the American wilderness not knowing he plans to remain there. Will he choose love over his own liberty?

The Perfect Daughter: ***Book Two of the Longleigh Chronicles***. - When a fascinating gentleman rejects perfection, what must a young lady do to gain his love? Perhaps, seduction.

Daughter of the Rainbow, Book Three of the Longleigh Chronicles. – Shy but lovely Iris Longleigh is passionate about only two things—painting and Lord Valls, who will not marry her due to a secret he harbors.

The Double Dilemma, Book Four of the Longleigh Chronicles – The Longleigh twins wish to marry only twins and find them in an isolated castle on a forbidding coast. The adventure begins!

A Taste of Bayou Water - a prequel to *Blessings and Curses*. When Celine Landry refuses to leave Cajun Country to marry billionaire Jonathan Hartz, what else can a brilliant techno-geek do but try to become Cajun?

__Blessings and Curses__ - Adrienne and Pete—is their love real or are they the victims of an old traiteur's love potion?

__The Courville Rose__ - Can four souls find love in two bodies?

__A Place Apart__ - A wounded warrior and a society girl both seek seclusion on the same deserted island.
Sparks fly!

Letter to Our Readers

Enjoy this book?

You can make a difference

As an independent publisher, Wings ePress, Inc. does not have the financial clout of the large New York Publishers. We can't afford large magazine spreads or subway posters to tell people about our quality books.

But, we do have something much more effective and powerful than ads. We have a large base of loyal readers.

Honest Reviews help bring the attention of new readers to our books.

If you enjoyed this book, we would appreciate it if you would spend a few minutes posting a review on the site where you purchased this book or on the Wings ePress, Inc. webpages at: https://wingsepress. com/

Visit Our Website

For The Full Inventory
Of Quality Books:

Wings ePress, Inc

Quality trade paperbacks and downloads

in multiple formats,

in genres ranging from light romantic comedy to general

fiction and horror.

Wings has something for every reader's taste.

Visit the website, then bookmark it.

We add new titles each month!

Wings ePress Inc.
3000 N. Rock Road
Newton, KS 67114

www.ingramcontent.com/pod-product-compliance
Lightning Source LLC
Chambersburg PA
CBHW070644100726
47907CB00007B/2101